### "They say opposites attract."

Cade pushed up out of the chair and Retta's breath caught in her chest. Tall, dark, and handsome came to mind, right along with sexy, sweet, and kind. "Think there's any truth in that?" he asked.

Then he tipped his cowboy hat toward her and was gone before she could reply.

*Yep, I could really like this fella.* She heard her father's voice in her head as clear as if he were standing right next to her. *He loves kids, cats, and he goes to church on Sunday.*

"So could I, Daddy, but..."

There are too many buts in the world, she remembered him always saying.

"I know, Daddy, but life is complicated."

*Life is what you make it and quite simple if you just listen to your heart.*

# High Praise for Carolyn Brown

"Carolyn Brown makes the sun shine brighter and the tea taste sweeter. Southern comfort in a book."
——Sheila Roberts, *USA Today* best-selling author

"If you like cowboy romances, you can never go wrong with a Carolyn Brown book."
——Romancing the Book

"Like a good piece of chocolate there's nothing more delicious, memorable and addictive than a Carolyn Brown story."
——Fresh Fiction

## THE HAPPY, TEXAS SERIES

"Wonderfully charming characters…This sweet, heartwarming romance is sure to increase Brown's fan base."
——*Publishers Weekly* on *Luckiest Cowboy of All*

"Carolyn Brown's cowboys are as real as they come…Luckiest Cowboy of All shows that there is always a second chance for true love, forgiveness, and a happily ever after. This series is fascinating, well developed, and satisfyingly sexy."
——*RT Book Reviews* on *Luckiest Cowboy of All*

"Goes down like a cup of hot cocoa—warm and sweet."
——*Entertainment Weekly* on *Long, Tall Cowboy Christmas*

"A truly romantic cowboy story...full of love, hope, loss, and second chances. Top Pick."

—Fresh Fiction on *Long, Tall Cowboy Christmas*

"One of the best feel-good reads I've had the pleasure of reading yet this year! It tugged on your heart strings and had you cheering for true love."

—Once Upon an Alpha on *Toughest Cowboy in Texas*

# THE LUCKY PENNY RANCH SERIES

"A nice blend of warmth, down-home goodness, humor and romance."

—*RT Book Reviews* on *Wicked Cowboy Charm*

"Full of Christmas magic, good times, great storytelling, and blazing romance. This is a book to make you laugh and swoon."

—Fresh Fiction on *Merry Cowboy Christmas*

"A charming tale, packed with plenty of heat, heart and hilarity, *Hot Cowboy Nights* is a must read for fans of contemporary western romance."

—Romance Junkies

"With an irresistibly charismatic cowboy at the center of this story, Brown's latest is a sexy, fun read."

—*RT Book Reviews* on *Wild Cowboy Ways*

# Also by Carolyn Brown

## The Happy, Texas series

*Luckiest Cowboy of All*
*Long, Tall Cowboy Christmas*
*Toughest Cowboy in Texas*

## The Lucky Penny Ranch series

*Wild Cowboy Ways*
*Hot Cowboy Nights*
*Merry Cowboy Christmas*
*Wicked Cowboy Charm*

# Cowboy Bold

## A Longhorn Canyon Novel

# Carolyn Brown

**FOREVER**

**New York  Boston**

Copyright © 2018 by Carolyn Brown
Preview of *Cowboy Honor* copyright © 2018 by Carolyn Brown

Cover design by Elizabeth Stokes
Cover copyright © 2018 by Hachette Book Group, Inc.

Forever
Hachette Book Group
1290 Avenue of the Americas, New York, NY 10104
forever-romance.com
twitter.com/foreverromance

First Edition: May 2018

Forever is an imprint of Grand Central Publishing. The Forever name and logo are trademarks of Hachette Book Group, Inc.

The publisher is not responsible for websites (or their content) that are not owned by the publisher.

The Hachette Speakers Bureau provides a wide range of authors for speaking events. To find out more, go to www.hachettespeakersbureau.com or call (866) 376-6591.

ISBNs: 978-1-5387-4486-4 (mass market), 978-1-5387-4487-1 (ebook)

Printed in the United States of America

OPM

10  9  8  7  6  5  4  3  2  1

*To my granddaughter,*
*Makela Robinson.*
*With appreciation for all the love and*
*support that you shower upon me.*

Dear Reader,

I'm asked pretty often where I get ideas for stories. Sometimes they come from nothing more than stopping at a burger shop on a research trip.

Mr. B and I were sitting in a fast-food place waiting for my number to be called when this couple came in with a dozen children, both boys and girls, who sat down in a long booth not far from us. It was evident that they weren't brothers and sisters and that the couple was not their parents. Several of them were talking about the day they'd had—evidently they'd been to a park—but one little guy kept his eyes in a book and didn't talk to anyone unless they asked him a question.

When we left, a cowboy popped into my mind. He told me that he'd been bringing children from the big city to his ranch for a couple of years and was planning to do so again that year. But he was in desperate need of a bunkhouse counselor for the girls, since his previous one couldn't do it that year.

That became the little mustard seed that grew into the Longhorn Canyon Ranch series. And that little boy with a book in his hands became a character in the story. I already had visited with Retta Palmer earlier, and she needed a job, so I simply sent her to visit with Cade Maguire, and *Cowboy Bold* was under way.

I have so many people to thank for helping me take that idea to the book you hold in your hands today. Huge thanks to my editor, Leah Hultenschmidt. I gave her a manuscript and she helped me bring out every emotion and detail, and I love her for that! Also to my whole Forever team—Beth, Amy, Raylan,

Bob, Gina, Mary, Barbara, Estelle, Lexi, Elizabeth, Melanie, Monisha, Jodi, and everyone else who makes my books happen. I'm grateful for each and every one of you!

My agent, Erin, and I've had a working relationship so long that we feel like family. We've been together for close to twenty years and that's longer than most Hollywood marriages. So big hugs to Erin and the whole Folio Literary Management team.

And my undying love to Mr. B. I couldn't make it through my hectic schedule without his support. He's a keeper for sure.

Don't put your boots and hats away when you finish Cade and Retta's story. Levi is about to meet a sassy lady named Claire in *Cowboy Honor,* which will be arriving this fall.

Happy Reading to all y'all.
Until next time,
*Carolyn Brown*

# Cowboy Bold

# Chapter One

Retta felt as if she was entering forbidden territory when she rapped on the door frame and glanced up at a carved wooden sign above the door that said BOYS.

"Come on in." It was the same deep voice she'd heard when she called to ask about the job and then again when she Skyped with Cade Maguire.

She took a deep breath and opened the door. He was sitting on the sofa staring at a laptop on the coffee table in front of him. Without looking up, he raised his hand and motioned to her.

She quickly crossed the room and held out her hand. "I'm Retta Palmer. I'm a few minutes early for our appointment."

He stood up, towering above her five feet eight inches, and flashed a smile as he shook her hand. "Cade Maguire."

She'd figured that he'd be a cowboy—after all he owned a ranch—and from his picture, that he'd be close to her age.

She had seen that he had dark hair, a sexy little cleft in his chin, but seeing the whole package in person was a totally different thing. There was no way that flat image had done justice to those mesmerizing blue eyes. Dammit! She'd always been a sucker for blue eyes.

He led the way from the middle of the floor to a small seating area. His wide back and biceps stretched the knit of his blue shirt. Her gaze drifted down the taper toward his waist and on farther to his butt. Those worn jeans looked made for him. He turned around and nodded toward a comfortable chair on the other side of the coffee table in front of the sofa.

She sat down and crossed one leg over the other. She should have dressed more professionally, but all of her business clothes were at least two sizes too big these days, leaving her with casual outfits.

*But I could have at least worn a skirt instead of boots and jeans,* she fussed at herself silently. *I'm probably making a horrible impression.*

"It's goin' to be a hot day. The weatherman is calling for high nineties," he said.

"That's summer in Texas." Always make a little small talk to put the person being interviewed at ease before the real questions start. She'd used that tactic before, so she wasn't surprised.

"So you drove down from Oklahoma?" He checked the laptop on the coffee table between them. "Waurika, right?"

"Yes, sir, Mr. Maguire."

"Cade." He chuckled. "No one even calls my father Mr. Maguire."

"Then Cade it is," she said with a smile, trying not to be distracted by his gorgeous blue eyes.

"Okay, Retta, I told you when we spoke previously about

our summer program, what the job entails and a little about the ranch, so now I'd like to know more about you."

"Sure. Fire away."

His eyes went back to the laptop. "You've got a degree in business and worked for a bank until three years ago and then there's nothing listed."

"My father took sick, so I went home to help out." This wasn't her first rodeo at being interviewed or the one asking the questions either.

*Don't talk too much. Answer his questions completely and honestly, but don't give away your whole life story. He's only interested in the job he's hiring you for, not anything personal.* That's the motivational speech she gave when the company sent her out to talk to college graduates looking for jobs in the banking business.

"Did he recover?" Cade asked.

"No, he lost the battle with cancer three months ago."

Again, his eyes locked with hers and there was that flutter again. "I'm so sorry for your loss."

"Thank you. It took a while for me to get things settled. The ranch auction was held last week and the new owners are eager to get into the house." She focused on that little tuft of dark chest hair showing at the top of his pearl snap shirt.

"And why do you want this job?" he asked.

"I'd love to have the opportunity to help children and I'm impressed with what you do here on the ranch for them. I'm not new to the idea of teaching leadership, since I've worked with people in that capacity in my previous jobs. The timing is perfect, since I only need something until midsummer."

"You've worked with adults. Ever had a bit of experience actually working with kids? Liking them and working with them are two different things. These are ten- to twelve-year-old girls from the inner city who are tough as nails. What makes you think you can control them?" He kept his eyes on the computer.

"I like kids, and a little love goes a long way with tough kids. I was a Sunday school teacher for girls in that same age range in the church my dad and I attended. Not all of those girls came from perfect homes or had sweet little temperaments. I helped with the Bible school programs all three summers while I was there. I've served as counselor, supervisor, and sponsor for two trips to summer church camp, and twice my girls and I went to southeastern Oklahoma for short missionary trips," she answered. "So I'd say I've worked with kids a few times."

"So what did you do on those trips?" He looked up and their eyes caught in the middle of the distance separating them.

"On the first one we painted an elderly couple's house for them. Second time we worked on a small farm, picking vegetables and fruit and selling them in a roadside fruit stand. It taught my girls to work and to help others," she answered, amazed that her voice sounded completely normal with those blue eyes boring into hers.

"Tell me about this ranch you sold?" he asked.

"It was small, only about two hundred acres. I was born in Waurika and lived on the place until I went to college and then came back to it to help when my dad was diagnosed. We couldn't afford to hire help so I did it all with Dad until he couldn't do it anymore, and then I did it by myself," she answered.

"Why didn't you stay there?" He blinked and looked down at the computer.

"The medical bills had to be paid," she answered honestly.

"Again, I'm sorry. Will you miss living there?"

"At times, I'm sure I will, but what I'll miss most is the memories." She shrugged and took a deep breath. "How many little girls will I be in charge of if you hire me?"

"Four."

She waited a full thirty seconds to see if he'd ask another question before she responded. "I'm sure there will be lots of giggling and whining, and I can expect it to lean more toward whining. Like I said, I've dealt with girls that age so I know what I'm signing up for, Mr. Maguire. Any more questions?"

"No, but I will be honest. I ran the references you listed," he said. "And your previous employers said that you'd be excellent in this position."

"So am I hired?" She shot another smile his way but avoided his eyes. If she got the job she had to remember to look at the cleft in his chin, or his ears or even his mouth but to never fall into those cool blue eyes again. On second thought, though, his mouth would be dangerous too. His lips were meant for kissing.

"Let me show you the bunkhouse and if you're still interested we'll talk salary." He stood, crossed the floor in a few long swaggering strides, and held the door open for her. "It's only a few yards from here so we'll walk."

"I saw it as I drove down here from the ranch house. Stopped to ask exactly where to go and met a sweet lady named Mavis." She passed close enough to him to get a whiff of the remnants of his shaving lotion. Without thinking, she drew a long breath and let it out slowly. Yep, the scent was woodsy and clean, reminding her of the fresh smell of morning when the dew was still on the ground.

*It's been way too long since you went out with a guy,* her best friend Tina's voice popped into her head.

"Amen," she muttered.

"I'm sorry, did you say something?" Cade nodded toward the next building down from the boys' bunkhouse. He shortened his step to keep up with her but it still only took two minutes to go from one building to the next.

"Just muttering to myself," she said. "One of my failings."

"Mine too."

He stepped up on the porch and opened the door for her. She scanned the large room. No television but there was a bookcase full of age-appropriate books.

"We have television in the ranch house and they can watch movies there, but we encourage them to spend time outside in the fresh air or reading books. We want this to be a learning experience."

"Teach them to like the smell of dirt and hard work. Sittin' in front of a television all day doesn't do anything but waste time," she said softly. "That's something that my daddy said all the time."

"Sounds like he was a very smart man. This is the living room and the little kitchen will be for you and the girls to prepare snacks."

"Does that mean I'm hired?" she asked.

"The job is yours if you want it. The kids arrive in three days. The quicker you can move in, the better, so you can get acquainted with the place and all of us before the children get here," he answered.

"I can be back by midafternoon." It might seem a little eager but she really wanted this job. It offered room and board and was tailor made for her for the next few weeks when interviews for her old job at Arlington Bank started. And besides that, the timing was perfect. She'd been vice president of the Arlington Bank and the next step on the ladder would have been president of a branch bank, but then her father took sick and she'd had to resign. If she was re-hired, she'd step right back into the job without having to start at the bottom and work her way up again.

"Great!" He stuck out his hand.

She shook with him and attributed the sparks to her excitement about landing the job.

"Let's do a quick walk-through of the rest of the place," he said.

"I can understand the Longhorn of Longhorn Canyon Ranch, but I don't see a canyon anywhere," Retta said as she followed him across the space to the first bedroom.

"My great-grandparents built this place from scratch and we've always had Longhorn cattle on it that we use for rodeo stock, but we raise Angus cattle. My great-grandmother lived on the edge of Canyon Creek, so they combined the two when they needed a brand. I'm a diehard Texas Longhorn fan so I love the ranch's name."

"I won't hold that against you," she said seriously.

"OU?" He almost groaned.

"Boomer Sooner!" she answered with a smile. "And this year we'll whip your butts."

"Want to make a bet on it?"

"Bettin' with the boss isn't a good idea. Besides, I'll be long gone by the second week in October."

"Hey, now! I don't want you to feel like I'm the boss. We work as a team when the kids arrive."

"Well, then if I were here, I'd gladly take your money."

"Dream on. Texas is goin' to whip Oklahoma's butt this year." He motioned into the room. "Each girl has her own room. All exactly alike so no one is special."

"That's a smart idea," she said, taking in the space. "Did you go to UT at Austin?" she asked as she followed him to the fifth door.

"Played for them. Helped bring home the Gold Hat in '09."

"And helped them give it back to Oklahoma in '10," she said.

"Ouch!" He grinned. "You know your football. Why would you live in Texas if you are an OU fan?"

"I went where the job took me," she said. "But evidently, I'm as diehard Sooner as you are Longhorn."

"I doubt it." He chuckled. "Don't tell me you're against the Dallas Cowboys too?"

"No, sir. I love them, but I'll always be a Sooners fan."

"Live in Texas long enough and you might change your mind," he told her.

"Honey, you'll be old and gray before there's even a possibility of that happening."

The slight cleft in his chin deepened when he smiled. "Kind of sassy, aren't you?"

"Been accused of it a few times," she answered.

"It'll take all of what you got to control these kids. Here's your quarters." He threw open the final door and stood to the side.

She expected him to show her a room like the other four but she was wrong—again. A queen-size bed took up a very small portion of the big room. Nightstands on either side, a big ten-drawer dresser, sofa and wooden rocking chair, walk-in closet, and a private bathroom with an oversize tub.

"Wow!" she whispered.

"This is the original bunkhouse. When it was built, the foreman at that time was about six and a half feet tall. He asked for a tub big enough for him to soak away the aches of the day. When we threw up walls and made this into a retreat type of bunkhouse, we left the tub. The boys' place doesn't have a tub, but it does have two shower stalls. It was built when the ranch outgrew this one. Nowadays the hired hands live in the surrounding towns and commute into work every day."

If he'd shown her the tub first thing, she would have already been in her old truck and driving back across the Red River to get her things. She envisioned bubbles and bath salts and reading a thick book every single evening that she was there.

"You haven't asked about a salary." He leaned a shoulder against the doorjamb and quoted a figure higher than she'd expected. "And in addition to that, you get room and board, which includes three meals in the big house."

The money was excellent. Benefits fabulous. And she got to work as a team. There were no cons—only pros.

"That sounds more than fair," she said.

"Contract is on the computer. I'll make a couple of adjustments and if you've seen enough we'll go back down to the boys' place and get it signed." He crossed the floor and held the door open for her.

If something sounded too good, then there had to be something wrong somewhere, right? Thinking about it overnight wouldn't hurt, but if she didn't take it now, then he might change his mind about her commitment and bring in one of the other candidates. "Why did you wait so late to hire someone?" She fell into step with him going from one bunkhouse to the next.

"The same lady who's always taken care of the girls had to back out last week. Her daughter had triplets and she had to go to Virginia to help out," he said.

Once inside, he went straight to the computer, hit a few keys, and then whipped the screen around to her. She read through the one-page contract. Payment upon completion of the program and would be forfeited if she left before the last day. Any accidents happening during the program would be covered by the ranch insurance. Pretty basic stuff really. She hit the sign here key and it was done.

"That does it. I'll print out a copy for you and give it to you when you return. Call me when you get back and I'll send some hired hands to help you unload." He rattled off a phone number and she plugged it into her phone.

\*       \*       \*

He walked out with her and frowned at her truck. It had probably been bright red at one time, but it definitely showed signs of being left out in the weather instead of in a garage.

Her dark brows drew down over brown eyes. "What? Are you regretting hiring me already?"

"Why would you ask that?"

"Your expression said you were having second thoughts," she answered. "I would love to have this job but if you've changed your mind…" She didn't finish the sentence.

"You are pretty good at reading people. I'm surely not having second thoughts. I wasn't expecting you to be driving a truck. With a résumé like yours I expected something different."

"I told you that I've been a rancher for three years," she said as she slung open the door and crawled inside the old truck. "What did you think I'd be driving?"

"Maybe a sports car," he answered.

"My cute little yellow Camaro went the same way as the farm—to pay off my father's medical bills, but I'm debt free and this old girl has a lot of miles left in her." Retta patted the steering wheel.

Cade held up his palms. "Hey, I like trucks. I drive one, and if you'll look up toward the house, you'll see three parked out front."

"Saw them when I drove in. They're nice." She fastened the seat belt and started the engine.

"Sounds like a new vehicle," he said.

"I keep her in good runnin' order. See you in a few hours," she said as she drove away.

With his long strides it only took a few minutes to get to the big house located about a hundred yards away. He circled around and went in through the back door, kicked off his good boots, and shoved his feet down into a pair of scuffed-up work boots and then headed to the refrigerator for a quart jar of sweet tea to take to the field for his brother, Justin.

"Did you hire her?" Mavis took a blackberry cobbler from the stove.

A short woman with kinky curly hair that went from brown to blond, depending on how long it had been since her last visit to the beauty parlor, Mavis had bright green eyes and loved gossip.

"I did," Cade answered. "And she'll be joining us for supper tonight."

Mavis lowered her chin and narrowed her eyes. "Not that I'm one to meddle, but—you better be careful, Cade Maguire. Those big brown eyes get you every time."

Mavis had been the cook at the ranch since before Cade and Justin were born and even though she was near seventy, she swore they'd take her out of the kitchen feet first. Her husband, Skip, had already retired as ranch foreman, but Mavis said there was no way she was staying home with him twenty-four/seven.

"Don't be fussin' at him, woman." Skip came through

the kitchen. "He's a grown man and knows not to mix business and pleasure. If he's hired her, then he ain't goin' to get all involved with her."

Skip was talk and lanky and favored bibbed overalls. His gray hair had been nothing but a rim around his bald head ever since Cade had known him. He might look like a gentle breeze could blow him away, but he was as strong as an ox and could do the work of three men on the ranch.

"He's a man and she's a woman. Business ain't got a thing to do with what happens between two people when they..." She stopped.

"What happens? Tell me," Cade teased.

Skip chuckled. "I'm listenin' and since we're both just men and don't understand anything, we'd like some details."

Mavis pushed a strand of hair behind her ear and narrowed her eyes. "Y'all ain't crazy. You both know what I'm talkin' about. Now, Cade, you take that tea to Justin and y'all get yourselves on back here by noon. And Skip Roberts, you get on back down to the boys' bunkhouse and fix that water leak."

"Better listen to her. She's the one doin' the cookin'." Skip bent to kiss her on the forehead.

"Yes, ma'am." Cade grinned.

"And if you can't be careful, then be sure you got some protection in your hip pocket." Skip chuckled again.

"I swear to God, you embarrass me every time you turn around," Mavis snapped at her husband and then turned back to Cade. "Boy, you watch that heart of yours. It's got a thing for brown eyes."

"Not a single thing for you to worry about, Miz Mavis." He stopped and bent down to hug her.

"Okay then, I'll set another plate for supper. I hope she likes pot roast," Mavis said.

"Me too, but she's a devout OU fan, so one never knows," Cade said in mock seriousness.

"Sweet Jesus." Skip crossed himself. "An Oklahoma fan in this house. God might shoot lightning right through the roof and zap us all."

Mavis shoved a finger up under his nose and started to say something, but Cade grabbed it and twirled her around in a swing dance movement. "You don't worry about me. I would never get involved with someone who's a Sooner fan."

"You rascal, you've messed up my hair." She patted at her short hair.

"You still got spring in your step. You and Skip should go with me and the boys out dancing some Saturday night," he said.

"Did that woman's brown eyes make you crazy? I'm too old for shenanigans like that. Lord have mercy! I'll be seventy in the fall."

"Don't you lie to me. You're not a day over fifty, and Skip can still two-step. I saw y'all at the last weddin' we went to. Put us young folks plumb to shame." He gave her another quick hug and headed out the back door.

"You are full of horse crap and you're forgetting your tea," Mavis yelled.

He came back, picked up the jar, and blew a kiss toward them on his way out that time.

But his step slowed as he thought about Mavis's warning. She wouldn't say Julie's name, but that's clearly who she meant. On the night before their wedding, he'd blown Julie a kiss when he walked off her porch at ten minutes until midnight. And the next morning she'd sent the engagement ring back with a note saying that she couldn't go through with it. Folks said that time would heal his shattered heart, but it had already been two years and he still felt the ache.

He got into the old work truck that didn't look a bit better than Retta's. He set the tea on the floor in front of the passenger's seat and shifted into low gear. He turned on the radio to take his mind somewhere else but that didn't help when "Deja Vu" started playing. Like Lauren Duski sang about, there were weeks when he didn't even think of Julie—and then it would all come back in a flash, especially when he saw a woman with beautiful brown eyes—like Retta's.

He parked the truck and picked up the quart of tea. A trail of dust floated out behind the green tractor coming toward him. The smell of freshly plowed dirt and hot sun rays beating down from a cloudless sky—this all came at the price of his heart, but he'd do it again without a doubt or regrets.

The tractor came to a stop a few feet in front of the truck and Justin hopped out of it. "I hope that tea is for me. I'm spittin' dust. Did you hire the woman?"

Cade held out the jar. "I figured you'd be ready for something to drink. And yes, I hired her. Her résumé says she's a city girl but she was wearing boots and jeans."

"Thanks. What's she look like?" Justin took the tea and had a long drink.

"Tall. Not skinny but curvy. Dark brown hair but I noticed some red in it when she was in the sun. Big brown eyes," Cade answered.

"Like Julie brown eyes?" Justin handed the jar back to Cade.

"Not the same," Cade answered. "Retta's are lighter, the color of a Yoo-hoo."

"Brown all the same." Justin slapped a hand on his shoulder. "Be careful, brother."

"She's an employee, for God's sake," Cade snapped. "Five weeks and she's gone. She's not Julie or anything like her."

Justin's shoulders shot up in a shrug. "Hey, I didn't mean to step on sore toes. I'm just sayin' to be careful. Tall, curvy, brown eyes. Hell, you'd have to be half dead not to flirt with that."

"I don't flirt," Cade said.

Justin laughed out loud. "Yeah, and the sun will come up in the west tomorrow mornin'. We are both Maguires. We flirt. It's in our DNA. You can have the tractor now. My butt was beginning to feel like it was grown to the seat. I'm going to go help Levi fix fence the rest of the day so I can stand up."

"I'll gladly plow a field or even string barbed wire not to have to listen to everyone on the ranch givin' me advice. You want to show Retta around the ranch tomorrow?" Cade removed his hat and used it for a fan.

"Nope. I'm working with Levi for the next three days. We want to get as much of the pasture roped off as we can. It's up to you—but since you don't flirt, we won't need to give you any advice."

Cade frowned. "Mavis has already been on my case. I don't need your smart-ass remarks."

Justin removed his hat and raked his fingers through his hair. His dimples deepened when he grinned. "We're just all lookin' after you. It's taken two long years for you to get over Julie, and you still go for the brown-eyed beauties when we go dancin' on the weekends. This isn't a one-night stand or even a weekend romp. She's goin' to be here for five long weeks."

"Holy hell, Justin! I just met the woman and hired her. I'm not going to sleep with her."

"Well, I hope not." Justin laughed. "See you at supper. Here, you take the rest of this tea. Mad as you are, you might need it to cool you down."

"Dammit!" he muttered as he got into the tractor cab and fired up the engine.

He'd barely gotten the tractor turned around when his bluetick hound, Beau, ran up beside him and barked loudly several times. He braked and slung open the door, and the dog scrambled up across him and took his place in the passenger's seat.

"Needin' a little air-conditioning are you? Let me tell you about this woman who's goin' to be with us on the ranch for the next five weeks. I think you'll like her, Beau, old buddy." He reached across and scratched the dog's ears with his free hand. "But don't get too attached. She's a city gal and she won't be stayin' with us."

# Chapter Two

Retta had lived in two places her entire life—the farm-house and the fifth-floor apartment that she rented in Dallas when she landed the job with Arlington Bank. Standing in the middle of the living room floor after she'd put her things in the truck bed, she didn't even try to hold back the tears. Slowly she'd walked through the whole house—the bedroom where she'd gone from a baby to a little girl to a teenager, where she'd leaned out the window and kissed her first boyfriend. The dining room where the family had always, always had supper together and discussed the day—and where she'd probably snapped a thousand bushels of green beans while she and her mother talked about everything. The master bedroom where her father had died surrounded by his memories of their family. And now the living room, which had been filled with laughter and love.

"It's time to move on," she whispered. "You told me

to do this, Daddy, but you didn't tell me it would be so painful."

She wiped tears all the way to Nocona and with a deep breath told herself that life was going to go on and she had to move with it. She stopped at the Dairy Queen for an ice-cream cone, but a mile down the road she still couldn't swallow past the lump in her throat so she tossed it out the window.

She had turned off the highway onto a farm road when she realized that someone was behind her. They stayed with her when she drove under the big wooden sign above the cattle guard proclaiming that from there on they were on Longhorn Canyon Ranch. When she parked in front of the bunkhouse, the other truck pulled in right beside her.

"Dammit!" she muttered. "My eyes are a mess and I'm not ready to talk to anyone."

Cade swung his long legs out of the truck and waved. "I'll help you get unloaded."

"Thanks, but I can take care of it," she told him.

He peered into the bed of the truck and asked, "Is this all? I thought you might be returning with a cattle trailer full of stuff. I was going to offer some empty space in the barn to store your things."

"Like I said, the medical bills are paid." She shrugged.

He hoisted two boxes onto his shoulders.

*Now that's one strong cowboy.* The voice in her head was Tina's.

She couldn't argue. The boxes that he carried were the ones that had taken all her strength to get up into the bed of the truck. She hurried ahead of him, set a couple of suitcases on the porch, and held the door for him. "Just put them in my room and I'll take care of getting the rest of it inside."

"I might be a grown man, but my mama would tack my

hide to the smokehouse door if I let a lady carry stuff. I'm already in hot water with her if she finds out that you opened the door for me." He grinned.

"Does she live on the ranch too?"

"No, ma'am. She and Dad moved out around Sweetwater three years ago, but they come home for Christmas and the whole family always meets in Dallas for the Texas-Oklahoma game every year." He set the boxes in the corner of the living area.

"I've missed the last three games. Watched them on television, but it wasn't the same. Oklahoma is good enough to whip Texas's butt this year. I'll be right there in the stands again to celebrate when we do." She wheeled the suitcases into the bedroom.

"In your dreams." He chuckled as he started back out for more boxes.

"Hey, now, this is serious business," she called after him.

"Don't I know it, and I'll be on the winning side," he yelled.

"And that, Mr. Maguire, is dreaming big," she hollered.

"Dreams do come true," he said as he made another trip inside. "What did you pack in these things, rocks?"

"Had to have something to remind me of the farm," she shot back.

"Are you serious?" He wiped sweat from his forehead.

"No, but if I'd thought of it, I would have gone down to the creek and gathered a few to keep as memories," she answered.

After another trip, he removed his hat and fanned with it. "We have supper at six o'clock. I'll be here about five-thirty to take you up to the house."

"You don't need to do that," she said. "I can find my way."

"Not saying you couldn't. I just wanted to be gentlemanly." He settled the well-worn straw hat on his head and then tipped it toward her. "See you there between five-thirty and six. The boys and I like a good cold beer before supper, but we can make you a drink if you want something different."

"Sounds good. I'll be there." The way she was flushing made her think that a cold drink would have been pretty good right then.

\*          \*          \*

A sweet southerly wind fluffed Retta's hair as she walked toward the house that evening. Her soft maxiskirt swished around her legs, making her feel all kinds of feminine. She'd paired the brightly colored skirt with an orange tank top and a pair of sandals, and even taken time to do her toenails in bright orange to match.

A big fluffy yellow cat met her at the yard fence, meowed a few times until she stopped to pet it and then followed her up on the porch. She wasn't sure whether to knock or just walk right in. *Better to be safe than sorry*, she thought. She raised her knuckles, but before she could rap on the door, Cade opened it.

"Good timin'. I was about to call the bunkhouse." He stepped to the side and his gaze raked her up and down, and he raised an eyebrow. "Orange like Texas colors?"

Her gaze dropped to his belt buckle embossed with a longhorn and slowly made its way up to his fitted T-shirt. "Hmmm…looks like you're in Sooner red to me. Did you change your mind and decide to go with a winning team?"

"Maybe we should change shirts," he said.

"Right here?"

"I'm game if you are." He grinned, mischief glinting in his eyes.

She caught his gaze and didn't blink. "I'm afraid you'd stretch this out way too much. But rest assured I will be wearing red at the game this fall."

"And I'll be the one across the field from you in orange cheering on the winning team. This way to the living room." He put a hand on the small of her back and guided her across the foyer into a huge living area with the cat running ahead of them. "I'll be glad to buy a Texas shirt for you if you change your mind about who you should be rootin' for."

"I'd love one. I'll need a nice dust rag for my new apartment. But if you'd like a Boomer Sooner shirt, I've got a couple of extra ones in my suitcases," she threw back without hesitation.

"What did I hear? Blasphemy coming from the new girl?" A tall guy who had to be Cade's brother waved from a recliner. "I'm Justin." He had deep dimples in his cheeks when he smiled, and though his eyes were blue, they had more gray mixed in than Cade's.

Another guy raised his beer bottle. "And I'm Levi Jackson, the lowly foreman on this big old ranch. Bear with her, guys. She'll learn that none of us will ever wear a Sooner shirt, and I'm not sure you can get into heaven if you use a Texas shirt as an old dust rag." He took a long drink of his beer and nodded toward Cade. "If you look closely, ma'am, you will see that Cade's shirt is clear red, and that stuff that Oklahoma wears is dark blood red...like what they bleed when we whip their butts on the field."

"Pleased to meet you both. And we Sooners wear red so that when we wipe up your blood with our shirts, they don't get stained." Retta shifted her gaze over to the other cowboy.

"Whoa! We got us a smarty-pants," Levi said.

"Got to be able to growl if I'm goin' to sit on the porch with the big dogs." She'd forgotten how much fun it was to banter with folks her age. For the past year, things had been pretty serious around her home.

"What can I get you to drink, Miz Retta?" Cade asked. "As you can tell, we're pretty informal around here."

"I'll have whatever they're having," she answered.

"Have a seat," Justin said. "Mavis is putting the food on the table and she'll yell when it's ready. She likes to be out of here by six, so believe me, it won't be later than that."

"And what about when the kids are here?" Retta asked.

"She'll stay in a spare bedroom. She's married to Skip, who'll be the supervisor for the boys, so they stay on the ranch during that time," Justin answered.

She settled down in the corner of the sofa. "My dad liked his supper at the same time, so I'm used to it."

Cade went to an antique side bar and opened a door to reveal a small hidden refrigerator. He pulled out a Coors longneck beer, popped the lid off, and carried it to her. "Do you want a glass?"

She shook her head. "Better right out of the bottle."

"Yes, ma'am, you got that right, even if you need some educatin' when it comes to football." Levi's green eyes twinkled.

His light brown hair floated on his shirt collar. She could imagine the women tangling their fingers in it during a makeout session. That thought made her glance over to Cade, who'd sat down on the other end of the sofa. His clean-cut dark brown hair was something she could sure enough imagine running her fingers through during a hot makeout session.

*Stop it!* She scolded herself. *Just because it's been a*

*while since you've had time for a man in your life is no excuse to be daydreaming about your boss. So get over it.*

The cat jumped up on the sofa and curled up in her lap. "What's its name?"

"That would be Gussie." Levi chuckled.

"Now ask him why," Cade said.

She glanced over at Levi as she stroked the cat's fur.

"Gussie was the name of my first girlfriend when I was in the third grade," he answered. "They say you never get over your first love. Anyway, I rescued the cat and her six kittens from the creek. Someone had tied them up in a plastic bag and tossed them over a bridge."

"That's horrible." She gasped.

"But there's a happy ending." Levi smiled. "I brought her home and she's kept us in barn cats for ten years. She'll be bringin' in a litter a couple of times a year and supplyin' the kids around here with pets for a long time."

"Levi is always draggin' in a stray of some kind. He rescued our ranch dog, Beau, about five years ago," Justin said.

"He was just a pup walkin' down the middle of the highway between here and Bowie. Been a good dog." Levi tipped up his bottle and finished it off, then glanced at his watch. "Five, four, three, two…"

"Okay, boys, food's on the table and I'm leavin'," Mavis called out.

Cade rose to his feet and held out his hand. "He hardly ever misses the exact second that she'll call us to supper, so never bet with him. She gets it on the table for us and then we're responsible for cleanup. It's my turn tonight."

Retta set Gussie to the side and her beer bottle on the coffee table before she put her hand in his. Careful not to let it linger after she was on her feet, she walked beside him out into the foyer, through a formal dining room and into a huge country kitchen. A table laden with food sat at an angle so that everyone could see outside through a window so big that it covered a whole wall and brought the outdoors right inside to them. She could see Mavis and a tall cowboy she guessed would be Skip getting into a fairly new truck and driving away as Cade pulled out a side chair for her.

When she was seated, Levi sat down across from her. Cade and Justin both took places at the ends and bowed their heads. Levi said a quick grace and then picked up the bread basket, took out two hot rolls, and passed it on to Justin.

"Pot roast was my dad's favorite meal. Mama made it for him on Sunday," Retta said as she laid a roll on the edge of her plate and sent them to Cade. Their hands brushed in the passing and she could swear there were vibes. Or maybe she was just hungry and the smell of a good, home-cooked meal caused the flutter in her stomach. She attributed it to hunger and not chemistry because no matter how much they'd teased about football or his saying that everyone formed a team, Cade Maguire was her boss.

"We don't have any complaints when Mavis makes it. We all love her home cookin' and we like whatever she puts on the table," Levi said.

"So tell us a little about yourself, Miz Retta," Justin said.

"Born and raised in Waurika, Oklahoma, a little town about twenty miles over the border. Went to OU." She glanced over at Cade. "I went to college at Cameron in Lawton, majored in business, and took a job for Arlington Bank when I graduated but I'm a Boomer Sooner fan to the death. Gave up my job as vice president when my dad got lung cancer a few years ago and I went home to help him. He passed about three months ago."

*        *        *

Cade loaded his plate with a thick slice of pot roast, pota-toes, and carrots and set the platter back on the table. Retta had answered Levi's question, but it sure enough had been an impersonal version—same as when he'd interviewed her. She had to be still hurting from losing her father. He couldn't imagine the pain if either of his parents passed away.

"So what about you guys? What's your story? Are y'all kin?" Retta asked.

"Well, it feels like they're both my brothers," Levi said. "But Mavis and her husband, Skip, raised me since I was a baby. He retired and I stepped into his shoes as foreman, but he still likes to help out. I'd been working here since I was about thirteen. When I finished high school, I moved out here to the ranch and have lived in the house ever since."

"And me and Cade were born in Bowie, but Mama brought us home to the ranch soon as she could and we been here ever since. Except for the four years when Cade was in college." Justin's voice held more than a little touch of pride.

"We thought he might go into the NFL," Levi said. "But he loved ranchin' too much to give it up. He's probably best remembered around these parts for the time he scored the winning touchdown that took us to the state playoffs and got him the scholarship to play for the Longhorns," Levi said.

"Tell me about it," Retta said.

"Ten seconds left on the clock. He's the quarterback, and a thirty-yard field goal would've tied the game. But he faked handing the ball to the kicker, shook off three guys, and ran it in for a TD himself to get the win," Justin said.

"Did you both play for the Longhorns?" Retta asked.

"No, ma'am. I didn't go to college. I'd had enough school when I graduated," Justin answered.

"Me, too," Levi said. "Me and Justin graduated on Friday night and went to work full-time right here. Ain't got a single regret in the world. But let me tell you Cade's still a hero around here."

"And it was all over for the other team," Justin said.

"I wonder if their coach yelled at them in the locker room like Coach Hamp would have us if Cade hadn't made that touchdown." Levi shook his head, seriously.

"Whew!" Justin wiped at his forehead and pretended to throw off the sweat. "Old Coach Hamp could do his fair share of hollerin'. Were you a cheerleader, Retta?"

"Oh, no, I was the kicker and shared the quarterback position with another girl," she said.

All three guys almost dropped their forks. Cade stared at her, not caring if it was rude.

"You're jokin', right?" Cade finally asked.

With her height and curves, Retta easily could have been a runway model. If she strolled down the red carpet, made a turn, and batted those brown eyes a couple of times, buyers would be flocking to the designer of that skirt and orange top to stock their stores in all sizes.

"Nope. I was on the girls' intramural football team. My field goal record is forty-five yards, and I threw more completed passes my senior year than anyone else," she answered.

"Tag or tackle?" His breath caught in his chest at an instant vision of her in a uniform with hips rounding out below a small waist and stuffing that chestnut brown hair into a helmet. He'd never been into role play, but his throat went slightly dry at the idea.

"Honey, in Waurika, Oklahoma, there is no such thing as tag or powder puff ball. We play for keeps."

"Did you borrow the Waurika team's uniforms?"

"Oh, no! We played in bikinis and helmets." She giggled.

"Now I know you are kiddin'," Levi said.

"Yes, I am. The school let us use the old shoulder pads and we wore jeans and knee pads, but I promise we were tough as the guys. We raised enough money to pay the electric bill for the football field every single time so no one had to sponsor us. And we had a load of fun doing it."

"Who did you play against?" Levi asked.

"Any area teams who wanted to suit up and play with us on Saturday nights."

Justin finally put his fork on his plate. "Saturday nights?"

"Most of us were farm kids. Our parents needed us to work, but they'd give us Saturday nights off to play most of the time."

"Did your father—" Levi started.

She butted in before he finished. "He came to all my games he could. It was Mama who had a fit. Her daughter could have been a ballerina but not a football player."

"Wow!" Justin said.

Retta shrugged. "Mama eventually got her wish. I left the farm and went into business, where I dressed up every day. But I never lost my love for a good game. Do y'all ever play ball with the kids, or is it ranchin' stuff?"

"Oh, honey, Cade always coaches the boys in how to throw a spiral and how to dance through a tackle every year that they've been here," Justin answered.

"Sounds fun," Retta said. "Maybe we should organize a game, girls versus boys this year." Cade loved the sparkle of the challenge in her eyes.

Levi picked up his fork and started eating. "Maybe you ought to be a boys' bunkhouse mama instead of a girls'."

"No, thank you. I do better with girls even when they get pissy and whiny," she said. "Boys at that age want to fight or strut around like they're all big and mighty."

"Got brothers?" Cade asked.

"No brothers or sisters, but got a few boy cousins." She followed Justin and went back to eating.

Cade did the same but couldn't get the picture of her in tight jeans and shoulder pads out of his mind.

\*      \*      \*

After they'd finished the meal, Cade brought out a fresh apple pie and a container of ice cream and four dessert plates. "Who wants pecans?"

Justin and Levi both nodded so he went back to the refrigerator and got a small jar of chopped pecans. "Anything else while I'm up? More sweet tea? Coffee?"

Retta held up her glass. "Yes, please to the tea. Got any caramel ice cream topping? My dad always loved pie, ice cream, a sprinkling of pecans, and then caramel over it," she answered.

"I want mine like that too," Levi said.

Cade put the pie on the table along with dessert plates. "I think I'll give it a try too."

"I've been meaning to ask all through dinner, who did those drawings on the wall?" Retta asked as she put four slices of pie on the plates.

Cade brought ice cream, pecans, and caramel to the table. "That would be Benjy's work. You'll meet him on Friday. Benjy is special needs in a really different way."

"How's that?" she asked.

"He's almost genius on the IQ chart, but he's what they call high-functioning autistic. He has limited social skills, but he retains everything he reads and believe me, he reads a lot."

"But with no social skills, he doesn't do well with others, does he?" she asked.

"That's right," Levi said. "And he's prone to blurting out facts, but he loves ranching, and his grandmother thinks the camp might teach him some people skills."

"Well, he's a fantastic artist. I recognize Gussie. Is that Beau, your dog?" she asked.

"Yes, it is, and the third one is Hard Times." Levi passed the caramel over to Retta.

"Is there a story about Hard Times the turtle? That sounds like a children's book." She applied the caramel to the top of a scoop of ice cream and handed it off to Cade.

"Oh, yeah, there is," Cade said. "Hard Times came up out at the barn with a cracked shell and like always, Levi came totin' him home. We applied some superglue to it and it got better. We figured he'd seen some hard times so that's how he got his name. He's shown up again every year for the past decade and stuck around through the summer months."

Levi took the first bite and made appreciative noises. "His favorite thing is watermelon but he'll eat Gussie's cat food or even Beau's dog food in a pinch. I'll have to see if he'd like a bite of this fancy apple pie sometime."

"We're just glad that elephants don't live in Texas or Levi would bring in a stray one and want to keep it in the house," Justin said.

"Can't help it. It's who I am and I make no apologies." Levi shrugged.

Beau, Gussie, and Hard Times. Retta committed the

names to memory. "Is there a story that goes with Beau's name too?"

Cade nodded. "Beau Beauchamp was quarterback for the Longhorns the year that Levi and Justin was born. My dad thought he was great and talked about him a lot so we named our pup that. He belongs to the ranch but he's mostly my dog."

"You're welcome for that," Levi said.

Retta hadn't sat at a dinner table with adults since the church dinner after her father's funeral. Since then she'd been so busy with the sale of the farm, the auction to get rid of all the stuff in the house and barns, and all the paperwork involved with medical bills that she scarcely took time to eat. And when she did, it was usually a sandwich or canned soup dumped into a bowl and heated in the microwave. Being able to do this three times a day would certainly warrant taking the job, even if the pay had only been half of what Cade had offered.

When Cade finished, he started clearing the table. "Y'all don't have to rush. I'm just gettin' things put away. Got someplace I need to be by seven-thirty."

Of course he did. A cowboy that sexy probably had a girlfriend in the wings.

"Me too," Levi said. "Only got a couple of more nights after this one before we have to be good for five weeks."

Justin rolled his eyes. "It's like Lent for cowboys. We give up drinkin', dancin', and women to take care of the kids. I love them, but it sure lets me know that I'm not ready for the husband and daddy role in my life just yet."

"It's a good thing you do here." Retta finished off the last of her dessert and carried her plate to the sink. "I'll be glad to rinse while you load to make the job go faster."

"I'd never hear the end of it from those two if you did.

They'd expect me to help them on their nights for cleanup duty because I had help." He grinned.

"Okay, then," she said. "It's been a long day. I'm going to the bunkhouse. You guys all have a good time tonight. See you tomorrow."

"Breakfast at seven," Levi called out as he left.

"I'll be here," Retta said. "Thanks for the dinner. This kind of cooking is a pretty fine benefit."

"Glad you liked the pot roast and apple pie. After breakfast I'll show you around the ranch. You used to a horse or a four-wheeler?" Cade followed her to the door.

"I'm okay at riding but enjoy a four-wheeler," she said as she left.

Beau followed her back to her bunkhouse and whined when she started into the house. "You are as spoiled as the cat." She bent to scratch his ears. "So you are named for a quarterback that I never even heard of, are you?"

Beau licked her up across her face. Her laughter rang out across the ranch and echoed back in her ears. It came straight from her heart, something that she hadn't felt in a long time.

When she straightened up and opened the door, Beau chased inside and curled up on the sofa. "Does Cade let you inside? I don't guess it matters what he does since this is my house for the next month. Besides I may register you as a service dog, one that helps little girls who wouldn't have room for a dog in the inner city. That way you'll have to be inside so they can pet you." She talked as she changed from her skirt and tank top into a pair of denim shorts and a faded chambray shirt that she knotted at her waist. She tossed her sandals into the closet and went out to sit on the porch in her bare feet with Beau right behind her.

The dog flopped down beside her and shut his eyes. She

rested her hand on his big head and gently rubbed it with her fingertips as she enjoyed listening to tree frogs, crickets, and a lonesome old coyote howling in the distance.

She'd leaned over on the porch post and was completely lost in her own thoughts when Beau jerked his head up, stood to his feet, and shook from head to toe like he was wet. Then he bounded off the porch and ran off into the dark toward the house.

"Hey, old boy, where were you? Out chasing coyotes or rabbits?" Cade's deep voice floated toward her on the night breezes.

With the light from the moon and stars, Retta could see his silhouette as he and Beau started toward the bunkhouses. His cowboy hat was practically touching the low hanging clouds, or so it seemed as she watched him slowly make his way toward her.

"Good evening," he said when he reached the porch. "Mind if I sit a spell?"

"Not a bit." She moved over to allow him to go past her, expecting that he'd sit in one of the two chairs on the other end.

But he sat down on the step beside her and stretched his long legs all the way to the ground. "Pretty pleasant evening."

"Peaceful." She wanted to ask why he was home before nine if he had a date at seven-thirty, but that wasn't a bit of her business.

"When the kids get here, it'll get a little bit noisier. Hey look, there's a lightning bug. The city kids are usually intrigued by them as well as the sounds of the night. Some of them are a little spooked the first time they hear a coyote howling in the distance," he said.

"The stars are never this bright in the city and all I hear

when I used to sit on my balcony was sirens and traffic noises."

"I sure missed the night noises of the ranch when I went to college. If it hadn't been for sheer determination, I wouldn't have lasted a month." He shifted his position so he could brace his back on the porch post.

Something about his deep drawl in the semidarkness sent tingles up her spine. She needed to get out, go to dinner with friends or even on dates. She'd been cooped up on a ranch with no outlet except church on Sunday too long if a cowboy she'd only just met could affect her like this.

Beau had run on past the boys' bunkhouse and returned with a rabbit hanging from his mouth. The sight jerked Retta out of her deep thoughts about dating, having fun, and men in general.

She gasped. "Did he kill it?"

Cade grinned. "You found him, old boy. Now it's catch and release time."

Beau gently dropped the cottontail on the ground and it raised up on its hind legs to touch noses with the dog.

"Meet Hopalong, another of Levi's strays. Hopalong has been with us longer than Beau, who was a big baby and didn't want to sleep by himself when we got him. So Hopalong crawled into his doghouse with him and they've been buddies ever since," Cade explained.

"So there's a cat, dog, turtle, and rabbit. Any more strays?" Retta asked.

"Not right now, but tomorrow is a brand-new day. Levi's looking at a miniature donkey in Nocona. It was born with a weak leg so the owners can't sell it and now they don't want the little thing. It's barely weaned so it could be coming to the ranch next week. The kids will probably spoil it rotten," Cade answered.

Hopalong eased up onto the first step and then the second. He sniffed Retta's hand when she held it out and then Cade picked him up.

"He likes this." Using his knuckles, he rubbed the spot between the rabbit's ears.

Retta could imagine those big hands working the knots from her neck and back, but it wasn't just her imagination— or the lightning bugs—that caused the sparks to flash between them when she caught his gaze and held it for a few seconds before looking away.

"Guess I'd best get going." He gently put the rabbit on the ground. "I thought I'd be out until bedtime, but I got a call before I left that my meeting was canceled. Now that I've got an hour or two of free time, I should spend it getting the tax papers together for the CPA."

So his date stood him up, did she? And she lived in Nocona or in that area.

"See you tomorrow then," she said.

He tipped his hat toward her. "Breakfast and then I'll show you around the ranch."

She watched those long legs stride away and felt a pang of something. It had to be regret at losing his and Beau's company for the rest of the evening. She liked having them there with her. She reached down and rubbed Hopalong's head like Cade had done, and the bunny snuggled down next to her.

"I wish you could talk and I'd ask you all kinds of questions about Cade. Like if he's got a girlfriend. And why he's such a flirt but I can see sadness in his eyes. I bet you could tell me all kinds of stories."

## Chapter Three

Cade hopped on the four-wheeler and patted the seat behind him. "Hope you don't mind riding double. One of our machines is in the repair shop and Levi needed the other one for the day, so that just leaves one."

"Not at all." Retta settled down behind him but there was no way possible to keep her knees from touching his thighs. His expression showed no indication that he saw or felt the vibes that she did.

"The ranch is two square miles, a little over twelve hundred acres," he said. "We've got most of it cleared and it serves as pasture for our Angus herd. We'll drive around the fence line first and kill two birds with one stone. You can get the lay of the land and I can make sure all the barbed wire is bull tight."

A lump formed in her throat as she nodded. Strange how she could go along for several days and think that she was finished with the mourning process and then a phrase could bring back a visual of her father when he was strong and healthy. He used to say that his fences had to be bull tight, and even though their farm was barely a tenth the size of the Longhorn Canyon, he'd always kept things maintained.

They'd only gone a short distance when the vehicle wheel ran over a rock and she instinctively wrapped her arms around Cade to keep from being bounced out into the knee-high pasture grass. With her hands splayed out on his rock hard chest and her breasts smashed against his back, it was no wonder she was instantly breathing hard.

"Better hang on. There's lots more rough riding," he yelled over his shoulder.

She'd braided her hair that morning and worn jeans and a soft chambray shirt over a tank top. Now she wished she'd brought her cowboy hat with her. Cade's sweat-stained hat looked just like the one she'd tossed in the trash when she'd left the farm. She hadn't thought her job description would involve riding on a four-wheeler for hours with the sun broiling her brains. Or that she'd enjoy hugging up to a cowboy's back as much as she did.

Several times he had to stop the vehicle to open a gate to a new pasture during the trip around most of the property. When they got to what she assumed would be the back corner, instead of following the fence line he made a turn down a rarely used path. Ruts showed where a four-wheeler had been.

He finally came to a stop at an old log cabin set back in a copse of mesquite trees. "Thought we might sit on the porch and rest a little while." He crawled off the machine and she followed him, glad to stretch her legs and even more so to get a little distance between them. The thoughts that flooded her mind as she was pressed against his back even made her blush a couple of times.

"This is about the halfway mark around the ranch. You want a drink? I've got water and a thermos of coffee in the saddlebags. There might be a leftover soft drink in the refrigerator inside the cabin," he said.

"Water would be good." She bent forward to stretch out her back.

He slid off to the other side. "Nowadays we use this place for a huntin' cabin. Sometimes we rent it out to guys who are avid deer hunters." He took two bottles of water from the saddlebags and handed one to her. "Looks like it's going to be another hot one today. I'm glad we're doing this in the morning instead of the afternoon. So if a kid got lost or ran away, do you think you could figure out where to look?"

She took a long drink of the water as she headed toward the porch. "I think so. You ever had that happen? A kid getting lost?"

"Not yet, but you never know, and I like to be prepared," he said.

She sat down on an old ladder-back chair on the porch without even brushing the dust from the seat. "Who lived in this cabin? Why is it here?"

"My great-grandparents lived here when they bought the original part of the ranch."

"Oh, I thought maybe it was the foreman's house at one time." She took a long drink from the water bottle.

"No, but when they built the house we live in now, they kept this in good shape. The story is that my great-grandma made my great-grandpa bring her back here every year for a week at their anniversary time."

"That is so sweet," she said. "So where did Mavis and Skip live?"

"We wanted to build a house for them on the ranch when

he was foreman, but Mavis had inherited her aunt's house in town and didn't want to move," he said. "Levi is biologically Skip's great-nephew."

"Where is his mother? Does she ever come to see him?"

Cade shook his head. "Levi's mama was Skip's niece and she was real young so Skip and Mavis took her in when she got pregnant in high school. It's complicated, but somewhere along the line, his mama remarried and let them keep him rather than moving him away from this area. She lives out in a little town in Pennsylvania called Green Castle. At first she came about once a year, but she hasn't been back since he graduated from high school. They'd become more like strangers or maybe distant friends instead of family."

"Most of life is complicated." She nodded.

"Ain't that the truth. You must still miss your dad something terrible. I can't imagine the hole that it would leave in my life and heart to give up my parents." Cade sat down in the other old wooden chair and propped his long legs on the porch railing.

"The grieving process is kind of strange. I thought I was over it already when my dad finally passed away. I'd witnessed all his pain and suffering, and when it was finished, I thought I'd hit the acceptance stage of grieving but I was wrong." She took another sip of water. "There's a line in a song that says something like the new life begins with death. My dad was a good Christian man, went to church every Sunday and most Wednesday nights when he wasn't too busy with the farm. But he was so ready to leave this life after three years of chemo and trial tests that I couldn't wish him back. But sometimes I get a flash of a memory that makes me miss him so much. To say that grieving is complicated is an understatement."

"And your mama?" he asked.

"Died in a car accident when I was eighteen. I got the news the first month I was in college. Almost quit and went home to help him then, but Daddy wouldn't have it," she answered.

"I'm sorry," he whispered.

"Want to sell this cabin?" She abruptly changed the subject.

"I thought you couldn't wait to get back to the city."

She raised a shoulder in half a shrug. "I can't, but it would be nice to have a little country place like this for vacation times."

"Can't sell it, but I might rent it out to you if you ever want to come back to the ranch." He removed his hat and fanned with it. "So you can take the girl out of the country but you can't remove every tiny bit of the country from the girl?"

"I'm not so sure of that. Even city girls like a little peace and quiet at times. I bet the stars are even more beautiful here than at the bunkhouses. Can we look inside?"

The chair fell forward with a bang and Cade was on his feet. "Sure we can. I need to check on things anyway. No one's been back here since last fall."

She set her water bottle on the porch rail and followed him. The place was bigger than it appeared from the outside. Two sets of bunk beds were set up on each wall with enough space in between for a sofa, a couple of rocking chairs, and a table with four chairs around it. She could see through a door into a bathroom with a shower and a vanity.

"This was the original cabin right here." He waved a hand around the single room. "They put in the plumbing later and added the bathroom after they'd had their first child—my grandfather."

"Cozy. How long did they live here?" She glanced over

at a two-burner stove, small refrigerator, microwave, and a wall-hung sink.

"Just a couple of years. My grandpa was about two years old when they built the new house. Great Granny had a wood-burning stove in here and a couple of what Mama called worktables to hold her skillets and stuff. They hauled their water up from Canyon Creek, which is about twenty yards behind us. It was pretty basic back then," Cade said.

She could hear the wistfulness in his voice. "You ever think maybe you were born in the wrong century?"

"All the time." He sighed. "How about you?"

"Well, I think I'd like a little bit bigger kitchen and bedroom with a door on it and I do like indoor plumbing," she answered.

"Folks who stay here aren't interested in making gourmet meals, so this works fairly well. Ready to go?"

She nodded. "Thanks for letting me take a peek at it."

"Anytime."

"Aren't you going to lock the door?" she asked when they were on the porch. "There's a road right out there." She pointed to a dirt road showing through the trees on the other side of the fence. "Aren't you afraid of vandalism?"

"Nope," he answered. "Never had a problem before. Don't expect one anytime soon. Mavis will have dinner on the table at noon and she's fryin' chicken so we don't want to be late."

"With mashed potatoes and gravy and hot biscuits?" Retta asked.

He nodded.

"How fast can you make that four-wheeler run?"

\*        \*        \*

Cade hoped that Retta couldn't hear his sudden intake of breath earlier when she bent over to work the kinks from her back. Or feel how hard his heart was pounding when she wrapped her arms around him on the four-wheeler. Or if she did notice, that she would think it was due to the fast ride back to the ranch house and not because her hands splayed out on his chest were causing all kinds of electricity. It was perfectly normal and didn't mean jack crap. Any woman who pressed her body up to his would cause that kind of reaction.

When they made it back to the house, she continued to sit on the four-wheeler after he was off and headed toward the porch. He turned and asked, "You comin' in to eat, right?"

"Yes, of course, but I've got a question. Is Mavis one of those stay-out-of-my-kitchen women?"

"I don't think so. Why?" He leaned against a post.

"You mentioned all kinds of activities for the kids, but maybe we should teach them a little responsibility to go with that fun stuff. I'd like for my girls to learn their way around the kitchen. They could use those skills when they get home. Maybe they could set the table and even make a dessert, nothing too fancy, once a week."

"Fantastic idea." Cade grinned. "But not only the girls, the boys too. They can switch off days and maybe help with one meal that day. Mavis loves kids but I'll ask before we put the plan into action. Don't want her to think we're stepping on her toes. Got any more ideas?"

"Well"—she inhaled deeply—"I noticed that the chairs and porch railing at the cabin could use a coat of paint. What if we let the girls do part of it and for their treat they get to camp out one evening? We could roast marshmallows and hot dogs for supper, and that would let the boys have a time away from the girls."

"And"—he picked up on the idea—"the boys could go to the cabin the next night and paint their portion. I love those ideas. It would teach them teamwork. Anything else?"

"Not right now," she said.

"Well, if you think of anything, just spit it out and we'll discuss it. For now we need to get washed up for dinner. We've only got ten minutes and I really don't like cold mashed potatoes." He grinned.

Yep, hiring her was going to be a good thing even if he would have to battle with the chemistry between them. She was innovative, and her ideas would be a nice addition to the things they'd already implemented in the program. Why couldn't she have been all that and not been so damned attractive? When she'd put her arms around him, he'd felt the sparks dancing all around them.

She threw a leg over the side and hopped off, started up the stairs beside him, and caught the toe of her boot on the second step. One minute she was going up and the next she was falling backward.

"Whoa!" he said loudly as he pulled her to his chest.

Her hands quickly circled his neck and she hung on to him until she got her balance. "Whew. I thought I was hitting the dirt for sure."

He looked down into her chocolate brown eyes and their gazes locked. She moistened her lips and he bent slightly. She rolled up on her toes and her eyes fluttered shut. Then Beau bounded around the side of the house and wiggled his way between them, and Justin stepped out on the porch.

"I heard the four-wheeler and figured y'all were home. Dinner is ready," he said.

Cade took a step back and rubbed Beau's ears. "Just got here and we were talking about some new things to teach the kids."

"If you'll show me which way the bathroom is, I'll get washed up," Retta said.

"First door at the end of the foyer to your right," Justin said. "We'll be in right quick."

"What's on your mind? I know that look. You're either mad or hungry," Cade said to his brother.

"You think it's real smart to flirt with Retta like you are doin'?" Justin asked.

"I kept her from fallin'. I was not flirting," Cade protested.

"That's not the way I see it, brother," Justin said.

"I flirt with women I meet at the bar on Saturday nights but not with my employees. And if I did, it wouldn't mean anything." Cade slapped a hand on his brother's shoulder. "I'm fully well able to take care of myself. Now let's go eat. We both hate cold mashed potatoes."

He met Retta coming out of the bathroom. Her hair had been smoothed back and if she'd been wearing makeup, it had either sweated off or been washed away. For the first time he noticed a sprinkling of faint freckles across her nose. Sure he liked being with her and there was a little chemistry there, but all he was doing was innocent flirting. It didn't mean a thing. What happened with Julie was enough to teach him a lesson. It hurt entirely too bad to get serious again.

# *Chapter Four*

It's good day to start a brand-new adventure, Retta thought as she stepped out onto the porch. The sun was peeking up over the horizon. No clouds hung in the sky. Beau was sprawled out on the porch and she'd slept better the night before than she had in ages. All in all, the promise of a bright, fun day lay ahead.

"Good mornin'."

The voice startled her and she whipped around to find Skip coming around the end of the porch. "You had coffee yet?"

"Yes, sir. I brewed a pot when I first got up. You want some?" she asked.

"Thanks, but I already had two cups. I was about to go up to the house for some breakfast. You goin' that way, too?"

"I can't ever turn down a good breakfast," Retta said.

"Then I reckon we can walk that way together. We ain't had time to talk much since you got here. So where do you hail from, Miz Retta?"

"Waurika, Oklahoma, but I lived down near Dallas before that and I'm hoping to go back that way when this job is done." With her long legs, it wasn't difficult to keep up with his stride. "You must like kids to do this for Cade."

"Truth is I miss Levi livin' with us, and this makes me and Mavis both happy to have kids around for a few weeks. Never could have any of our own, so we take what we can get. How about you? You like kids?"

"I do but I'm not plannin' on havin' any kids anytime soon, so this will be my dose of little girls," she answered.

Skip stood to the side to let her go ahead of him on the porch. "These younguns come from the hard city life and the first week ain't a bit easy. Except with Benjy. Now that boy is a real joy. He's different but he's got a heart of gold. I look forward to seeing him every year."

"Has he formed a bond with anyone here?" she asked.

"I know he likes me, but I don't try to hug him. Sometimes he hugs Mavis, but mostly she waits for him to come to her. He loves Levi and he really likes the animals, especially Beau and Gussie, but he's pretty much of a loner."

He opened the door for her and took a deep breath. "Ain't nothing better than the smell of bacon and coffee in the morning. Hello!" he called out. "Where is everyone?"

"In the kitchen," Mavis yelled. "And if another one of these pesky boys try to steal a piece of bacon, I'm going to stab him with a fork."

"Ah, come on, darlin', you know you love us," Cade teased.

"Forget the fork. I'll get out a steak knife if y'all don't leave the food alone until it's on the table," Mavis said.

"You wouldn't stick a knife in any of us," Cade said.

"Didn't say I'd stab a one of you with it, but I could take it to each of your bedrooms when I change the sheets today and do some damage on those things you keep in your nightstand," Mavis threatened.

"Mavis Roberts!" Skip crossed the room and slapped her playfully on the butt.

Mavis laughed and tiptoed to kiss Skip on the cheek. "Mornin', Retta. You ready for this?"

"What? Breakfast or what you're going to do in these guys' bedrooms?" Retta grinned.

"Either one." Mavis giggled.

"Yep, I'm starving. As as for the other, it doesn't affect me, so I couldn't care less but if I was them, I expect I'd leave the bacon alone until grace is said," Retta answered.

Retta's eyes immediately went to Cade. Droplets of water hanging on his hair testified that he'd just gotten out of the shower. His blue knit shirt hung on the outside of his snug-fitting jeans, and he wore his old scuffed-up work boots.

"Good mornin'." He scanned her from boots to hair. "You look great."

"Thank you," she said.

Suddenly she felt as if he'd slowly removed every bit of her clothing with nothing but his eyes. The blush started on her neck and traveled at warp speed to her cheeks. She wanted to fan them, but that would draw even more attention to the fiery red burning sensation. She headed to the coffeepot and poured very slowly as she counted backward from one hundred. When she got to fifty, she turned around and asked Mavis if she needed any help.

"Thanks. You could help get this food to the table before all these strappin' cowboys starve plumb to death," Mavis said. "And you guys can go on and get settled down. It'll only be another minute."

When they were out of the kitchen, Mavis lowered her

voice and said, "Cade told me about your ideas for teachin' the kids a little about cookin' and learnin' some teamwork at the old cabin. I think those are very good ideas."

"Thank you." Retta picked up a bowl of steaming hot biscuits in one hand and a platter of scrambled eggs topped off with cheese in the other.

Mavis carried a crock bowl full of sausage gravy to the table. "I hear you're a Sooner fan."

"Yes, ma'am."

"It ought to make for an interestin' summer around here." Mavis chuckled.

"What's going to be interesting?" Cade asked.

"Oklahoma versus Texas all under the same roof," Mavis answered. "Now y'all sit down and Skip can say grace this mornin'."

As soon as Skip said amen, the guys started passing food and talking about hay, cattle, plowing, and chores. It reminded Retta so much of the way days had started when her mother and dad were both alive that it brought tears to her eyes. She blocked out the conversation around her and enjoyed nostalgia for several minutes.

"I'm going to work on getting barbed wire stretched around that new pasture today," Justin said.

"I've got to go into Bowie for some tractor parts. Anyone need anything from town?" Cade asked.

"You could pick up a load of feed while you're there," Levi said. "I thought I'd go tomorrow, but you could get it and save me a trip. That way I can take half the hired hands to the back pasture and help them work that bunch of cattle before we turn them out in the new pasture that Justin's gettin' ready."

"Sure thing." Cade nodded. "Want to go with me, Retta?"

"Or you could stay here and vaccinate calves with me," Levi suggested.

"Or I can always use an extra hand stretching barbed wire," Justin added.

"With those choices, I think I'll go with Cade." She passed the basket of biscuits to Justin. "Great breakfast, Mavis."

"Thank you. I enjoy cookin' and I'll be lookin' forward to havin' the kids in the kitchen with me. All of them, boys and girls alike, need to know a few basic cookin' skills."

"I can sure agree with that. Daddy called it the goose and gander law. What was good for the goose was good for the gander, and I had to learn to do everything, no matter if it was considered boys' or girls' work." Retta glanced up and her gaze locked with Cade's. From the look in his eyes and the expression on his face, it looked as if he was about to ask her a question. But then Justin handed him the bowl of gravy and the moment, if there was one, ended.

He passed the bowl on to Skip. "So where do you want to go while we're in town, Retta?" he asked.

"Walmart will do fine. I could pick up all of what I want right there in one store," she said.

"There's a few things I could use too. I'll make a list. Here, Retta, have a blueberry muffin to finish off your breakfast," Mavis said.

Cade took the basket from Mavis and sent it on to Retta. Their hands touched briefly and she felt the same sparks that she'd known when she put her arms around him. Fate was a real witch for making her new boss such a sexy cowboy.

*        *        *

Cade hiked a hip on the porch railing and waited for Retta to go to the bunkhouse for her purse. Carrying a large cooler of iced tea in one hand and a sheath of disposable cups in the other, Levi backed out of the house. He took both to his truck, then turned around and came back.

"What's goin' on with you and Retta?"

"Nothing," Cade answered.

"Okay, then. If you want to play it that way, I won't get in your way," Levi said. "Ain't none of my business anyway."

"What do you think is going on?" Cade asked.

"There's chemistry. I can almost see the sparks dancin' around y'all, and when you look at her…well, there's something there that ain't been since Julie," Levi answered.

"Any more than between me and any of the sweet little blondes I meet at a bar?"

"Oh yeah, and this one ain't goin' home the next mornin', Cade. Just remember that." Levi settled his hat on his head. "Y'all goin' to be home in time for dinner?"

"More than likely. How about you?" Cade said.

"Not me. Skip is bringing sandwiches out to the corral for me and the boys so we can keep working. There's plenty of room for one more hand when you get back," Levi said.

"I'll be there." Cade nodded.

The dust from Levi's truck had barely settled when he noticed a movement in his peripheral vision. Turning that way, he watched Retta making her way toward the house with Beau in front of her and Hopalong bringing up the tail end of the parade. Mavis always said that you can't fool dogs or kids. If that was the truth, then Retta had definitely passed the test with flying colors when it came to the animals. When she reached the porch, she sat down on the bottom step, picked Hopalong up and kissed him right on the nose, and then scratched Beau's ears.

"You guys hold down the fort." She stood to her feet and turned toward Cade. "Do you know the girls' names that I'll be getting?"

"Not until they get here. We just know that there will be four boys and four girls and that Benjy is one of the boys." He opened the truck door for her. "Why did you ask?"

"I'm going to buy each of them a little welcoming gift. If I knew their names I'd be able to personalize it." She put her purse on the floor and fastened the seat belt.

*See there. If I was really interested in her, I would have taken care of that seat belt for her,* Cade thought.

"That's pretty nice of you," Cade said as he got into the truck. "But it's really not necessary."

"When my Sunday school class went on retreat, I always did this and it works two ways. It makes me feel good to do something for them and it shows them I'm interested in them," she said.

After only two days, he could already tell that Retta was an amazing woman. She fit in with Mavis and the guys. Beau and Hopalong loved her. And now she was buying presents for little girls that she hadn't even met. Maybe Levi and Justin were right—the chemistry between them might be more than fun flirting and a flash in the pan. But—and there always seemed to be one of those when he thought about relationships of any kind—if he was totally truthful, he wasn't over Julie. Sometimes he thought he was, but when just a simple memory of her carrying a quart of tea shot pain through his heart, then he had to be honest and admit that he had not completely moved on.

"Did you hate living in the country? Is that why you moved to the city?" He drove slower than usual so he'd have more time to talk to her.

"You wouldn't understand." She turned to look out the side window.

"Try me," he said.

"When you were in high school, what were your dreams?" she asked.

"I wanted to be a pro-football player. I got a scholarship to play for the Longhorns, and that set me on my way. The first couple of weeks were fine in the city, but then I got homesick for the strangest things. Like the sound of crickets and tree frogs, the smell of a roast in the oven. When I realized I'd rather be stretching barbed wire than throwin' a football down the field, I changed my dreams and my plans," he said.

"You been back to your class reunions?"

"Two." He nodded. "The five-year and then the ten-year a couple of years ago. Have you?"

She shook her head. "I got put down in high school. I was too tall, not thin enough, not pretty enough, not rich enough—you name it, and I fell short of the mark except when it came to playing girls' football. So I made up my mind that I was going to get a fancy job in the city and when I came back to Waurika for a class reunion..." She paused.

"That you'd show up in a low-slung sports car, wearing designer clothes, and show them all that you'd made it?" he asked.

"Something like that."

"But did you really love the city once you reached that goal?"

One shoulder popped up in half a shrug. "Liking or loving is a luxury. I threw myself into my work and didn't think about anything else."

"Then your dad got sick, right?" He parked at the tractor supply place but didn't make an attempt to get out.

"Yep, and I reassessed everything a dozen times. I knew from day one I'd lose the farm and accepted it. That meant I'd be going back to the city to work and I accepted that.

It's all in the mind-set, Cade. You do what you got to do for survival," she answered. "We'd better go get whatever you need for that tractor. What's the matter with it anyway?"

"The one I'll be working on needs a tune-up," he answered.

"I can help with that." She got out of the truck and was halfway across the parking lot before he caught up with her.

"Are you serious? You know how to work on tractors?"

"John Deere?"

He nodded. "That's right."

"I can do basic stuff like tune-ups."

The automatic doors swung open and he stepped to the side to let her go first. "I'd appreciate the help. When I get ready to work on it, I'll give you a call?"

"Sounds good."

He shouldn't compare because they were two different women with two different backgrounds and lifestyles. But Cade couldn't fathom Julie ever even going into a tractor supply store much less knowing where to go once she was inside or worse yet, getting her hands dirty working on a tractor.

# Chapter Five

Retta had bought four baskets filled with all kinds of things for bathtime—different colors and fragrances. She'd signed a card welcoming each girl to Longhorn Canyon Ranch and laid both on the dresser in each girl's room. She was glad she'd had the three days with Mavis and the guys and gotten acquainted with the ranch, but come morning she'd have four little girls who didn't know her or one another. Suddenly, she had a case of nerves. What if they didn't like her? What if they were hardened little girls who hated being part of a team?

Hoping that being outside would ease her jitters, she kicked off her boots and socks and wandered out to the porch. Beau had been lying on the top step, but when she opened the door, he rose to his feet, tail wagging, and came to meet her. She'd bent down to kiss him on the head when Cade's chuckle startled her.

"You spoil him," Cade said from the porch swing in the shadows.

"It's easy to do when he's so lovable," she said.

He patted the swing seat. "Join me. I was trying to make up my mind whether to knock on your door or not."

"Did you need something?" she asked.

"Just some conversation. I get nervous on the night before the kids get here," he said. "They always make life exciting on the ranch. Seeing things through the eyes of a child—well, it's not something so easy to explain. But I get to worrying about whether or not the experience will really be good for them, if they'll enjoy getting out of the city and living on a ranch."

"I'm jittery too. I loved working with my Sunday school girls. Some of them came from broken homes but they all lived right around Waurika. I just hope I've got what it takes to help these kids," she admitted.

"Just love 'em and let them come to you when they're ready. For the most part they're pretty tough and some of them haven't had a lot of affection or rules to live by."

The swing stopped so she kicked it off again with her foot. She drew her knees up to her chest and wrapped her arm around them. "My biggest failing is rushing in too fast with anything. If there's a problem, I think I have to fix it right now. Daddy always told me to sleep on things before I made a decision."

"Good advice," he said. "Want a beer? I brought a couple."

"Love one," she answered.

He picked up two bottles from beside the swing and handed one to her. "Nothing like a good cold beer on a hot night."

"Amen." She twisted the top off and took a long gulp.

"Daddy didn't like beer, but he did like a shot of good whiskey every now and then."

"Sounds like my mama. She turns up her nose at beer, but she does love Pappy Van Winkle or Jack Daniel's. That's the only two she'll have." He smiled.

Talk went from parents, to living in small communities, and the moon was sitting high in the sky when Cade pulled his phone from his pocket to check the time. "It's after midnight, Retta. I should be going." He stood up and wiggled the kinks from his shoulders.

"Thank you for taking my mind off things." She pushed out of the swing.

He took a step forward and she did the same. So sure that he was about to go beyond just staring into her eyes and kiss her, she moistened her lips with the tip of her tongue. But then he blinked and the moment was gone.

"Thank you for the same thing. See you in the morning." He spun around and was off the porch before she could answer.

"Dammit!" she muttered. "I shouldn't even think of kissing the boss, but I wanted to so bad."

\* \* \*

Cade opened the top drawer in his dresser, took out a small black velvet box, and flipped it open. The diamonds still sparkled in both the engagement ring that Julie had worn all that time and the matching wedding band that had never been on her finger.

He sat down on the edge of the bed and remembered the day he'd proposed. They'd gone to dinner at a fancy restaurant in Dallas and when the waitress brought out Julie's favorite dessert—a thick slice of turtle cheesecake—the ring was lying on the top. He'd dropped down on one knee and proposed and she'd said yes without a moment's hesitation.

Two years later, on their wedding day, the ring came back to him, and his heart was broken. He remembered the humiliation of having to tell all the guests who arrived for the wedding that it was off. He snapped the box shut and moved it and the note that he'd never read again into the bottom drawer. Someday maybe he could get rid of both of them. Right then, it was a baby step in the right direction just relocating them to a different place.

Even though it was late, he wasn't sleepy, so he headed down the hallway toward the kitchen. Surprised to see a light on, he peeked around the doorjamb to see Justin sitting at the table with a glass of warm milk.

"Come on in. Peanut butter is in the cabinet if you're hungry. You were down at the girls' bunkhouse pretty late," Justin said.

"Yes, I was." Cade set about making a PB&J sandwich and pouring a glass of milk for himself. "Want me to top off your glass?" he asked Justin.

"No, I've had enough. You've been spending a lot of time with her," Justin said.

"Yes, I have," Cade answered. "We talked. Not that it's any of your business but there was no hand holding, kissing, or sex."

"I didn't ask." Justin grinned. "She's a pretty woman and fits in right well with all of us. It's way past time for you to move on from Julie, brother. But until you do, it's not fair to lead Retta on."

"Not leadin' her on." He sat down at the table. "And I keep tellin' all of you that I'm over Julie. It's been two years."

"I might believe that someday, but not this one." Justin

pushed the chair back and carried his dirty dishes to the sink. "Good night. See you in a few hours. Don't be late to breakfast. You know that upsets Mavis."

Cade gave him a thumbs-up sign and mumbled, "Good night."

He'd wanted to kiss Retta but she wasn't a bar bunny and she'd just recently lost her father, her farm, and practically everything she owned. It wouldn't be fair to her to take advantage of her vulnerability.

"But, I wanted to hold her in my arms and feel her mouth on mine so bad," he whispered.

*         *         *

The sun was bright that morning when two vans came down the lane from the paved road, throwing a cloud of dust behind them. Retta shaded her eyes with her hand and could almost see the excitement bouncing around among everyone on the porch with her. It was like Christmas day when she was a little girl and her parents could hardly wait for her to open her presents.

The door slid open on the first van and a lanky, red-haired kid got out first. His eyes darted around, taking in the area. Finally, a half smile broke out when he saw Beau. The dog ran toward him and the boy dropped down on his knees to hug the animal.

"Hello, Benjy," Mavis called out.

He ducked his head and cut his eyes up at her. "Hi, Mavis."

Retta stepped off the porch. "I'm Retta. You are quite an artist."

"Thank you." He rose to his feet and with Beau right beside him, slowly made his way up the porch steps. "Hi,

Skip. The sun is shining and it's a hot day. It'd be a good day to bale hay."

"Yes, it is, son. We like it when the sun shines, don't we?"

Benjy nodded, serious. "I'm hungry. The stomach growls when it needs food and I didn't eat breakfast, which is the most important meal of the day. Kirk is mean and I don't like him."

Skip smiled down at the boy. "Then why don't we all go inside and have a snack. Mavis has made some real good muffins. She's got blueberry and chocolate chip."

"I don't like blueberries. They look like ticks on dogs. I saw that on the Discovery Channel and read about it in a biology book. Chocolate is better." Benjy opened the door and went inside.

Cade whispered to Retta, "He'll be sitting at the table when we get there with his hands folded in his lap."

Three more boys scrambled out of the van in a hurry but then stopped to try to take in the whole place with eyes as big as saucers.

Skip motioned them inside. "Hey, all you guys, just stow your stuff here on the porch. We'll have a snack before we take it to the bunkhouse."

Retta's pulse kicked up a little as she waited for the next van to park. The first person out was a short lady with long brown hair. She wore a cute little suit and serviceable heels. When she opened the back door four girls piled out and, like the boys had done, tried to take in the surroundings with a single glance.

Cade left the porch and stood in front of the three other boys and the four girls. "Welcome to Longhorn Canyon. This is my brother, Justin, right here." Cade pointed to his left and then to his right. "And Levi, our friend and foreman.

They will unload your things onto the porch so these good drivers can be on their way. While they do that we'll all go inside for a morning snack and get acquainted. So follow me and I'll show you to the dining room."

Levi and Justin stood to one side as they filed in with Cade leading the way, and then they hurriedly moved the kids' sacks, suitcases, and duffel bags to the porch.

"Aren't the drivers coming inside?" Retta asked Skip.

"No, they're on the clock. We hire the two cars to pick them up at the Department of Human Services in Dallas and drive them here. Right now we'd best get on in the dining room so we can put names to all these new faces," he said.

When Retta and Skip reached the dining room, the kids were standing back, girls huddled together in one area and the boys in the other. The only one that seemed even semi-comfortable was Benjy, and he was sitting there like a little statue, looking straight ahead.

Cade sat down beside him. "So you think it's a good day to bale hay, Benjy?"

"A small square hay bale weighs about fifty pounds. Kirk is mean."

"Why do you say that?"

Benjy turned his head toward Cade but kept his eyes on the boy who was standing with his arms crossed over his chest. "That's the weight of a bale on this ranch. Some can weigh a hundred pounds but I can't lift that much. Kirk says I'm an idiot but my granny says I'm smart."

"You are weird," Kirk said.

Skip clamped a hand on Kirk's shoulder. "You could learn a lot from Benjy if you just listen to him."

"Yeah, right." The kid shrugged off Skip's hand and swaggered toward the table in jeans that were a couple of inches too short and shoes that slipped up and down on his heels.

Justin and Levi arrived as Mavis was putting two plates of muffins in the middle of the table. Skip brought in two pitchers of milk and put one on either end and then went back for a bowl of fresh fruit.

Mavis followed him and brought out a tray of sliced cheese and crackers. "Now boys on that side with Skip and Levi. Girls on this side with me and Retta. And Cade and Justin will have the end chairs. You'll see a little card in front of the chairs where you are supposed to sit."

"And that's the way we'll sit every time we come to this table," Cade said.

The girls moved slowly toward the table and found their places. Retta sat down in the place that put her next to Cade. Justin took the other end with Benjy next to him. Levi sat down next to two of the other boys. That left Skip and Kirk between him and Cade.

"Thank you for not letting Kirk sit beside me," Benjy said.

"I didn't want to sit by you," Kirk smarted off.

Benjy didn't even look his way. "Where is Gussie? I didn't see her or Hard Times."

"They're around," Levi said. "When they hear that you are here, they'll be comin' to see you for sure."

"Okay, remember where you are right now," Cade said. "We won't keep the name cards except today."

"We've got a lot planned for you while you are here and we want you to have a good time," Justin said.

"This is a real ranch and we'll be doing some work and having a lot of fun," Levi chimed in.

"And I'll be staying with you boys in the bunkhouse," Skip said.

"I want an apple, please," Benjy said. "You need to plant an apple tree. Apples have vitamin C and no cholesterol."

Cade reached and got a shiny one from the top of the bowl and handed it to Benjy. "I'd like it if you gave me a picture of the bunkhouse. I'll frame it and put it on the wall with the others."

Benjy nodded. "Thank you. Oranges have more vitamin C, but they are messy."

"He really does remember everything he reads," Retta whispered to Cade.

"Yep." He nodded. "Retta is going to start the introductions. Please stand up and tell us your age, name, and anything else you'd like us to know."

Retta pushed back her chair and stood to her feet. "My name is Retta and I'm the supervisor for you girls, and the lady who made these wonderful muffins is Mavis. Now it's your turn to tell us your names, starting right here." She pointed at the little girl next to her.

"I'm Faith. I'm eleven and that's all any of you need to know about me," she said with a hard look at Retta. Purple streaks in her blond hair, blue eyes that flashed more than a little anger, and the tattoo of a heart on her shoulder. Retta could already tell that she'd be the one who would require watching.

"Gabby, and I'm eleven, too," the next one said. She was dark haired and looked Hispanic, with big brown eyes and cute little dimples when she smiled nervously.

"Alice, and I'm ten." The third one's voice was barely above a whisper. Freckles across her nose. Light brown hair in braids and green eyes.

"Sasha, and I'm twelve." The last one looked like she might break into tears. Cute little thing with red hair that kinked all over her head. Retta was not looking forward to helping her take care of that.

"Boys?" Justin said.

Benjy's eyes went to Cade, who nodded at him.

"I am Benjy and I'm twelve. I like coming to this ranch and my granny told me to be a good boy and I will." He pronounced each word distinctly.

He was average height for a twelve-year-old boy and built on a fairly slim frame. Retta saw shyness and wished that she could do something, anything, to help him.

"I'm Nelson. I'm ten." He had blond hair, green eyes, and a fair complexion that would burn in the sun.

"Ivan and I'm ten, too." Mixed race with that kinky black hair and dark brown eyes.

"Kirk and I'm eleven." He almost growled. Brown hair cut short and hazel eyes that looked like they could cut steel with a glance.

Retta memorized their names. According to her former employer, the ability to learn names so fast was a gift, but in truth her father had taught her the art when she was a little girl. Thinking of him being young and strong brought about a fresh lump in her throat.

"Okay, now that we know everyone, Justin, you can start that plate of chocolate chip muffins around the table, and, Skip, you can take care of the cheese and crackers. I expect that Cade can reach the fruit bowl easiest," Mavis bossed. "And for all you kids' information, Skip is my husband and we've been part of this ranch for more than fifty years."

"We'll have break time every morning," Cade said. "We'll meet right here or if we're out too far on the ranch to get back, we'll take a snack with us. Today you have the rest of the morning to get your gear stowed away in your rooms, and after lunch we'll begin to learn about workin' together as a team."

"I don't give a damn about cows and pigs." Faith crossed her arms over her chest. "I'll just stay in my room."

"Did you read the paper that you signed?" Cade asked.

Her eyes cut around toward him in defiance. "No, I didn't have a choice anyway. It was this or juvie hall for the whole summer."

"Well, the document said that you will obey orders, do what you are told, and be a team player, so that's exactly what you will do or you can go back to juvie right now," he said.

Cade's tone wasn't cold but it left no room for wiggling. He stared right into Faith's eyes and said, "Your choice, but you have to make it now. If you decide to stay with us, you will do whatever the rest of us are doing. You will participate in the events and the work."

Her chin dropped to her chest. "I'll stay, but I don't have to like it."

"No, you do not," Retta said. "But you might learn to like it if you give it a chance. Now I see the muffins are coming your way. Don't take all of them. I'm next in line and chocolate is my weakness."

*       *       *

Cade appreciated Retta taking the initiative. That let her girls know that she wasn't going to back down from them and that she would uphold what he called house rules. He took the plate from her hand, took off two, and passed it on.

"I'm a sucker for chocolate too, and I'll get you a copy of what each kid signed before they came here. The social workers who chose the kids explained it to them in full," he whispered.

"Appreciate it," she said.

Yes, sir, he'd sure hired the right woman for the job, all right.

At the end of the break there wasn't a crumb or a piece of fruit left. Cade wouldn't be a bit surprised if a few apples and oranges had been hidden away in their pockets. That wasn't at all unusual for the first few days, but then as time went on, they'd begin to see that there wouldn't be a time when they would go hungry, and hiding food would stop.

"Okay, ladies." Retta stood up. "Break time is finished. Now let's go down to our cabin and get our things put away. After that is a hay wagon for a tour of the ranch."

"Whoopee," Faith said sarcastically.

"I give demerits for bad behavior. When you get ten you get extra cleanup duty. That little remark is your warning. Next time it's a demerit, so suck it up, lady, and make up your mind to enjoy being here," Retta said.

The girl opened her mouth but snapped it shut without saying a word when Retta held up her forefinger.

"Do you do that too, old man?" Kirk sneered at Skip.

"Nope. If you sass me or act out, I take you out to the back woods, give you a pocketknife and let you find your way home. The knife is to use to catch your food and cut kindlin' with so you can eat it cooked and not raw. And from now on, that's yes sir and no sir, not old man," Skip said.

Kirk glared at him.

Skip removed a knife from his pocket and held it out.

"Yes, sir," he said coldly.

"Okay, then, guys, we've got work to do before we come back here for some of my wife's smothered steak and mashed potatoes at noon. And you'd better eat good because the hay ride will take a while." Skip put the knife back in his pocket and winked at Cade.

There was always one rotten apple in the barrel at first. But without exception so far, they'd managed to turn that bad one into a good kid by the time they all went home in July. However, it was usually only one surly kid they had to contend with, not two, so this year might be a challenge.

"She's proving her salt," Levi said when they were all gone.

"Yep," Cade said.

"But I can see the way you look at her."

"I'm a big boy and I can take care of myself," Cade shot back as he grabbed his hat and headed out the back door.

He started down to the boys' bunkhouse but kept walking when he got there. Skip needed to establish his role, and if Cade stepped in to help, it could undermine his authority. This wasn't a boot camp for errant kids, but getting things running smoothly always took a few days. To do that both Skip and Retta needed their own methods and time.

\*     \*     \*

The girls had barely gotten inside the cabin when Gabby picked up a plastic bag and Faith, most likely with a bad taste still in her mouth from being called down, started yelling.

"That's my stuff and you don't touch it," she screeched.

"It's my bag because I tied all mine with a pink ribbon and you don't have any right to holler at me." Gabby bowed right up to her.

Alice and Sasha cowered in the corner of the room, evidently afraid to touch any of the baggage in the middle of the room.

Retta stepped between them. "Take the ribbon off the bag and dump it on the sofa."

Gabby carefully untied the narrow ribbon and shoved it into her pocket. "See, it's all my stuff. Shirts, bras, and panties that my foster mother put in there for me."

Faith picked up another bag, made a big, dramatic production of showing Retta that it didn't have a pink ribbon on it and said, "I'm not bunking in the same room with her."

"You would if we had bunk beds but as it is, you each get your own room. You do have to share a bathroom, and it will be for showers or using the toilet. You have a small sink and mirror in each of your rooms to brush your teeth and primp by," she said.

"You mean we get our very own bedroom?" Sasha asked.

"Exactly." Retta had planned on letting them choose their rooms even though they were all alike but she changed her mind. "Faith, you get that one." She pointed. "Sasha is next to her, then Alice and then Gabby."

"And whose is that one?" Faith pointed to the last door.

"Mine," Retta said. "Now get what belongs to you and get it taken care of. I want underwear, bathing suits, and everything that isn't supposed to be on a hanger folded neatly and put into drawers. Anything that needs hanging up should be neat and not sloppy. I'll have a room check every day for the first week before we go to breakfast. Beds will be made and the room in order."

"This is like prison," Faith muttered.

"No, darlin'." Retta giggled. "The food is better and you get more than an hour a day in the sunshine. And you get a nice bed instead of a cot in your own private room rather than sharing it with someone else."

"Yeah," Gabby said. "So stop your bitchin'."

"Cussin' gets demerits," Retta warned.

"Sorry about that, but I've been waitin' for weeks to get

to come here. I ain't never been out of Dallas and I'm not goin' to let her ruin it for me," Gabby declared.

She watched as they carried their baggage to their rooms and then went out on the porch to catch a breath of fresh air. This wasn't like any leadership conference she'd ever held and she'd never had a Faith in her Sunday school classes.

"Got 'em unpackin'?" Cade asked as he sat down on the porch steps.

Retta nodded. "I already settled argument number one."

"I heard some pretty loud yellin' when I passed by a while ago." He chuckled. "They just think they're tough. We know we are."

"I'm not so sure I've got enough tough in me," she whispered.

"Then bluff and never let them know. Little bit of advice. Take the two that square off to argue and fight the most and put them together when you need a two-person team for events."

Retta's eyes felt like they might pop right out of her head. "Are you kiddin' me? I put Gabby and Faith as far apart as I could when I assigned rooms. They'd scratch each other's eyes out if I paired them up."

"Give it a try. Make them depend on each other. Better get back to the house. I've got a little paperwork to do in the office before Mavis calls dinner. I stopped by to tell you that everyone has to be in the living room thirty minutes before dinner today for a little group session. I ask them each to tell me something about themselves kind of like an ice breaker. Today it'll be what part of Dallas they're from and who they lived with," he said. "See you at noon."

"How often do you do the group thing?" she asked as he was walking away.

He turned around and smiled. "Whenever I think we need it."

She marched back into the bunkhouse. "Hey, you girls come on out here in the living room when you finish."

Alice poked her head out of her door. "Why? Did we do something wrong?"

"No, darlin', you didn't. I just wanted to get to know each of you a little better and thought maybe we could have a visit."

Alice came out of the room and sat down in a recliner. "Is that basket of stuff on my dresser really for me? I can open it up and use it?"

"Yes, it is. I chose a different color for each of you so you wouldn't get things mixed up," Retta answered.

Gabby came out next. "Thank you for the basket and that note. I'll keep it forever. I still can't believe that I get my very own room."

The other two joined them and stood in the middle of the floor. They eyed the sofa but none of them took a seat on it. Fear? Stubbornness?

Retta pointed to the end of the sofa. "That's your spot for our group visits, Faith. Gabby, you sit in the middle, and Sasha can have the other end."

"I'm not sitting beside that . . ." Faith's mouth was pursed to say bitch but she stopped.

Gabby moved to the sofa and plopped down in the middle. "She's afraid of me, Retta."

"I'm not afraid of anything." Faith quickly sat down but moved to the corner so that she wouldn't touch Gabby.

Sasha shyly eased down on the other end. "I love my room and purple is my favorite color. Did you know that when you got the basket for me?"

"No, I didn't but I'm glad that I chose it," Retta said. "Alice says she's happy to have her own room. I want each of you to tell me if you share a room at your house."

Alice nodded. "I share with three sisters."

"Share, he...heck," Faith stammered over the cuss word. "I sleep on the sofa in the foster home where I stay."

Sasha went next. "I share with my sister. She's sixteen but we got a baby bed in our room too, because she's pregnant. Mama says she can't marry her boyfriend because they're too young."

"Gabby?" Retta asked.

"I sleep on the sofa like Faith does. Me and Mama only got a one-room place with a twin bed," she answered.

"So are you going to like having your own space?" Retta asked.

"It's like heaven. I already wish I never had to leave," Gabby answered.

One child wanted to stay on the ranch forever. Retta looked forward to maybe getting her old job back in the city. It was a crazy world for sure.

# Chapter Six

Cade needed to get a new tire on the tractor before the hayride with the kids that afternoon. Seeing the ranch for the first time through the eyes of the kids was an experience that he loved, but when he went to hitch the wagon up to the tractor, he'd discovered a flat tire.

If Retta hadn't been busy with the girls he might have called her to help him. The whole attraction he felt for the woman was a lot like the kids who came there for a few weeks. They arrived, had a good time, and went home. Anything that would develop between him and Retta could be just like that—have a good time and then wave good-bye the day after July Fourth.

They both knew what they wanted, and their paths were as far removed from each other as Longhorn Canyon and the moon. He was thinking about that almost-kiss when the wrench slipped, splitting the skin on one of his knuckles and making him swear loud enough that it almost blistered the paint off the side of the old tractor.

He quickly wrapped his hand in a handkerchief and hurried back to the tack room where he ran cold water over it. A little cleaning with hydrogen peroxide and some antibiotic ointment and a Band-Aid fixed it right up. Levi was leaning on the side of the tractor when he returned.

"I heard that yellin' all the way out in the yard. My poor little donkey don't know whether he's welcome in this barn or not," Levi said.

Cade held up his hand and growled. "Donkey can't take a little cussin', he's comin' to the wrong ranch. So you brought him home, did you?"

"Yep, I did, and the kids are goin' to love him. It's goin' to be an interestin' summer," Levi said. "You think Benjy is better or worse than he was last year?"

"Too early to tell. Help me get this tire on and the wagon hitched and I'll give you a ride back to the house," Cade said.

"You got it." Levi pushed his cowboy hat back on his head and shoved his hands down into a pair of work gloves.

When the job was done, they drove across the pasture to the house in the old truck. They barely had time to wash up before it was time to sit down to the table. Skip said grace and immediately after the last amen, Benjy took a hot roll from the platter in front of him and bit into it.

"Yes, Mavis. Just like I remembered. Sugar mixes with yeast and that makes carbon dioxide and that makes the dough rise," he said.

"Thank you, Benjy." She smiled.

"How do you know all that stuff you know?" Alice asked.

"I read books," he answered.

"You smell like tractors, Cade," Benjy said.

"I've been workin' on one all mornin'," Cade told him.

"Will you teach me to do that?" Gabby asked.

"Why would you want to do something stupid like learn about tractors?" Faith popped off.

"If I know how a motor works then I'll be able to fix my mama's car so she don't have to walk to work every morning," Gabby answered.

"Sounds like a smart girl to me. I wish I would have made my daddy teach me about cars," Mavis said.

"I'm glad he didn't." Skip chuckled. "If you'd known anything about cars, you might've left this old cowboy that first year we were married."

"You got that right." Mavis nodded.

Faith cocked her head to one side and frowned. "So y'all had some arguments?"

"Honey, marriage is a partnership and sometimes it takes a while to get all the whats, hows, wheres, and all the rest ironed out," Mavis answered. "It's teamwork like you kids are going to learn while you are here."

Cade forked a steak onto his plate. "Anyone who is interested can come to the barn next time I work on a tractor." Being surrounded by kids would sure enough curtail any bad language.

"And those that don't want to do that can help me fix fences," Justin said.

Benjy raised his hand. "I will help Justin. One post every twenty feet for barbed wire fence with two spacers in between and a wood post every fourth one so the fence don't sag."

"You really are smart," Gabby said.

Benjy ducked his head and set about eating his steak, laying his fork and knife down between bites and wiping his mouth with his napkin.

"I've got a pasture full of small bales of hay that need brought in..." Levi started.

"Slave labor," Kirk smarted off.

"No, it's not," Skip said. "And you best get that kind of thinkin' out of your head, son. Anyone who wants to do a little farmwork in their free time will be fairly compensated."

"You mean we get paid if we work?" Faith asked.

"Sure you do," Mavis answered.

\* \* \*

Cade passed out straw hats to everyone as they filed out to get on the hay wagon, and Retta was more than glad to settle her new straw hat on her head. It didn't feel as good as the one she'd left behind at the farm but with sweat and time it would shape up and fit right well.

"I like my hat. It's like Cade's." Benjy plopped the one with his name on the inside down on his head.

"Me too." Alice crammed hers down on her braids. "Do we get to come back next year?"

"I need to draw the wagon. Some hay wagons have wood wheels." Benjy walked away and chose a seat at the back of the wagon.

"Once you turn thirteen, you don't get to come back," Retta explained in a low voice.

"I'm only ten so that means I might get to do this again." She beamed as she skipped down the porch steps.

The tires on the old wooden wagon made the ride a little less bumpy. But the wagon itself was the same as she'd been in dozens of times as a kid. Open air, benches on two sides, and hay strewn on the floor. She spotted a cooler at the back and figured that it was full of either water bottles or cold drinks.

She sat down beside Alice, and Sasha quickly sat on the other side of her, which meant again that Gabby and Faith had no choice but to sit together. Maybe Cade was right about making them learn teamwork.

Skip pointed toward the pasture where Levi was baling hay. "This is a self-supporting ranch as much as possible. We grow our own hay for the cattle in the winter."

Retta listened with one ear but if she leaned far enough to one side, she could see Cade's face reflected in the side mirror on the tractor pulling the wagon.

"Those are some whompin' big hunks of hay to be picking up," Faith said.

Retta quickly jerked her head back. "Those will stay in the field. They'll line them up against the far fence line and then bring them to the cattle as they are needed."

Skip nodded. "Look over in that field at those small bales. Those are the ones that we take into the barn. We don't make a lot of the little ones, but sometimes they're needed in the stalls if we've got a cow or a bull that has to be kept up for a while."

"I could get them bales to the barn," Nelson said.

"Yeah, right," Kirk smarted off.

"I can and if I do, then I make money to take home, right, Skip?" Nelson asked.

"That's right, and we can always use all the help we can get."

Retta could see dollar signs dancing in all of their little eyes as they thought about helping haul that hay to the barn the next day. When she looked at the mirror again, she caught Cade's eye and he winked at her, causing a blush so deep that she removed her hat and fanned with it.

"Little warm back there?" Cade called out.

"Hot as hell. That's what Levi says," Benjy said.

Nelson pointed a finger. "He cussed."

"He ain't smart enough to even know that he cussed," Kirk sneered.

Benjy turned his head and shut his eyes. "Kirk is an idiot. Statistics say that an idiot is someone with an IQ of less than twenty-five."

"I am not!" Kirk raised his voice. "And besides what's an IQ?"

"It's a number that shows how smart you are," Skip said.

"What's Benjy's number?" Kirk growled.

"Way higher than an idiot," Skip said.

"Then why don't he act like it?"

"He does," Alice said. "He's been tellin' us lots of things. You just need to listen to him."

Benjy's expression didn't change a bit but he did nod slightly.

"Now all of you look that way." Cade raised his voice and pointed behind the boys. "That's Justin and his crew puttin' up fences. We have to keep good fences up so we can control the pastures for the cattle. Do any of you know why we stagger the planting?"

No one answered.

"Benjy?" Cade asked.

"To give the cows good green grass all summer. When they eat what's in one pasture then it's all gone so they move them to another place."

"Smart answer, Benjy. Thank you," Cade said loudly.

"See, he's smarter than you are." Alice glared at Kirk.

"Yeah, did you see them pictures in the house that he drew? I bet you can't draw like that," Gabby said and turned toward Faith. "I can bring in more hay than you can."

"But not me. I'm strong." Kirk puffed out his chest.

"Bullsh...crap," Faith hissed. "I can outwork all of you if I want to."

Kirk stretched his foot out across the space separating the benches and touched her toe. "You're just a girl. I can do more than both of you put together."

"Yeah," Nelson agreed.

"Us girls will work together tomorrow," Sasha said. "And we'll show you that girls are just as tough as boys."

"Yes, we are." Gabby did a head wiggle that dared them to say anything else.

"When we get done, y'all girls will be whinin' like puppies with no mama," Kirk bragged.

"Well, y'all will be passed out colder'n a homeless drunk man down in the ghettos," Gabby said.

"Right," Sasha agreed.

"I can help," Benjy said.

Ivan barely nodded. "Me too. Me and Benjy will work together."

"Y'all can do that. I want to help Mavis in the kitchen and have food ready when y'all come in the house," Alice said.

Faith shrugged. "I'm going with Alice to the kitchen."

"No fair," Gabby said. "That means there's four boys and only two girls."

"You can have Benjy and Ivan, and me and Nelson will still beat y'all," Kirk said.

"Good. I don't want to work with you," Benjy said.

Skip chuckled and nodded at Retta. It didn't take much to read his mind. The hay ride had already begun to whip the kids into shape.

Retta glanced at the mirror but Cade had turned around slightly so she couldn't see his face. Then suddenly he made a wide turn, started back toward the house and yelled above the noise of the tractor engine. It was midafternoon when they got back and Retta's girls made a beeline for their bunkhouse where Gabby and Sasha plopped down on the sofa to figure out ways that they could work harder than the boys. Faith stormed off to her room and slammed the door. Alice picked out a book and carried it to her room but she didn't shut the door.

Retta moved out to the porch where Gussie was sprawled out on the top porch step with Hopalong right beside her. Beau came bounding around the corner but neither of them even opened an eye. She sat down in a chair and propped her feet up, and Beau sat down beside her. But then his ears perked up and he jumped over the cat and the rabbit and headed toward the house. That's when she saw Cade coming toward her with two bottles in his hands.

"Thought you might like a cold root beer," he said when he reached the porch. "It'd be even better if it was real beer, but..." He shrugged.

"Thank you. Can't be havin' what we can't let the kids have." She took it from him and ran the icy cold bottle over her forehead. "Settin' an example isn't always easy, and those are my dad's words, not mine."

"Wise man." Cade sat down on the shady side of the porch in one of the two rocking chairs. "Did you go back and visit often after you'd left home?"

"Every time school was out for holidays and all summer. He needed the help." She twisted the lid off and drank deeply. Cold soda pop and a hot cowboy sitting with her. It didn't get better than this. "Tastes pretty good on a hot day like this."

"It really does." He nodded. "Levi wants us to take the kids out to the barn after supper and let them see the new little donkey."

"Sounds good to me. Right now I've got two in there plotting against the boys, one who can't wait to get in the kitchen, and another one slammed the door to her bedroom. I hope she's reading." She eased down into the rocker, kicked off her boots, and propped her feet up on the railing.

"Faith will come around. She just needs time to find her calling," he said.

"You ever had one like her or like Kirk before this bunch?"

"Last year we had two girls and two boys who were complete hellions the first couple of weeks. Thought for sure I'd have to send them home, but they did a complete turnaround when they found their place. Guess who cried the most when it was time to go home?"

"Those four?"

"Yep. It just takes some of us a while to figure out what we really want," he said.

"And sometimes when we do figure it out we don't get it." She nodded.

"Want to explain?"

"I was going to get out of the rural life and make everyone sorry they'd treated me like they did. After that three-year battle with my dad, it seems like a silly goal," she answered.

"I understand. I left with one goal in mind—pro ball. Only it got changed when I figured out that my heart wanted to be a rancher no matter what my mind wanted. And that until I gave in and became what my heart wanted, I wasn't going to be really happy with anything or anyone," Cade told her.

"The heart will have what it wants for sure." She nodded in agreement.

He pushed up out of the chair with a groan. "That old tractor has got the worse ride of anything on the place."

She almost opened her mouth to say that she'd rub the aches from his body but caught herself. The vision that went with the thought flushed her already hot and sweaty cheeks. "It wasn't much better ridin' in the hay wagon."

"Life on the ranch, huh?"

"Yep."

"See you at supper."

"We'll be there with bright shiny faces and ready to eat, I'm sure. And thanks for the root beer." She grinned up at him. His dark lashes fluttered almost shut and she was sure that this time he would kiss her, but Alice yelled from the door and broke the moment.

"Hey, Retta, is it all right if we get into the refrigerator and get a cold soda pop?"

"Yes, it is," she answered.

When she looked up Cade was already several feet from the porch on his way back to the house. She fanned herself as she watched him all the way across the distance, but the heat wasn't all because of the hot weather.

# Chapter Seven

Cade laced his fingers behind his head on the pillow and stared at the ceiling of his bedroom. Clouds scooted across the full moon, leaving an array of designs, but his thoughts weren't on the flitting shadows above him. They were on the attraction he had for Retta. Finally he sighed and crammed a pillow over his eyes, but sleep was a long time coming that Friday night.

The alarm on his cell phone went off the next morning and he hit a button to snooze a little longer but when it sounded the second time he slung his legs over the side of the bed. After rolling his neck to get the kinks out, he headed to the bathroom only to find Justin standing outside the door.

"Levi beat us and Mavis has taken over the second bathroom while she's here," he said grumpily.

Levi opened the door and a fog of hot steam rushed out to meet them. "Looks like Justin is ahead of you this mornin'.

That's strange, since you're usually already in the kitchen by now. Havin' nightmares about them two kids who are so feisty or were you dreamin' about Retta and didn't want to wake up?"

"You two are crazy." Cade rushed into the bathroom, locked the door, and rubbed the fog from the mirror with a hand towel. The same cowboy was looking back at him like always. But there was something different there and if felt really good.

*     *     *

Cade was sitting on her porch that morning when Retta ventured outside before the sun was fully up. He was holding an empty cup.

"Want me to refill that? I just made a pot."

"Yes, ma'am." He held it out toward her.

A few minutes later she backed out of the screen door and handed his cup back to him. "So you're a morning person too?" she asked.

"Yep. Looks like you are too." He sipped the coffee. "Strong and black. Perfect."

"That's the only way to drink coffee, as far as I'm concerned. I'm used to getting up early. Daddy was always up before the sun. The work is never done on a farm, so I was up with him. I never could break the habit." She sat down beside him on the top porch step.

"I've got a question," she said. "I thought every minute of the days would be filled with activities like a summer camp."

"Nope, we like to let the kids kind of find their place and then go from there. There'll be fun things for them to do, but basically we like to build leadership and teams with a fairly flexible schedule. It takes a few days but they'll settle in."

"I'm a little worried about the Alice-and-Faith combination in the kitchen. Alice is so young and shy."

Cade sipped his coffee. "Alice might need a protector and Faith might need someone to protect. One day in the kitchen won't hurt them, and if they don't like working together then they can always change their minds."

"How about the boys?" she asked.

"Skip says that Kirk and Nelson are plotting against the girls. I'm a little worried about Benjy. He gets distracted easily. He may be helping with hay and then suddenly he'll decide he needs to read for a while," Cade said.

"The sun isn't shining. Where is Hard Times? Did you know that turtles can live for years?" Benjy rounded the house and joined them on the porch.

"He's probably hiding under a bush somewhere. I bet you get to see him before the summer is over, though. Are you ready to haul hay today?"

"Yes. Gabby is nice but I like Alice better. Did you ever read *Alice's Adventures in Wonderland*? That is a weird book. One time she's big like a giant and another time she's itty bitty. I wonder if that's possible. I'd like to be big like a giant someday but not today because if I was I might hurt Kirk and that wouldn't be nice." He turned around and crossed the lawn back to the boys' bunkhouse.

"Looks like he really doesn't like Kirk," Retta said.

"Hopefully by the end of the time they're here, things will change for both of them." Cade finished his coffee and stood up.

"How's that?" She followed his lead and stood to her feet.

"Kirk will learn to be less aggressive and Benjy will

learn to like him. Thanks for the coffee." He tucked his fist under her chin and brushed a sweet kiss across her lips.

"You're welcome."

"See you later." He turned around and whistled all the way back to the ranch house.

She touched her lips to see if they were as warm as they felt but they were surprisingly cool. "Well, I'll be damned. So all it took was a cup of coffee." She took a few steps off the porch to watch him until he was out of sight.

The grass was damp and cool on Retta's bare feet but it wouldn't be that way for long once the sun came out. That was one of the things she missed when she lived in the city—the feel of wet grass early in the morning, and the scent of freshly plowed dirt.

"And neither grass nor dirt was as good as that kiss," she whispered as she whipped around and went back inside the cabin.

Faith looked up with accusing eyes and asked, "You been out doin' Cade?"

"No and how do you even know that kind of language? You are twelve years old for goodness sake," Retta scolded.

"In my world that's old enough to know that kind of thing. And I see the way you look at him. Might as well go on and do him and see if it's any good." Faith shrugged.

Retta plopped down in one of the recliners. Lord have mercy! When she was twelve she hadn't even had a boyfriend yet. "I was on the porch with Cade. We had a cup of coffee together because we are both early risers. I see that you are too. So have you had sex?" Retta asked, bluntly.

"No, I'm waiting until I'm thirteen," Faith answered.

Retta was glad she was sitting down. "Don't you think that's a little young?"

"Nope. One of the girls in the foster home where I stay is thirteen and she's pregnant but I plan to get on the pill before I do it. I don't want no babies, not ever."

And this kid was going to be with Alice, who was only ten years old. Retta would take Mavis aside and talk to her so she could keep an eye on them.

"When did you give up your V-card?" Faith asked.

"What?"

"Virgin card," Faith answered.

"Not until I was in college and only then because I loved the guy," Retta answered honestly.

"Man, you must've been old-fashioned." Faith giggled.

"No, just brought up by a God-fearin' father."

"There ain't no God. If there was I'd have a mama who cared enough about me to not do drugs and get me put into the system when I was only five years old." She bounced up from the sofa. "Is it time for us to get dressed and go up to the house for breakfast?"

"You got your bedroom put in order?" Retta asked.

"Yep, did that first thing. I always get up early so I can watch the sun come up. It's the only quiet time I get in a house with so many kids in it," she said.

Retta nodded and started toward Alice's bedroom door, but it swung open and the little girl came out rubbing her eyes. Her brown hair was flying every which way. No wonder she wore braids. It was so curly that it would be hard to manage even in a ponytail.

"Good mornin'. Want me to braid your hair today?" Retta asked.

"Yes, please. My biggest sister fixes it for me every day before she goes to work. I'll get the brush." She ran back into the room and returned with it in her hand.

"So you like purple?" Retta asked as she carefully worked the tangles from Alice's hair.

"No, I like pink," Alice said. "Why would you think I like purple?"

"Your brush is purple," Retta answered as she parted her hair and whipped the strands into a French braid.

"Katy, that's one of my sisters; she let me borrow it," Alice whispered. "We have to share at my house but my other sister, Tamara, she got a new one and said she'd share with Gloria. That way I got to bring this with me."

Retta's eyes filled with tears but she blinked them back. "Well, that's mighty nice of Katy."

"She's my favorite. She works at McDonald's and sometimes she brings hamburgers home for us."

"How old is Katy?" Retta asked as she finished the second braid.

"She's seventeen and she goes to high school. Mama says that she has to graduate so she can get a good job. Katy says she's even goin' to college," Alice told her. "I want to learn to cook so I can get a job when I'm old enough."

"What does your mama do?"

"She works in a factory where they sew all day. She brings home scraps and I make doll clothes out of them. When I get all growed up, I'm going to make fancy clothes for models like you see on television."

Alice caught sight of her braids in a mirror hanging on the wall and squealed. "I love them. Can you do this every day? I'll even get up early if you will."

"Of course." Retta hugged her tightly.

She squirmed loose and ran back to her room. "I got to get dressed and make up my bed and brush my teeth. I hope Mavis likes my new braids."

Gabby and Sasha came out of their rooms, fully dressed, hair pulled up in ponytails and their hats settled on their heads. Their jeans were faded but clean and their tank tops hung on their slim bodies.

"I'd suggest you throw a lightweight shirt on over your tops or you'll both sunburn," Retta said.

"Good idea," Sasha said. "Kirk and Nelson wouldn't never let us hear the end of it if we got blistered. If they come out all without no shirts, let's don't tell them about sunburns."

Gabby put up a fist and Sasha touched hers to it in agreement.

"Okay, everyone ready for breakfast?"

"Yes!" Alice pumped her fist in the air. "And then I get to learn to cook. I really like that Mavis."

"I'll give this cookin' stuff one day and if I don't like it, I'll do something else," Faith muttered.

Alice cocked her head to one side. "Really?"

"Yes, really. You got a problem with that?" Faith looked down on the girl that barely came up to her shoulder.

"Not if you don't get in my way," Alice shot back at her.

Alice might be small but she had three older sisters and evidently she'd learned to be tough when she had to be. Faith might have bitten off more than she could chew. Question was, with Cade's kiss had Retta bitten off more than she could chew too?

# Chapter Eight

Cade was headfirst into the tractor with grease on his hands and face when he felt a presence behind him. He knew it was Retta before he even straightened up. Even before he'd ever kissed her, there was a little kick in his heart that told him when she was near. But since the kiss, it had deepened into a pretty hard thump in his chest.

Cade backed away, wiped his hands on a red cloth, and held it up. "See this?"

"Sure. It's a red shop rag," she answered.

"It's the color of OU football uniforms. That's what we think of that color. We use it to wipe grease off our hands," he teased.

"In Oklahoma shop rags are orange," she shot back at him.

He laughed out loud. "So you ready to get your hands dirty?"

"Can I see the donkey first?" she asked.

"Not unless you want to walk over to the other barn where the stalls and corrals are. This is basically the tractor barn with only a few bales of hay for Gussie to keep her kittens in. Want a bottle of water? I'm ready for a break."

"Sure." She nodded. "I'll get them. Tack room?"

He leaned forward so he could watch her all the way back down the center aisle. Her butt filled out those faded jeans really well. She'd tied the tail of a chambray T-shirt in a knot in the front so it accentuated her small waist and even left a tiny bit of back skin showing. She wore those cowboy boots and the straw hat with ease and she even knew what a tack room was and where it was located. That woman was a rancher. She might not know it yet, but the time would come when what was in her blood and her heart would win over what she thought she wanted.

She returned with a couple of bottles of icy cold water and handed one off to him. "Nice tack room. Saw a bunch of well-maintained saddles. You got horses?"

"Just a few old guys we put out to pasture. I keep them for the kids. Did you have horses?" He twisted the cap off the bottle and took a long drink.

She did the same. "Couple of gentle old mares for me to ride when I was a kid. Daddy got rid of them when I went to college."

"Dogs or any other pets?"

"Daddy's old cattle dog died a week before he did. I buried him behind the barn and covered the grave with stones. Then I took Daddy out there in his wheelchair—God, he hated that thing but he wanted to see where Rusty was buried. We both cried so hard that our eyes were swollen when we got back to the house." She paused and took a deep breath, as if centering herself to keep from weeping again.

He could visualize the picture that she'd painted so well that it put a lump in his throat.

"How can I help with this job?" she asked. "I'm at loose ends, with my girls either in the hay field or the kitchen."

He swallowed hard before he answered. "You can hand tools to me so I don't keep hitting my head when I raise up to get them. I'll be the surgeon if you'll be the nurse who takes care of the equipment." He finished up the water and threw the bottle like a football toward a trash can. "Touchdown!"

"Oh, no. You don't get to throw the ball over the goal line, you have to run it or kick it, like this." She laid her empty bottle on the floor, took two steps back, and shook the kinks from her shoulders and then expertly kicked the thing right over the top of the trash can.

Cade bent forward and made the referee's sign that meant "no good."

She bowed up to him, nose to nose. "That cleared the top of the goalposts and sailed right smack through the middle. It was good for three points, so now I'm ahead in this game. It's not my fault that you thought you were playin' basketball and threw the ball over the goal rather than carried it."

"Are we keeping score until July Fourth?"

"Sure, and right now you are down by one," she told him. "Now let's get this operation over with so you'll have a spare tractor when you need it."

The air in the barn reminded Cade of the feel just before a tornado or a bad storm rolled over north central Texas. It was something felt, not seen, and words couldn't begin to describe it.

"I guess you helped your dad with tractors?"

"If it's a John Deere, I can tear one down and put it back together with my eyes closed. Since Daddy thought that someday I'd inherit the farm, he made sure I knew a spark plug from a distributor cap. But if you want to play surgeon, I'm glad to hand you whatever you need."

He bent over the engine. "Crescent wrench."

She slapped it into his open hand.

Man it was great to be working with a woman who knew the difference between a screwdriver and a torque wrench. "I guess you can do about anything when it comes to ranchin'."

"Yep," she answered.

Her head was so close to his that when she moved, her hair tickled his cheek. He had to think of something other than that kiss and the heat between them. Baseball—that would do just fine.

"I thought the boys might like a baseball game this afternoon."

"Count us girls in. It'll be fun." Her warm breath on his neck put a little pressure behind his zipper.

He nudged her on the shoulder and the sparks flitted around even more. "We don't want to encourage too much competition between the sexes because that doesn't make for good teamwork, but we could make a little side bet that no one knows about."

"Oh, yeah! What are we betting?"

"If the boys win, you get to name your prize. If the girls win, you can join me and my family in October in our private box at the OU-Texas game."

She stuck out her hand. "You are on, cowboy, but that's taking a big risk. You realize I'll be rooting for Oklahoma right there in the midst of all you Texas fans."

"I'm not planning on losing." He shook with her and wished he didn't have to let go of her hand.

"Now let's work together. I'll get the plugs in and you torque them."

When they finished, she rubbed her hand on the seat of her jeans and headed for the tack room.

"You're goin' the wrong way," Cade called out.

"I'm goin' to wash up in the tack room. I don't want Mavis yellin' at me for gettin' either the kitchen or the bathroom sink all greasy." She threw the words over her shoulder and kept going.

Sounded like a good idea to him so he followed her. The sink was full and her arms were lathered to the elbows when he arrived. She stepped to one side and he sunk his hands into the warm water. He picked up the bar of soap and started to work on his hands and arms.

"Do I have dirt on my face?" she asked him.

With soapy hands, he reached for a paper towel and wet it. "A little on your nose and some under your pretty brown eyes on both sides where you've wiped sweat away." He gently cleaned it away and then took her chin in his wet hand, turning her face both ways to make sure it was all gone.

Her eyes locked with his for a few seconds before hers fluttered shut. He bent slightly, and their lips met in a fiery kiss that obliterated the rest of the world, leaving them as the only two people left in the universe. Her arms snaked up around his neck and his went around her waist to draw her closer to his body.

When he tried to pull away, she tangled her fingers in his hair and deepened the kiss even further. Finally, with a groan from both of them, they took a step back.

"We'll be in trouble if we aren't at the house in exactly five minutes." She pointed at the clock hanging on the wall.

"That thing is always fast." He dried his hands and put his hands on her shoulders.

She looked up at him and he brushed a sweet, gentle kiss

across her lips. "I'm just glad you didn't put your wet hands on my chest. Now that would have been hard to explain."

With a giggle, she jerked the tail of her T-shirt around and checked the back to see if his handprints were there.

"Nothing but a wet streak." He tucked her hand in his. "We'd better get going."

He'd rather stay right there in the tack room all day and make out with her like they were a couple of teenagers. He felt as if he'd only gotten a tiny taste of a sweet dessert and he wanted more.

# Chapter Nine

Two girls with clean faces but with bits of hay sticking out of their hair took their places at the table at noon that Saturday. Sitting with them were two other girls with flour in their hair, and Faith was actually smiling.

"I set the table," she said proudly. "Mavis showed me how to do it. And me and Alice made the chocolate cake for dessert."

"Well, our team won in the hay field," Gabby said.

"Did not!" Kirk declared from across the table.

"It was a close tie," Levi said. "The girls were ahead all day but the boys rallied at the end and they helped get the exact same number of bales from the field to the barn."

Cade caught Retta's eye and sent a sly wink her way.

*He's flirting with you,* her friend, Tina's voice was in her head. *Flirt back and have a good time. You'll be chained to that job in the city soon enough.*

*But anything we would start would have a big stop sign at the end of this job,* Retta argued.

*Hey, it doesn't have to be a commitment or a relationship. Maybe you both just need a little fun to let off some steam and then you can say good-bye when the job is over like a couple of adults. No tears. No long-distance crap. Just a summer fling.*

"And our team finished tuning up a tractor. Who won? Me or you?" Cade's warm breath sent tingles chasing down Retta's spine when he whispered in her ear.

"It was definitely a tie but there's a smudge of grease on your ear," she said.

"You could return the favor and wipe it off for me." His blue eyes glittered.

"What are y'all whisperin' about?" Faith asked.

"I was tellin' him that he didn't check his ears when he cleaned up for dinner."

Faith leaned forward and nodded. "But you got some in your ear too."

"Guess we both better find us a mirror after we eat." Cade grinned.

"Or put one in the tack room," she muttered.

"Not happenin'." He handed her a platter of hot rolls.

Flirt with Cade? A summer fling? It all sounded good, but the warning sirens were going off loudly in her head.

*If you start something, finish it. Every choice you make has consequences.* That was her father's advice. She'd made the choice to leave the farm and pursue her plan. It had its consequences for sure because she missed her dad.

*So if I don't start anything, will I regret it later? And if I do, what would the consequences be?* She mulled over that as she dipped two spoons full of green beans onto her plate.

"I heard that there might be a baseball game this afternoon for anyone who's interested," Skip said from across the table.

Four boys' forks went down and their hands went up.

Retta glanced down her side of the table. "You girls want to play?"

"Only if we can have Benjy on mine and Sasha's team," Gabby said.

Benjy looked right at her with a shy smile. "I can run fast."

"I know you can," Sasha said. "You can load hay better than anyone."

He ducked his head but the smile didn't fade.

"Then we get Faith," Kirk piped up from across the table.

"I ain't goin' to get on your team if Alice can't be on it," Faith declared.

"Oh, all right." Nelson sighed.

"We want Ivan too," Gabby said.

"Looks like we got us two teams." Skip grinned. "I'll be the umpire. Cade you've got the team with Kirk, and Retta, you can have the one with Benjy."

Benjy cut his eyes around at her. "If a ball is going sixty miles an hour and you hit it at the right angle, it will go way far out into the pasture and you can make a home run. You are tall and I bet you can do that. I could draw you with a bat in your hands."

"Thank you, Benjy." She smiled at the boy and then whispered to Cade, "What does that mean?"

"That he likes you. If I could, I would draw you." His knee pressed against hers under the table and she pushed back. She might not have had much time for dating over the past three years, but if he wanted to flirt she sure didn't have to get out a how-to book.

\*       \*       \*

After lunch, she and her team started for the pasture where Levi and Skip were measuring out a place to put the bases. They hadn't gone far when Cade and his team caught up to them. The kids ran on ahead, leaving them behind.

"Guess it's not boys against girls after all," he said.

"I've got a good team and you've got a cocky one. Good beats cocky every time," she said.

"Sounds like your team has a cocky coach. Maybe mine has a good coach," he said.

"When my team beats yours, you may not want to draw my picture." She slung a hip against his. In all the responsibility of the past three years she'd forgotten how much fun it was to simply flirt with a guy. Or share a few kisses with one, either.

The bases were laid out. It was decided that Cade and Retta would serve as catchers. Retta's team lost the coin toss, so Cade was first up to bat. Gabby was the pitcher, Sasha was on first, Ivan on second, and Benjy on third base.

Cade was first up to bat and Gabby wound up a fastball that whizzed past the tip of his bat. "Holy hell," he swore under his breath.

"Weren't you the one who said they were street-smart and tough?" Retta said from behind the catcher's glove.

The next time he was ready and managed to get a pop-up that Sasha missed and landed him on first base. Then it was Kirk's turn, and Gabby gave it her best. He hit the ball high and Cade took off for second base, but Benjy's hand shot up and caught the ball, so Kirk was out and Cade had to return to first.

Kirk kicked the dirt and went back to the area they'd decided would be the batter's box. "He's not supposed to be able to do that."

"Never judge a book by the cover," Retta told him.

There was no score by the time Retta's team came to bat. Kirk wound up dramatically and threw the ball faster than Retta expected. She swung hard and missed.

"Strike one," Skip yelled.

"You got to hit the ball and then run," Cade taunted.

"You just hush and hope I don't kill a cow with the next hit." Kirk threw it just like the first one and she connected wth it, and took off for first base.

*       *       *

One minute Cade was on his feet, looking right at the ball with his glove held high. The next he was falling backward like a rag doll. He could hear noises and people talking but they were in a tunnel. Someone yelled at him to open his eyes and they popped wide. White light—was he dead?

"Are you okay?" Retta's voice was high and squeaky.

"It only grazed him," Levi said. "There's no blood."

Who shot him? Cade opened one eye to see all the kids gathered around him.

Tears flowed down Benjy's cheeks. "Don't die, Cade. Please don't die."

"He's alive, Benjy. See, his eyes are open. Dead people can't open their eyes." Ivan touched Benjy on the shoulder but he moved away.

Cade focused on Retta's face first and she looked like she was about to cry.

"He's had worse injuries than that playin' football," Skip said. "Let's take him to the house and put an ice pack on it."

"I knew he wouldn't die," Kirk declared. "He's too tough to get killed by a baseball. It'll take a bullet to do him in."

Cade managed a chuckle at that compliment and looked up at Retta. "Did you break the bat?"

"It splintered," she whispered. "You sure you're okay?"

"Oh, honey, I'm fine. You might need to massage my temples to get rid of this headache but I'll be ready for church tomorrow mornin'. Were you showin' off when you hit that ball?" He sat up, rolled up on his toes, and then came to a full standing position. "I could use a good cold drink. What's the score? Who won?"

"Tie," Levi said.

"We'll have to practice and have another match later. Bet still on?" he asked Retta.

Her brown eyes glittered. "You don't get out of the bet by pretending to be knocked out."

"Pretending, nothing. The least you can do is let me lean on you until we get back to the house."

To his surprise she didn't argue but walked right up to his side and put her arm around his waist. He slung his arm around her shoulder, and they started toward the house with a parade behind them.

"You make a good crutch," he whispered.

"I've had lots of experience," she said softly.

"Did you train Gabby to throw like that?" he asked.

"Not me. She learned that on her own," she answered. "But I'll keep the team I've got when we play again."

He stumbled and leaned on her a little harder. "I hope the kids aren't disappointed that we have to quit now."

"They're just glad you aren't dead."

"So am I," he said, wondering if this was a wake-up call telling him to let go of the past and move on with his life.

# Chapter Ten

Retta, Mavis, and the girls sat on a pew right behind Cade, Levi, Justin, and the four boys in church the next morning. It was one of those little white nondenominational churches that often spring up in small communities. Two rows of pews with a center aisle and a choir section behind the pulpit. The preacher sat on an old oak deacon's bench, tapping his foot to the congregational music.

Faith had a lovely soprano voice, clear with a little breathlessness. Alice, God love her soul, couldn't carry a tune, but she sang with gusto. Gabby and Sasha harmonized well together on the two hymns, giving testimony that they'd been to church before.

The preacher took his place and read scripture from the book of Ruth and then told the story of how she'd left her country without looking back to follow her mother-in-law to a faraway country. It was those three words—*without look-*

*ing back*—that made Retta's mind start to stray and think about things other than Ruth and Naomi.

Her father had left instructions on what to do when he was gone. Sell everything to pay the medical bills so that she could start over and live her life without looking back.

Mavis nudged her from the end of the pew and whispered, "These little children have left their homes and they're living in a strange land. I want to be like Naomi to them."

"You already are," Retta told her.

She tried to pay attention but Cade was sitting right in front of her. Back straight. Hair neatly combed. Big football player's muscular neck. One ear just slightly larger than the other. Shirt collar starched stiff. No one would ever guess that he had to lean on her to get from the pasture to the house the day before. Her father would approve of Cade, but then he could talk cattle, hay, and maybe even a little country music, so that would appeal to Harry Palmer a lot. The only guy she'd brought home to meet her father had been afraid to take a step outside the yard fence for fear he'd step in a fresh cow patty and ruin his Italian leather shoes. When she saw the guy through her father's eyes, it didn't take her long to figure out that she didn't want a long-term relationship with him.

"Remember if we're content with our lot, then peace will be ours," the preacher said. "Now if Levi Jackson will give the benediction we'll all go home and have our Sunday dinner with our families."

*Family.*

The word stuck in her mind. She'd be going to the ranch. Not home because she didn't really have a home. And family? She looked down the pew at four little girls. She'd been with them less than a week but they were a temporary family. The folks in the church either agreed heartily with Levi's prayer or they were glad he'd made it a short one because everyone said, "Amen," and jerked her back into reality.

"Good lookin' crew you've brought with you, Miz Mavis," the preacher said when they reached the door. "I'd forgotten this was camp month."

"Yep," Skip said right behind her. "We're gettin' settled in pretty good."

"Well, we sure like havin' the kids here in church." The preacher smiled.

Cade laid a hand on Retta's shoulder as they crossed the parking lot where Mavis's van and two trucks were parked to take the "family" home. "I'm starving. How about you? Wonder what it is about church that makes us hungrier than just a normal day."

"It's biblical," she said.

"How's that?" He removed his hand.

"'Blessed are they who hunger and thirst after righteousness,'" she quoted. "We've been sitting in righteousness, so if we got the blessing then we're hungry and thirsty."

The laughter came from down deep in his chest. "Testify, sister."

"You okay? Is Cade makin' fun of you? If he is, I'll spit in his food 'cause I'm helpin' Mavis." Alice slipped her hand into Retta's.

"No, darlin' girl. I'm fine. Honest. He was laughing at something I said, not at me," Retta said.

"What did you say?"

She hugged the little girl to her side. "Something my daddy used to say that I thought was kind of funny. He died three months ago and he loved to go to church and I miss him."

"I never knew my daddy. He left before I was born but my sister tells me about him some of the time. I don't think he was very nice to my mama."

Poor little girls. Not a one of them knew the love of a father like she'd had. She wished every one of them had known a Harry Palmer in their lives.

*      *      *

Sunday afternoons were set aside for two things. The kids had to write a letter home to their family after Sunday dinner and then they were supposed to do their laundry. That included bedsheets, towels, and their clothes to get everything ready for the next week.

"Okay, ladies, you have pens, pencils, and paper in the top drawer of your dresser, so it's time for letter writing," Retta said.

"I ain't never wrote a letter before," Alice said. "What do I say?"

"You tell them all about the ball game and makin' food with Mavis and everything that you can think of," Faith said as she headed toward her room.

"We can tell about hay haulin', Sasha," Gabby said.

"And how that Kirk is a jack...I mean a jerk." Sasha went to her room and closed the door.

Retta used the time to change from her Sunday sundress to a pair of cutoff denim shorts and a sleeveless western-cut shirt that she tied at her waist. She wandered out to the porch to think about her father and how he would have put his blessing on what she was doing for the girls.

She sat down in one of the rocking chairs but it wasn't her father who came to mind—it was Cade Maguire and the way his hand felt on her shoulder and the heat his kisses caused in her body. How could something that brought about so much inner turmoil still create a sense of peace?

"Did you write a letter?" Benjy sat down on a porch step. A lock of red hair was stuck to his forehead and the fine hairs on his upper lip were plastered with sweat.

"Not yet. How about you?" she asked.

"Yes. I told my granny that Cade is alive."

If only he would look at her when he talked so she could read his expression even a little bit.

"So have you ever drawn Cade?" she asked.

He nodded. "I like Cade a lot and Skip and Mavis. And I like Beau too."

"Think you'll like the new little donkey?"

He looked up at her, his green eyes full of life. "I'm going to draw him. He'll be smaller than some dogs."

"Will you make two pictures so I can have one?"

The corners of his mouth turned up slightly. "Yes, I will. Good-bye, Retta."

He got up and tucked a sketch pad under his arm. When he reached the boys' bunkhouse he sat down on the steps and took a pencil from his pocket. Intent on watching him, she didn't even feel Cade's presence until he was only a few feet from her.

"Benjy talked to me and even smiled," she said.

"He usually doesn't take to people that fast so you must be special." Cade settled into the rocking chair. "I guess the girls are writing letters?"

"Supposed to be. If my dad was still alive, I'd write one to him."

"Justin and I still write a letter to Mama on Sunday afternoon. I thought it was a good practice for the kids to learn to write letters," he explained.

"Do you really think foster parents will read the letters?"

He patted her on the arm. "It's not only for the one getting the letter. It's for the one writing it."

"Want a glass of iced tea, lemonade, or a soda?" she asked, amazed that her voice wasn't high and squeaky. His every touch made her pulse race.

"No, I'm good but thank you. I was going to check on Skip and the guys and saw you sitting out here with Benjy."

"He seems eager to sketch the new donkey. When are you going to let the kids go see him?"

"Soon as Levi says it's time. We're having pizza delivered tonight for supper. Sunday is usually Mavis's day off, but when the kids are here, she insists on working until after Sunday dinner."

"How about next week the girls and I take over the kitchen for Sunday supper. Faith and Alice are happy there, but I'd like for Gabby and Sasha to get in a little bit of teamwork with them," she said.

"That would be great," Cade said. "I should be going." He pushed up out of the chair. "See y'all later."

She leaned forward so she could watch him until he disappeared into the boys' cabin. She'd learned to read people by their body language and their walk. Slumped shoulders meant that they were shy and unsure of themselves. Cade Maguire's swagger said that he was bold and confident in his place in the world.

*A man's man.* Her father was back in her head again. *The kind of feller who wouldn't even look down at his boots if he was walkin' across a pasture.*

"Okay, Daddy, I hear you," she said.

She pushed up out of the chair and went inside the cabin, got out a piece of paper and a pen, and took it to her room. If this letter-writing thing was for the author as much as for the reader, then maybe she'd give it a try.

Letters were nearly extinct in this day of texts, emails, and Twitter, and she couldn't remember the last time that she'd handwritten anything other than a grocery list. With pillows propped against the headboard in her bedroom, she leaned back and began her letter:

Dear Daddy,

I don't know what to write or how to begin. I got everything sold and taken care of just like you told me to do. Selling your land was hard and I'm still angry at the doctors for charging so much and then not curing you. I'd thought we'd have years and years together, that you would live to enjoy your grandchildren. My life plan includes two children, one when I'm forty-one and the second at forty-three. They will never know you except through my memories and that's not enough for me so I'm angry.

They say that grief comes in stages. The first is denial. I went through that when you called me to say that you needed help. Surely God wouldn't give a man as strong as you such a horrible disease. I have to admit that I lost all my faith and it was only through your patience and love that I found it again these past three years.

I've taken a temporary job on a ranch that lasts until my interview with the bank where I worked before in Dallas. You'd love it here and you'd be such a good influence on these poor kids. They are starving for love and a sense of belonging and I only hope that I can dig deep into all the things you taught me and help them discover themselves and confidence. It would be a lot better if you were here with me.

She stopped and shook her aching hand. Writing in complete sentences was so much harder than typing on a keyboard. After staring at the wall for several minutes she picked up the pen again, but when she put it to the paper she wasn't sure she wanted to write anymore. Maybe that was enough for one Sunday. A memory flashed through her mind—when she was a little girl and bedtime rolled around, she used to remember one more thing she had to tell her dad. It happened so often that he nicknamed her the one-more-thing girl for a whole year.

Picking up the pen, she started to write again.

One more thing, Daddy—Cade Maguire and his brother own this ranch and their best friend, Levi, is the foreman. You'd say that they are all good men and you'd like them. Daddy, I'm drawn to Cade and it's not a good thing. He's a rancher. I'm a businesswoman with my plans written in stone. I've known cowboys my whole life and none of them ever made my heart race, but he does. Is it just a physical attraction or is the universe telling me that life does not offer guarantees and to ditch my plan and live for today? I don't know but I sure wish you were here to talk to me about it. Until next Sunday, I love you, Daddy.

She folded the letter and put it into an envelope. It didn't need a stamp or to go to the ranch house for someone to mail the next day. Heaven didn't have a post office box.

Alice came in with her letter and asked, "Who do I give this to?"

"Put it in an envelope, seal it, and take it to Mavis. They've got all of your addresses. You might put your name in the upper left-hand corner. Ever written a letter before?"

"No," Alice answered. "Not one that was goin' to be mailed but we did write one in school last year to one of the kids who got cancer. Our teacher took them all to him in the hospital. He never did come back to school but the teacher said he was in 'mission."

Retta wished that she and her dad had written long letters or even simple post cards to each other through the years instead of depending on phone calls and emails. Then she'd have something to hold in her hands and to read over and over again. Cade didn't realize what a precious gift he was giving his mother.

Sasha came to the door, and the very expression on her face said that there was trouble brewing. Retta slid off the bed and hurried to the living room where Gabby and Faith were squared off. Hands were knotted into fists and a machete couldn't have cut through the tension.

"We got a problem here, ladies?" Retta stepped between them.

"Tattletale," Faith hissed at Sasha.

"Sasha didn't say a word." Gabby's voice raised an octave and she spouted off some rapid-fire Spanish. *"Perra estúpida. Esta provocó para que no yellin' a Sasha."*

"One demerit for calling Faith stupid and another one for calling her a bitch." Retta went to the whiteboard and wrote Gabby's name, then added two black checks behind it. She'd figured that Faith would have ten before the other girls even got one, but it was Gabby with her quick temper that had gotten her into trouble. "Now what's this all about?"

They all four started talking at once and Retta couldn't understand any of them. Finally, she whistled shrilly, and silence filled the room. "Faith, you go first," she said.

She pointed at Gabby. "She wanted to put her clothes in with mine to wash and I said no."

Retta glanced at Gabby.

She shrugged. "We have to save water where I live. We all do laundry together and it don't matter if my stuff is in with another girl's. And what she said about me was worse than what I called her."

"You can put my stuff in with yours," Alice said. "I just want to get all this laundry done so we can go outside. Just tell me what to do and I'll even help fold everything."

"Sasha?" Retta asked.

The girl threw up both palms. "I don't care how we do laundry. At our house, it's all piled in together. We got our sheets done but now we've got to do our clothes. None of us has got much, since we only been here a few days."

Retta looked at the tiny piles in the floor of the small area of the kitchen where the washer and dryer were located. "Looks to me like y'all got a choice. Either put all your white things together and then your dark things in another load and get done so you can go outside or be here until supper time or beyond. It's your choice, but you have to do it without yelling bad words or calling anyone names. And you Faith." She wrote Faith's name on the board and added a check behind it. "You get one demerit for calling Sasha a tattletale. Learn to get along or else you'll be cleaning a lot this next five weeks to work off those bad marks. If you ever want to beat those boys at anything you'd better learn to work as a team."

She turned around and walked to the front door. "If there's going to be blood, take it outside or else you'll be cleaning it up on your hands and knees."

"Had a little problem, did you?" Cade was back, but this time he was on the swing.

"How did you know?"

"I been sittin' here for a little while. Heard the Spanish

and it didn't sound like she was telling her that she loved her. I'd love a cold Coke if there's any left in the refrigerator," he said.

"Comin' right up and you're right. She got two black marks behind her name for what she said. She'll be more careful, now that she knows I understand her language." Retta grinned.

"Thanks and seemed like you settled it in a hurry and that part about the boys was pretty good." He smiled back at her.

"Little competition might make them decide to work as a team." She glanced at the girls, who were busy resorting clothing, grabbed a couple of cold Cokes from the refrigerator, and left them to their laundry.

When she went back to the porch, Gussie was curled up in her chair. Cade quickly picked the cat up and put her on his lap.

"She's between litters right now and spends more time up around the house. When she has kittens in the barn, she tends to stay out there most of the time." He took one of the Cokes from her hands. "Did you have cats on your farm?"

"Oh, yes." Retta sat down in the rocking chair and took a long drink from the can. "Daddy got such a kick out of watching kittens play or the goats or the new lambs."

"So you had livestock as well as crops?"

"Had a bit of everything," she answered. "Daddy said it took that to make a living, and then in the end he lost it all."

"But he enjoyed it all when he was healthy, didn't he?"

"Yes, he did." She'd been so angry that it had taken every bit of the money from the farm, the house, and even her car that she'd forgotten to think about what that had bought him—a lifetime of doing what he wanted and loving every minute of it. He couldn't take a bit of what he'd accumulated with him so it had been worth it.

"And your mother? Did she like the country life?"

"She loved it. They had something pretty special. Daddy never even considered dating another woman after she was killed in a drunk driving accident on the way home from the grocery store." Another thing that she could be thankful for—she'd never had to endure a stepmother.

"The kids who come here don't have that, Retta," he said softly. "Not a one of this group has two parents in the home unless they're being fostered. Benjy has neither. He lives with his ailing grandmother. Two of yours have a single mother. Two of the boys are in foster care and the other one lives with an aunt."

"What do you expect to accomplish with this camp?" she asked.

"Teamwork, maybe a little responsibility and to learn to make good decisions on their own but to be accountable for the bad ones and learn from them."

She thought about what he'd said. The black marks on the whiteboard would stand because both of those girls had to be accountable and they were learning all of the other things he'd mentioned with nothing more than dirty laundry.

Gussie hopped from Cade's lap over to hers and butted her nose against Retta's hand. She got the message loud and clear and began to rub the cat's ears. "Are you going to get along with the new donkey as well as you do with Beau?"

"She's already looked him over and the jury is out on that one." Cade chuckled.

"Maybe you shouldn't name him until she's passed judgment." She stopped rubbing and the cat nudged her hand again.

"She's got a little more than a month. If she don't like him by then, they'll have to agree to keep away from each other. Levi is pretty taken with the critter."

"Awww, her feelings are hurt that he'd put another animal before her and she's been so good to take care of Hopalong and the turtle," Retta teased.

"Life is complicated." Cade finished off his Coke and set the can beside his chair. "I probably shouldn't take that inside to the trash. See y'all at supper and before I forget, I told Levi, Justin, and Skip that you were taking over Sunday night supper. They wanted to know if you'd do Sunday dinner and let the boys have Sunday supper. That way Mavis could have the whole day off."

"No problem. What about breakfast?"

Cade slapped his leg. "I hadn't thought of that. We can have cold cereal that morning or maybe the ladies could make muffins on Saturday and set them aside."

"We'll need to be in the kitchen on Sunday morning to get things ready for dinner, so we'll take on breakfast too. I make some mean pancakes and I've been known to fry bacon one time without burning it," she said.

"Fantastic!" He nodded. "Well, that's settled and I've still got a couple of hours' worth of work in the office to do. I'd rather plow forty acres in an open tractor as spend an hour looking at a computer."

"And I'm right the opposite. I love book work and accounting."

He pushed up out of the chair and her breath caught in her chest. Tall, dark, and handsome came to mind right along with sexy, sweet, and kind. "They say opposites attract. Think there's any truth in that?"

"Maybe." She nodded.

"See you at supper then or maybe in the barn before then if you go with the girls to see the new stray." He tipped his cowboy hat toward her and was gone before she could say anything.

*Yep, I could really like this feller.* Her father was back in her head. He loves kids, cats, and he goes to church on Sunday.

"So could I, Daddy, but..."

*There are too many buts in the world.* She remembered him saying even before she heard his voice.

"I know, Daddy, but life is complicated."

*I never have liked that word.* He'd said that many times before also. *Life is what you make it, and if you listen to your heart, it's a simple thing, not a complicated one.*

# Chapter Eleven

Cade hated paperwork. He stared at the notes Levi and Justin had taken through the week, data that needed to be put into the computer. But he couldn't keep his mind on any of it, and besides all that, he needed to install a brand-new program, which would require hours of reading directions. Finally, he got up and went to the window to stare out toward the barn. Benjy and Ivan were on their way across the pasture and Ivan was telling Benjy something using all kinds of hand gestures.

If he and Julie had gotten married, he could have had a son by now. He wanted children, lots of them, but he also wanted a wife who'd be content on the ranch.

"Then why am I drawn to women who don't want any part of it?" he asked out loud.

No answers came crashing through the window, so he went back to the computer and got back to work. When he finished it was four-thirty and the pizza would be there at five o'clock. Timing was perfect. He had time to catch his breath before eight hungry kids arrived.

Justin rapped on the office door and opened it a crack. "You about done in here?"

"Just finished."

He came on into the office and slumped down into a wingback chair. "How's the head?"

"Fine. I did pop a couple of pills a while ago but it was from the computer stuff, not the ball game," he admitted.

"How's the infatuation with Retta? You've been droppin' by there more than you did with the other bunkhouse mamas."

"I'm not going there with you again. I told you that I can take care of myself," Cade said, gruffly.

"Not tryin' to start a fight. I like Retta and she's probably the best bunkhouse mother we've had for the girls. But I know you, brother, and you are attracted to that woman."

"I've been attracted to lots of women since Julie and you haven't meddled in that." Cade picked up a pencil from his desk and flipped it back and forth through his fingers.

"Like I said before, there's a difference between barroom bunnies and Retta, and I'm goin' to look out for you whether you like it or not. A poor old cowboy's heart, no matter how big and bold and mean he is, can't take two breaks like what you went through with Julie. But if this would turn out to be something real and get you movin' on, I'd be the first one to shake your hand."

Levi came into the office without knocking. "Hey, Skip and the guys are in the livin' room. Benjy has a new drawing to give to us and he's waitin' on you both to get there. And heads-up, it looks like Kirk is a little jealous of Benjy."

"Already knew that." Cade stood up at the same time Justin did.

They'd made it out of the office when the girls all trooped into the house, their faces aglow with excitement.

Alice left the others behind and went straight to where Benjy was sitting cross-legged on the floor. "Whatcha got there, Benjy? Can I see it?"

He held up a picture of Alice standing on third base.

She clamped a hand over her mouth and squealed through her fingers. "That is so good. Can I have it?"

He ripped it out of his sketchbook and handed it to her. "I like to draw animals better. Do you like it, Cade?"

"I love it. When you draw the donkey, we'll have it framed and put it on the dining room wall with the others."

"Wow!" Nelson exclaimed. "You ought to be an artist when you grow up."

"Anybody can draw," Kirk grumbled.

Skip shot a look his way that made him clamp his mouth shut and then said, "But not everyone can do it as well as Benjy. That takes understanding the subject."

"I'm going to give this to my mama." Alice held it close to her chest.

"Pizza!" Justin said. "Who's ready for a pizza supper? Afterward we can all go out to the corral and learn how to sling a lasso."

"Do we get a peek at the donkey?" Retta asked Levi.

"Maybe a peek but he's not familiar enough with things to pet him. Give him a few more days."

\*     \*     \*

Retta had learned to handle a rope when she was a teenager and she'd seen her dad lasso a rangy old cow from the back of a horse many times. She'd never been that good, but Levi,

Cade, and Justin were excellent. Cade didn't miss a single time when he threw it at a fence post.

"He and Justin team roped when they were in high school." Skip walked up beside her and leaned his elbows on the top rail of the fence. "Didn't know for a while if he was going to go pro-rodeo or if his love of football would win out. He couldn't do both justice and in the end he chose football."

"Was Justin disappointed?" she asked.

"Nope, Levi stepped up and helped him with the team ropin' and they both rode saddle broncs at the rodeo. Don't think his mama liked it none too good. I know Mavis didn't. She lived in fear that Levi would get hurt and he did a few times, but it toughened him up," Skip answered. "What about you? I hear you played a little football. Did you ever do much with a rope?"

"Little bit. But nothing like those guys are doing." She put a boot on the bottom rail and leaned forward like Skip. Cade was sure enough a fine specimen out there with a rope in his hands. For a few moments she was downright jealous of that damned fence post and her mind conjured up all kinds of delicious scenarios where he'd rope her and drag her toward him for more of those steamy kisses they'd shared in the tack room.

Cade nodded toward the fence where eight ropes, all cut to the same length, were hanging. "Okay, kids, each of you claim one of those and then show me if you've been payin' attention."

"First thing you have to do is tie the knot," Levi said.

Cade wound up his rope and tossed it over a nail on the back of the barn. He put a hand on the fence post nearest to Retta and jumped it without any effort at all. "Who do you think will get the knot tied and the fence post under control first?"

"Probably Benjy. I'm amazed at how good he is at physical things," she said.

"If he likes something, he's good at it. If he doesn't, wild mules couldn't make him do it. He likes animals, ranchin', and drawin' and he loves to read. Want to bet on who'll be next?"

"Faith, because she's got something to prove."

"I think it'll be Kirk for the same reason. About that bet?"

"What are we betting? We've already got one going about the OU/Texas game, remember?"

"Five bucks," he said.

She held out her hand. "You're on. Faith can take Kirk standing on her head in hot ashes and blindfolded. That girl has a stubborn streak."

His big hand wrapped around hers firmly. It didn't matter if it was only a bet, it still sent a flash of heat through her body. "Now I've got this picture in my head of that little girl upside down with a bandanna over her eyes."

She dropped his hand reluctantly. "She could run Attila the Hun some competition."

Cade propped a leg on the bottom rail so close to hers that she could actually feel the sparks jumping back and forth. "So tell me, Retta Palmer, in one word, what do you want out of life? When you come up to the end of your last words, what do you want to think?"

"Want to explain that a little more before I choose one word?" she asked.

"If you were looking eternity in the eye how would you finish this sentence, 'I have been a success because I was'? Happy? Successful? Rich?"

"Happy," she said without hesitation. "And you?"

"Happy," he said. "Now what makes you happiest?"

"I'll have to think about that. Is there a time limit on this?"

"No, ma'am." He pointed toward the corral, grazing her shoulder with his finger as he did so, and sending more sparks flitting around. "Look at that. Faith and Kirk have their knots done and are both about to see if they can master the art of a sling."

They slung the lassos around their heads, kept their eyes on their individual posts, and let them fly at the same time. The moment the lassos fell, Faith drew back on it hard to tighten it up and Kirk did the same. If there was a millisecond's difference in their timing, it was unnoticeable.

"You two should work together as team ropers," Cade yelled. "Your timing is great. Now let's give Benjy and Sasha a chance to show us what they can do."

"I'm not betting with you anymore. It's always a tie when I do," Retta teased.

"And I was depending on that five dollars to buy you a hamburger on the half-price night at a greasy burger joint in Bowie," he flirted.

"Tough break, cowboy. Now I'll just buy two and eat both of them myself."

"You'd let an ugly old cowboy starve while you eat two burgers?"

"No, but I might let a tall, dark, and sexy one go hungry until supper time," she shot back at him.

He cut his eyes around, caught her gaze, and held it. "So you think I'm sexy?"

"Oh, come on!" She laughed. "Don't give me that shy crap. You're as bold as a big Angus bull. I bet you can run fast too."

"What's that got to do with anything?" he asked.

"You're not married so you must be able to outrun all the women in north central Texas."

His expression said that she'd driven a sharp needle into a raw nerve. "Maybe they don't want damaged goods. At least not on a long-term basis."

"What was her name?"

He nodded. "Julie and everyone in this part of the state knows all the gossip about the breakup."

"Did you love her?"

He nodded. "I did, but looking back I'm not sure I was in love with her. We'd dated since junior high school, went to college together, lived together the last year we were in college, and I came home to run the ranch and she worked in Dallas at a big law firm. I proposed but she didn't want to get married right then so we had a really long engagement. We spent more than a year planning the wedding."

"What's the difference in loving and being in love? Aren't they the same?" She moved from the fence to sit on the grass.

He followed her, leaving a foot of space between them. "They are similar but one goes so much deeper than the other. In love is one of those things that goes all the way to eternity and beyond. We were happy the whole time we were dating and really got along well that last year in Austin. She loved the city life and having everything right there."

"So what happened?" She nodded toward the corral. "Benjy won that round. Gabby will be practicing for a re-match. She's almost as competitive as Faith."

"I'm proud of him. To answer your question, she gave Justin a note to give me on the morning of our wedding. It said that she simply could not live on a ranch and that she'd been offered a job in Hawaii with her firm. She left that day and I stayed here to face all our friends and families. I haven't seen her since then," he said.

"How cruel." Retta gasped.

"I thought so that day, but since then I've come to realize that real cruelty would have been going through with the wedding when she would have hated the ranch and we'd have both been miserable."

She laid her hand on his knee. "You are a good man, Cade Maguire."

"I've had two years to think about it and I think I'm starting to move on." He laid his hand over hers and held it there. "She's done the same. Married some high-powered CEO last December."

"Good for you, and I hope she thinks of you every day and regrets what she did," Retta said.

Cade cocked his head to one side. "Why?"

"Because that was downright mean. She knew what you were and who you were. To wait until your actual wedding day? Come on, Cade. That's criminal. She should have done time in the county lockup for a crime like that," Retta fumed.

His grin widened, deepening the cleft in his chin. "Maybe you and Faith share DNA with old Attila."

"We just might at that," she said. "But that is wicked. I bet you had to be responsible for returning everything while she went off on a lark to a tropical island. And the embarrassment. She should be shot."

"Look!" he pointed. "Nelson and Sasha are competing. And would you look at that, Faith is cheering her on. This lasso business might teach some teamwork after all."

"And you are changing the subject," she said.

"To be honest, I wouldn't have made it without Ruby and Mavis. They got all the gifts returned and I didn't leave the ranch for a month because I didn't want anyone's pity. Still don't." He looked her right in the eyes. "And yes, I changed the subject, but I do appreciate that you'd like to shoot her."

"She'd best stay in Hawaii as long as I'm on the ranch," Retta said. "Now back to the kids. I believe they are learning a little bit of teamwork. It's magic that Faith is cheering anyone on."

Cade nudged her with his shoulder. "The Longhorn Canyon has been known to work a little magic in the past."

When they'd each had a turn, Cade praised the kids for their quick learning. "Before the summer is over, we'll run some real calves in here and you can each choose a teammate for the roping contest. A boy and a girl on each team, so be thinkin' about who you trust enough to work with them."

"I call Benjy," Alice said.

One of his shy grins said that he liked that idea, but he just shrugged and handed Skip his rope.

"And now," Justin said. "The new little donkey told me that he was ready for y'all to meet him after all, so I'm going to let him loose in the corral. Remember his little leg doesn't work right yet so be easy with him. And while Levi is getting him out of the barn, I've got another announcement. He's not named yet and we're going to have a little name-choosing contest. Each team, boys and girls, can come up with two names that they really think fit him. Skip and Retta will choose one name and then Levi gets to choose from the two finalists."

"What do we get if we win?" Kirk asked.

"The team that wins gets the braggin' rights to having their name chosen," Justin said loudly. "Sometimes that's even more important than a prize."

"Yeah and the girls are goin' to get them." Gabby bowed up to Kirk. "Boys don't know nothing…"

Levi returned to the barn and turned the little donkey, no bigger than a small collie dog, into the corral with the kids.

"Ohhhh." Gabby clamped a hand over her mouth. "He is so so cute. I could just take him home and let him live in my bedroom. My foster sisters would just love him."

Braggin' rights. Retta pulled her dark hair up into a ponytail and secured it with a holder from her jeans' pocket. What did she want braggin' rights to when she came to the end of her life? For being successful, even if it cost her happiness? For being happy, even if she had to pay for it by giving up her life plan? It was a lot to think about but that could wait until later. Right now she wanted to be out there with the children, loving on a tiny little donkey.

*          *          *

Cade still couldn't believe that Retta wanted to go back to city living. The way she climbed over the fence and then dropped down on her knees in front of the crippled donkey with kids all gathered around her screamed that she was a country woman at heart.

Skip scooted over next to Cade and leaned his elbows back on the fence. "That woman will make a fine mother someday. Look at the way the kids are gravitatin' toward her. And the donkey has lost that scared look with her right there beside him."

"Yep," Cade said.

"You got a thing for her, don't you, son? I could see it from the first time I saw you with her." Skip shooed away the flies with the back of his hand.

"Yep, but that don't mean anything can happen," Cade answered.

"Never know what Miz Fate has in store for you until

it happens. Just don't slam any doors until you're sure you don't want to see what's behind it."

Cade nodded. "Nice for the first Sunday in June, ain't it?"

"I see you ain't in the mood to talk about Retta so I'll change the subject. What movie are we watchin' tonight?"

"*Because of Winn-Dixie*. We got it in the closet and it's fit for their age."

"I like that one and it's so old that they probably haven't seen it. You goin' to let 'em watch *Old Yeller* while they're here?"

"Absolutely not!" Cade said. "The boys would cry just like the girls and then the girls wouldn't let them live it down."

"How about *Ferris Bueller*? Didn't we let them do that one last year on Sunday night movie time?"

"That would be a good one for sure." Cade nodded.

"Can't keep your eyes off her or your mind on the kids, can you?" Skip laughed.

Cade slapped his forehead. "What movie did you say?"

"You heard me. I'm sure the boys would get quite an education with that one. What're you going to do about this thing with her?"

"Probably nothing."

"Why?" Skip asked. "You ain't looked at a woman like this since Julie."

"It all boils down to what she wants and ranchin' ain't even on the list," Cade said.

Retta left the donkey in the children's care and climbed back over the fence. "Don't tell Gussie because she really likes me, but that little donkey's the cutest thing I've ever seen. You should hear the names they're throwing around out there. Everything from Buttercup to Beastie."

Skip laughed out loud. "He don't look like a Beastie to

me and if Levi names him Buttercup, it might be the first time I've ever seen a donkey blush. Beau and Gussie would tease him something terrible."

"You should write children's books with your imagination, Skip." She plopped down on the grass and watched the kids through the railings.

"I ain't smart enough to do that but I used to tell Levi stories when he was a little kid. Me and Mavis, we sure did like havin' him in the house. Missed him when he moved to the ranch permanently. Even though we see him every couple of days, it ain't the same."

A soft breeze carried the remnants of her perfume to Cade—a tantalizing scent that brought visions to his mind of her sleeping beside him after passionate sex. He focused on the donkey to get the picture out of his mind. "So what would you name him?"

"Elvis, because when he brays, it's kind of like he's trying to sing," Retta answered.

"Or maybe Willie after the great Willie Nelson," Skip said.

"That's even better." She laughed.

"Movie time in fifteen minutes," Levi finally called out. "Popcorn and cookies will be served along with the leftover pizza while we watch a movie about a dog called Winn-Dixie."

"That's a crazy name for an animal," Ivan said.

"Isn't that a grocery store?" Alice asked.

"Wait and see. Be thinkin' of a name for this little feller but make sure it's one that he'll like. Until then let's call him Little Bit." Justin made his way through the crowd and led the donkey back inside the barn.

Kids scrambled over, through, and under the fence and headed back to the house in a dead run with four adults coming along behind them at a slower pace. Cade's hand brushed against Retta's and the electricity was greater than anything he'd ever experienced with Julie or any other woman.

*     *     *

Four boys lined up on the floor in front of the television. Elbows on the floor, heads resting in their hands. The girls were two feet away sitting in a row with their chins resting on their drawn-up knees. A bowl of popcorn and a platter heaped high with chocolate chip cookies sat between them.

Levi and Justin had begged off from watching it again and had gone out to check on a prize cow about to give birth. With Skip in a recliner over by the boys, that left the sofa for Retta and Cade.

He placed a bowl of popcorn and a small plate of cookies between them. Then he passed out bottles of root beer to everyone. "Get comfortable because the movie is about to begin. Lights out."

Retta jumped when the room went totally dark but then the movie began and the lights from the television lit up the place somewhat. It was an old movie about a little girl and a big, scraggly mutt, who brought a whole new level of friendship to a small town. The lessons in it would hopefully speak to the children's young hearts and they'd find the joy, not only in it, but also with each other.

Without taking her eyes off the television, Retta reached into the bowl but instead of wrapping her fingers around a handful of popcorn, she closed it around Cade's hand. She jerked it back and glanced at him.

He picked up a double handful. "Let me help you."

She cupped her hands and he filled them. Holy smoke! No make that holy blasted fire. Every time he touched her, heat rushed through her entire body. It had to be because she hadn't had so much as a dinner date in three years. She'd feel the same if Levi or Justin had either one put popcorn into her hands.

Halfway through the movie she leaned over in the semidarkness to be sure Cade didn't have a hand near the cookie plate. He'd done the same thing and their faces were only inches apart. His dark lashes fluttered and she moistened her lips. His hand moved to her cheek and she leaned to the side. Her eyes were almost shut when the lights came on and she jerked all the way back to her side of the sofa.

"Intermission for five minutes." Skip laid the remote to the side and lowered the recliner's footrest. "Bathroom break or stand up and stretch. I don't think any of you've moved a muscle since the movie started." He groaned as he got out of the chair and headed down the hallway.

Alice reached for a cookie and stood up. "Man, this is a good show. I think maybe we should name the donkey Winn-Dixie."

"Silly girl." Ivan laughed. "That's a dog's name. Our cookie plate is empty. Can we have some of yours?"

"If we can have some of your popcorn." Faith answered for her. "You haven't even touched it."

"We can get popcorn any old time. We can even make it for ourselves in the microwave but we don't know how to make cookies like these," Nelson said.

"Let 'em have the cookies that are left. I want some more popcorn." Gabby stretched out her legs and bent her head forward to touch her knees.

"Me too." Sasha piped up as she stretched out on her back and then did half a dozen sit-ups.

"You're blushing," Cade whispered for Retta's ears only.

"Yes and with good reason," she said. "We shouldn't start something..."

He nodded. "No, we shouldn't but..."

She shook her head. "No buts."

Before he could say another word, Skip had settled back into his chair. "Intermission has ended. Everyone ready for the second half of the movie?"

The kids resumed their positions on the floor without a word.

Retta settled into the corner of the sofa. "No buts" meant keeping her hand away from the popcorn. She glanced over at Cade just moments before the lights went out, and he gave her one of his sly winks that said the conversation definitely was not over.

# Chapter Twelve

One week down, Retta thought that Wednesday morning as she poured a cup of coffee and carried it to the porch.

"Mornin'," Skip said from one of the rocking chairs. "Your kids movin' as slow as mine this mornin'? I'm goin' to light a fire under my boys' butts after breakfast. I'm going to put Nelson with Benjy and Ivan with Kirk."

"Why?"

"They need to learn to work with someone else. I switch them up every week and give them different things to do. Up until now we've let them choose but now it's time for them to learn to work with someone else and to follow instructions." He chuckled and took a sip of coffee. "It'll be miserable today but that's the way I do things and it all pans out in the end."

"So what are they going to do?"

"Nelson and Benjy are going to help me weed the garden and gather in the vegetables. Kirk and Ivan will be with Levi today, moving cattle from one pasture to the other and whatever else he needs done. Breakfast in fifteen minutes." He eased his tall, lanky frame up from the chair. "Bones are gettin' stiff. I reckon a day in the garden might loosen 'em up a little."

"Don't forget your hat and a few bottles of water," she said.

"Essentials of any outside job in Texas this time of year. Here comes my boys, divided into their little chosen couples. They ain't goin' to like me much today." Another chuckle and he was gone.

Sasha and Gabby were both yawning when they finally made it outside. Retta nodded at them and they headed off toward the house, where Faith and Alice were already helping in the kitchen. Poor little darlins had no idea that she was about to implement Skip's plan into their lives, too. Teamwork required getting to know all the team and working with each one, and it was beginning today.

With a sigh, she stood up and started toward the house. Beau bounded out from between the two bunkhouses and hurried on ahead of her. Gussie was right behind him, but she kept winding herself around Retta's legs, trying to talk her into some serious petting.

"I'll miss animals when I'm in the city," she muttered, taking time to squat down for a minute to rub Gussie's fur. When she realized that someone was right behind her she gasped and jumped to a standing position.

"Didn't mean to startle you," Cade said as he joined her from the shadows. "And yes, you will. Didn't you miss the farm animals when you moved away from Waurika?"

"At first I didn't because I was so busy getting adjusted, but then I went home for Thanksgiving and my cat had died while I was gone. Daddy buried her with my other pets out by the pond and..." She let the sentence hang.

"We've got a place out behind the barn," he said.

They stepped up on the porch at the same time and his hand brushed against hers again. It seemed like there was a magnet in each of their bodies that drew them together.

*If you can't fight 'em, join 'em*—she could almost hear Tina saying that and then picking up a third margarita on girls' night out. But this was more than wanting another drink and yet, did it have to be? Couldn't it simply be two consenting adults who had some chemistry between them? Two grown-up people who could shake hands at the end of a fun summer and say good-bye with no regrets.

"Your mind is a million miles away, Retta." He chuckled as he opened the door for her.

"Yes, it was, but I'm back in the present now."

"Retta, guess what?" Alice ran to meet her. "Me and Faith, we got to make the scrambled eggs all by ourselves this morning. I can't wait to make breakfast for my sisters when I get home."

"That's wonderful. Maybe I can help y'all finish up and get it on the table," Retta said.

"You'll have to get your orders from Mavis. She's the boss of the kitchen," Alice said seriously.

"Only if you are under thirteen years old." Mavis giggled. "Mornin', Retta. I can see by the glow on your face that you're settlin' in on the ranch really good."

"I thought that something else made a woman glow," Skip said.

"I love the smell of a big breakfast." Retta's face burned with a crimson blush.

"Most important meal of the whole day," Mavis said.

"Faith, you keep stirring that gravy. It's almost done. And Alice, you go on and help Retta set the table."

Mavis pointed toward the clock. "Five minutes and we'll call in all the guys. Gabby, you'll find napkins in that drawer by the sink. And Sasha, you can take those biscuits off the cookie sheet and put them in the basket."

"See," Alice whispered. "She's the boss of the kitchen but I love her."

*       *       *

Cade filled a coffee cup and carried it to the living room where the other guys waited with four boys. "So what's on the agenda today, guys?"

"Kirk and Ivan are going to be with Levi," Skip said. "Think you boys can learn how to get cattle from one pasture to another?"

"But...," Ivan stammered.

"I'm with Nelson. I don't care what job you give us. We'll do whatever you say, but he's my partner," Kirk argued.

"He was your partner, son," Skip said. "But in order for a team to work, they have to learn to work with everyone in it. So today, you and Ivan are going with Levi. Benjy and Nelson are going to the garden with me."

Faith stormed into the room and flopped down on the sofa. "I'm supposed to tell y'all that breakfast is ready. I don't like this switching us around. Me and Alice was doin' fine in the kitchen and now we have to go work in the garden. I hate getting my hands dirty."

"Do you good to figure out where the food you eat comes from," Cade said.

"I don't give a..." She shot a dirty look toward Cade and started over. "I don't give a darn where it comes from, out of cans or jars or microwave containers. I don't like this one bit."

"You have the option of not doing anything at all today," Cade reminded her.

"You okay working with Nelson today, Benjy?" Retta asked.

"Skip said for me to so I will," he said. "I like Skip—a lot. Vegetables are good for you. They have fiber and vitamins. Meat has protein and that makes good muscles. You should eat both."

"And I like you a lot." Skip patted him on the shoulder.

Benjy didn't shy away from him like he did when other people got too close.

"Good spirit," Retta said. "We could all learn from Benjy."

Faith huffed. "Well, we might as well eat breakfast and get on with it."

"So how do you feel about working with Skip today?" Cade leaned toward her and asked.

"If the boss man says that's where I need to be, then that's where I'll go," Retta said.

"The boss man would rather work on tractors with you, but you and Skip might both be needed to settle arguments today," he said.

"Truthfully, I enjoy gardening, so this is no hardship."

"Are you absolutely sure about not stayin' in the ranchin' business?"

She shrugged. "I sold the farm, remember?"

"Time to eat. I'm hungry and then it is time to pull the weeds. Weeds rob the roots from the water they need to make vegetables, which need lots of water." Benjy put his hand in hers and tugged her toward the dining room.

Retta felt like she'd just been given a jeweled crown.

*     *     *

With her hat firmly on her head, Retta joined Faith and Sasha in the garden that morning along with Skip, Benjy, and Nelson. The girls both gave her dirty glances, but if looks could kill she'd already have been nothing but a greasy spot on the kitchen floor when she told Gabby that she would be joining Alice in that area.

She held up a huge blue plastic bowl. "Mavis says that she needs this bowl full of green beans for dinner. If y'all will help me pick them, Gabby and Alice and I will take them inside for Mavis to snap. And we also need at least a dozen good ripe tomatoes and a few radishes for a nice salad for lunch today."

"I hate green beans," Faith grumbled.

"Mavis makes good green beans," Benjy said.

"I'll help you girls. You want to pick the ones that are about the length of your finger. Leave the little ones for another day." Retta set the bowl in the middle of a row, bent over, and started to gently pull the beans from the vines.

"Want to pull weeds?" Benjy asked.

"No, thank you!" Faith said. "And me and Sasha, we can pick enough green beans for dinner real quick."

"Good." Retta straightened up. "And if you fill the bowl up two or three times, we can get some ready for later in the week. I'm looking at my phone. Let's see if you can do the job in less than thirty minutes."

"If we win?" Sasha asked.

"Then you get to keep picking," Retta said.

"If we lose?" Faith asked.

"Then the guys can pick the next bowl full and you can pull weeds," Retta answered.

"Get busy, girl," Sasha said as she began to lift the broad leaves and pull beans.

"Don't tell me what to do," Faith said, but she didn't waste a bit of time following Sasha's lead.

Skip stepped back into the shade and leaned on a garden hoe. Retta removed her hat and fanned herself with it as she joined him.

"Some folks might think we're gettin' free labor with these kids, but I swear, I could do the work in half the time if I wasn't havin' to show them how to do stuff or else settlin' arguments," he said.

"They get paid for what they do, so that's not free labor," Retta said.

"We don't just give them all their paycheck in money. We take them to town and they have to use part of it for school clothing, shoes, and supplies. About half of it goes home with them or less if they want to spend it wisely. We hesitate to give it all to them for fear that it winds up in their parents' hands and is used for something other than for the kid who worked for it," Skip said in a low tone.

"Yep, that's right," Cade said right behind them.

Retta was getting used to him appearing out of thin air, but it still startled her. "How do you do that?"

"What?" Skip asked.

"Twice today Cade has snuck up on me and made me nearly jump out of my skin," she answered.

"He learned it from his daddy." Skip grinned.

Cade moved around her to watch the kids. "I was really expecting a bigger argument than we had from them."

"It's amazing how fast two enemies can become workin' buddies," Retta said.

"Your dad teach you that?" Cade asked.

"No, sir." She shook her head. "My first boss sent me to

leadership class with a woman that I could not tolerate even for five minutes. We might not have been best friends when it was over, but we did learn to work together."

Skip wandered back out into the garden, leaving them alone. Retta checked her phone. "They seem to have worked out a plan. Faith is working one side of the row of beans and Sasha is working the other so that they do a good job."

Cade pushed his hat back on his head, leaving a mark on his forehead where it had been. "I figured you told them how to do that."

She tried to focus on the puffy white clouds, the garden, or anything else, but she really wanted to sink into his blue eyes and never even come up for air. He removed his hat, raked his fingers through his hair, and then resituated the hat back to the original position. What would it feel like to have his hands on her body for more than a short little makeout session in the tack room? She shivered in spite of the heat and looked down at the phone in her hands.

"Expecting a call?" Cade asked.

"No, just checking the time again."

"How much longer have they got and what's the stakes?"

She nodded and told him what was happening.

"Don't expect they'll be pulling weeds as fast as they're going," he said. "Think they'll learn to like it."

"Now that part might take a miracle. But I believe in them, especially after Benjy held my hand this morning," she said.

"You are good with them, Retta. I figured Faith would spend her day in the bunkhouse rather than get her hands dirty. That's magic," he teased.

"No, darlin', that's the root of all evil workin' out there pickin' them beans," she flirted.

"What?"

"The love of money," she said.

"Done!" Faith raised both hands in the air.

Sasha pushed a few red curls away from her sweaty fore-head and held up a hand. Faith slapped her hand against it and brought the bowl to Retta.

"Good job, girls. I knew y'all could do it if you worked together," Retta said.

"You want us to pick the rest of them all the way to the end of the row?" Sasha asked.

"That would be wonderful. Y'all get a bottle of cold water from the cooler over there and I'll empty the bowl and bring it back," Cade answered. "Magic, pure magic," he whispered for Retta's ears only while they were getting the water.

*       *       *

The cattle had been moved. The garden looked great. The girls in the kitchen had snapped two big bowls of green beans. Lunch had been served, and they were ready to go outside and learn how to throw a spiral football through a tire suspended from the frame of an old swing set. And then a flash of lightning and rolling thunder brought in a heavy rainstorm. The kids barely made it back to the ranch house without getting soaked. The thunder stopped in twenty minutes but the low-hanging dark clouds brought a nice slow drizzling rain that, at any other time, Cade would have appreciated. But he'd looked forward to playing football, not only with the kids, but also maybe seeing what Retta could really do when it came to throwing the ball.

"Well, rats," Nelson grumbled. "I betcha I could put a

football through that tire if I could practice and then I might be able to play in school next year."

"What do we do when it rains?" Faith asked.

"Well, me and Justin are going to the barn and clean it up. Tack room is awful and the stalls need a good cleanin'. There's always something to do whether it's sunshine or rain," Levi answered.

Kirk raised his hand. "Can I go with you?"

Another hand went up. "I'll go if I can pet Little Bit," Alice said.

"Well, y'all ain't goin' without me," Gabby declared.

Then five more hands were in the air and Faith glanced over at Retta. "What are you going to do all afternoon?"

"She's going to help me in the office with a ton of computer work," Cade answered. "You did know that she has a college degree in business, right?"

"Really?" Sasha asked.

"Yep." Retta nodded.

"And that she yells for Oklahoma at the OU/Texas games." Justin chuckled.

"No!" Faith clamped her hands on her cheeks.

"I like baseball better. Don't matter who is playing. It makes more sense. Hit the ball and run. Football has too many rules. I know them, but I like baseball better," Benjy said.

"I like football better," Kirk said. "But you are shhhh... kiddin' me, about yellin' for the Sooners aren't you?"

"'Fraid not," Retta said. "I'm Boomer Sooner all the way."

"And I was just beginnin' to like you." Nelson groaned.

"We might convert her," Skip offered.

"Not for a million bucks," she said and added *and a sexy cowboy* in her thoughts.

"Cade, does that mean you can't marry her? Marriage is a contract between two people and they promise to live together forever until they die, but if she doesn't like the Longhorns, then you can't marry her, can you?" Benjy asked.

"Well, shucks." Cade grinned. "I'd already found an engagement ring in a Cracker Jack box that I was plannin' on givin' her, but you're right, Benjy. I'll save it for a girl who is a Longhorn fan."

"Well, there goes my chance at a big fancy wedding but I could never marry someone who yells for Texas." Retta sighed dramatically.

"And on that note, we'd better load these kids up in a couple of trucks and get them out to the barn while this rain has slacked off a little bit," Skip said. "We'll see y'all at supper time."

Mavis shooed them out the back door and then said, "There's a slow cooker full of baked potato soup and one of chili on the counter. Hot dogs are in the refrigerator if anyone wants a chili dog. Loaf of fresh bread is already sliced. I'm going home for the afternoon. Retta and the girls can get supper on the table tonight." She took off her apron and got her purse. "Our Sunday school class is playin' poker this afternoon. They do it once a month and I never have gone because we don't want to leave you boys in a tight place, but with Retta and the girls helpin', well, I'm goin' this time."

"Sunday school class?" Cade could hardly believe his ears.

"Poker?" Retta gasped.

"Got you two goin' didn't I?" She slapped her thigh. "I need to do some bankin' and investment business. Been needin' to take care of it for a while but didn't quite have the time. Today I'm gettin' it done. Y'all get on about your business now. Supper ain't goin' to be no problem at all."

"You sure you're all right. You aren't sick are you? You're not just tellin' me this because you are going to the doctor," Cade asked.

"She's fine. Fit as a Stradivarius fiddle," Skip said. "Now go. Shoo. I been tellin' you for weeks that these boys could eat bologna sandwiches one day and they wouldn't die from it. And besides the way she whines about something simple as an ingrown toenail, if she was sick you'd have known about it a month ago."

"Oh, hush." Mavis threw her apron at him. "Don't you talk to me about whinin'. Ain't nothing worse than a sick man."

Skip caught it midair and hung it on a hook. "That's the first time you threw something at me since way back when you wore high-heeled shoes."

"She threw a shoe at you?" Retta asked.

"She got mad at me and threw it at me. I fell down on the floor and it whizzed past my head and stuck in the wall," Skip said.

Mavis slung her bright red purse over her shoulder. "You never did flirt with that woman at the feed store again, did you?"

Cade chuckled. "I can't believe it."

Retta couldn't contain the giggles. "They remind me of my mama and daddy, always goin' on at each other."

Cade laid a hand on Retta's back. "Don't laugh. It makes them worse."

"I heard that and I won't forget it," Mavis yelled.

Retta giggled again.

He could have listened to the sound for an hour. "Pure delight," he said.

"What?" she asked.

"Did I say that out loud?"

"Yes, you did and I agree with you. They are both a delight. You'd be lost without them on the ranch."

"Don't I know it," he said quickly, thankful that she'd misinterpreted what he was talking about.

"So this is the new program?" She picked up a box from the top of the desk. "Piece of cake. I installed and used this at the farm. It's simple once you get the hang of it. Even Daddy could use it, and he was all thumbs on the keyboard and definitely computer challenged. When he got to the point when he couldn't get out much, he took care of that end of the business."

"But how do you move all the data from the old program over into this one?" He seated her behind the desk, then pulled another chair over and sat down beside her.

"It takes a little time but it's not complicated." She opened the box and started to work.

*A little time to sit close to you and figure out if this attraction is a good thing,* he thought.

She rattled a few keys and then leaned back. "Now it's a matter of waiting and then following the prompts on the screen."

"And then you transfer the old stuff over to it without losing anything?"

"That's the plan." She turned her head slightly and their gaze caught in the foot of space that separated them. He sunk into her eyes and suddenly they were the only two people in the universe. His hands went to her cheeks, while his thumbs made lazy circles below her ears. The tip of her tongue darted out to moisten her lips. The first kiss was barely more than a brush. Then her hands went around his neck. Her fingers splayed out in his hair and she pulled him forward for more.

The second kiss deepened, and his arms circled around her shoulders. He teased her mouth open with his tongue on the third one and then she moved from her chair to his lap and pressed her upper body tightly against his chest.

They were both panting when she pulled away and went back to her chair. "We can't start something that could lead to heartache for us both."

"Why does it have to lead to anything?" He leaned toward her and nuzzled the side of her neck. "Why can't it just be two adults who are attracted to each other?"

"Because…" She seemed to be thinking about it but then she sighed. "Because it's not fair to either of us. What if one of us ended up wanting more and the other one didn't?"

He kissed her on the cheek. "Fair enough, but you will admit that there's vibes between us?"

"Oh, honey, the sparks have been there since I first walked into the interview," she admitted.

Cade nodded. "For me too. I don't think the attraction is going away, now that I've had a taste of your kisses. What happens now?"

"Now, I'm going to install this program and we're going to work together without giving in to our hormones," she answered.

"Where's the fun in that?" He grinned.

"No fun. No magic. Just plain old work."

*Maybe for now, but if you feel what I do, you won't want to stop with only a few kisses,* Cade thought.

# Chapter Thirteen

Retta tossed and turned, beat her pillow into submission, got up and drank a glass of milk and even tried reading, but it was still after one o'clock in the morning before she finally drifted off into a troubled sleep. But then it was only to dream of Cade.

She awoke the next morning to high-pitched voices in the living room and by the tone and the volume, there was an argument going on. She slung her feet over the bed and rubbed her eyes to erase the vision of Cade with his broad bare chest right there beside her. When she opened the door three of them were squared off and Alice was sitting on the sofa with the cat, Gussie, in her lap.

"What's going on out here?" she asked.

"They're fighting about who gets to use the phone first tonight to call home," Alice said. "Me and Gussie, we're stayin' out of it."

With very little sleep and even less patience, she made a

snap decision. "Alice calls first tonight. Alphabetical order by first name. Next week, Alice goes to the bottom of the list and Faith calls first. After that it'll be Gabby's turn and then the following week, Sasha's. Whoever is last gets five extra minutes to make up for having to wait. Do y'all have to argue about everything?"

"It's what sisters do," Alice said with a shrug. "Me and my three sisters fuss about everything. Mama had to make rules about who gets to be in the bathroom first in the mornin's and my oldest sister is a real witch when it's her turn. She takes too long and almost makes me late for the school bus."

"I am not your sister," Faith said with clenched teeth as she glared at Gabby. "Or yours." Her gaze shifted to Sasha.

"If I was your sister, I'd run away from home," Sasha said. "And I'd take Gabby with me."

Retta left them to their banter and went straight for the coffee machine. Thank goodness she'd programmed it the night before and the pot was full because she needed something other than bickering girls to wake her up that morning.

Alice set Gussie to one side. "Well, me and Gabby got to go help Mavis if we want money at the end of this camp. So y'all better get done with your fussin'."

Retta poured a cup of coffee and took a sip. Leave it to the youngest one in the whole bunch to take charge and end the fight.

She carried the mug to her room and set it on the dresser, stopping to take a sip in between getting dressed and putting her room to rights. She tossed the shirt she'd been wearing the day before in the hamper and got a whiff of Cade's shaving lotion. Dragging it back out, she pressed it to her nose, and all the emotions of that steamy makeout session came flooding back.

"Retta, it's almost time for me and Gabby to leave. Can you braid my hair? I can do it, but it's not very pretty." Alice's voice came through the closed door.

"Of course," Retta said. "I'll be right out."

She had one side of Alice's hair done when her phone rang. She dropped the brush and worked the phone up from her hip pocket. There was a picture of Cade that she'd secretly snapped a couple of days before.

"Good mornin'," she said.

"We've got a major problem. Mavis sprained her wrist last night. Can you and the girls help out in the kitchen? She swears she can do it with just two girls, but I don't want her to have to."

"Of course we can. Are you sure it's not broken? Did she see a doctor?"

"Skip took her to the emergency room and they did an X-ray. It's just a bad sprain. It was late when they got back or I would have called then."

"No problem. I'll be there in five minutes with my whole crew of girls," she said and hit the end button.

"What was that?" Alice asked.

"Okay girls." Retta raised her voice. "Listen up. Mavis sprained her wrist and needs help, possibly for the rest of the time we are here, but that does not mean you won't have other things to learn to do. This morning we're all going to work together to get breakfast on the table for everyone, and if I hear one mean word, the black marks behind your names will double."

Gabby's eyes went to the board where she already had a couple of big fat checks. She nodded without a word and jerked on her sandals. "I'm ready. I already got my hair put up 'cause we can't work in the kitchen unless we have it out of our faces."

Faith came from her room with her purple-streaked hair in two high dog ears that had been braided. "I heard you and I'm ready."

"I expect you all to work together. You know your way around the kitchen a little bit so be nice to each other and do what Mavis says without attitude," Retta said.

"Yes, ma'am," All four voices said at the same time.

Mavis fussed the minute they all paraded through the back door. "I told Cade I could do this with just two girls."

"We like helpin'." Alice tiptoed and got an apron from the hook and tied it around her tiny waist.

"Yes, we do, and we need to learn to work together," Retta said.

"Okay, then, let's get to it." Mavis nodded. "Sausage gravy, biscuits, scrambled eggs, and pancakes, and when breakfast is done, we'll start dinner. Then you'll have a few hours before we put supper on the table."

Mavis gave orders and they followed them. Everything was under control when Cade popped his head in the kitchen. "How's it goin' in here, ladies?"

"We got this," Mavis told him. "Don't worry."

Faith looked up from the table she and Sasha were setting. "You just keep them boys out of our kitchen."

"I think I can manage that." Cade grinned.

"Good," Mavis said. "Now let's get busy or they'll all be whinin' about starvin' to death."

"Thank you, again," Cade whispered to Retta.

Mavis pointed at Faith. "Okay, girl, you get out two pounds of sausage and the big cast iron skillet. Gabby, you and Alice put out the jellies, jams, syrup, and picante sauce for the eggs. Sasha, you get three dozen eggs from the refrigerator and crack them into a bowl, then get out the whisk and work on them until they are fluffy. Retta can make biscuits and then stir up pancake batter."

"Yes, ma'am." Faith nodded, seriously.

The morning flew by because she and the girls went straight from cleanup after breakfast to helping Mavis get meat loaves and blackberry cobblers ready for the noon meal.

"You really do have magic hiding somewhere," Cade whispered in Retta's ear on one of the several trips he made through the kitchen that morning. "I'm wonderin' if you'd be willin' in a couple of days to shift things around and put two of the boys in the kitchen. That way they can learn a little about cookin', too."

"Great idea," she said.

"We don't like it when y'all whisper," Faith said.

"Why?" Cade asked.

"Because it means you don't want us to hear and that you're plannin' something we ain't goin' to like," Faith said.

"It's a surprise that I'll tell you about later," Retta told her.

Faith groaned. "I hate surprises."

"Would you get on out of here?" Mavis popped him with a dish towel. "We've got work to do. This afternoon you can teach them how to throw a football or whatever else you got planned. But right now they're all busy, including Retta."

"So you girls still want to learn to play football?" Cade slowly made his way out of the kitchen.

"Of course they do," Retta answered, but they were all nodding.

"You going to step in as quarterback?" he asked.

"Maybe. Depends on whether any one of these four can throw a good spiral," she answered. "How about you?"

"Oh, honey, I intend to lead my boys to a victory over your

girls. It'll be as exciting as winning the OU/Texas game." The cleft in his chin deepened and her pulse shot up a couple of notches. "See y'all in the pasture about two o'clock?"

"We'll be there, but get ready to lose." Retta managed to get the last word in.

*       *       *

Cade stood about twenty yards from the tire dangling from ropes on the old swing frame. "Okay, kids, you've got to hold the ball like this. Get a firm grip on the end with either one or two fingers on the laces and the other two toward the end. Leave some air in your hand. And when you let go of the ball be sure that your thumb is down after the snap. When you play baseball you want your thumb up, but with football it's the opposite. Like this." He showed them the correct way to hold the ball so that it wasn't touching the palm of his hand and then he threw a perfect spiral through the middle of the tire.

Justin caught the ball from the other side of the tire and threw it back to Cade.

"You see that, guys. That was a perfect throw," Cade said.

"That's what I've been doin' wrong," Kirk said. "Nobody told me about the air or the thumb. Can I try?"

"Line up, boy, girl, boy, girl," Cade said. "Kirk can go first and then he goes to the back of the line. The ones who aren't throwing can learn from the other's mistakes or victories."

Kirk took the ball from Cade and held it just like Cade said but he forgot to snap it with the thumb down and it went wide. Justin ran to the other side of the tire and slung it back at Cade.

"Know what you did wrong?"

"It was the thumb." Kirk nodded.

"You can do it, Kirk. You got to remember, that's all," Benjy said. "You can read a football book or watch it on YouTube."

"Can you do it?" Kirk asked.

Faith had a turn and almost made it through the tire, and then it was Benjy's turn. Cade thought for a minute Benjy might ask for a tape measure to get things exact, but he did just what he'd been told and the ball went through the tire.

"Yes, I can, Kirk, but it was not perfect," Benjy answered.

When they'd all had a turn and missed, Cade handed the ball to Retta. She palmed it and turned around to the kids. "This is not a basketball but remember you control it with your fingertips just like you do a basketball. You don't dribble with your palm, do you?"

Man, that woman could steal his heart for sure, Cade thought. She could cook and she knew the finer details of football and evidently basketball too.

"No, ma'am," Faith said.

Retta drew back and the ball went smack through the center. "If this had been a real game, it would have sailed right into my man's hands and he would have run it all the way for a touchdown."

"Hummph." Gabby giggled. "Is Cade your man?"

Cade chuckled and glanced over at Retta to see two high spots of color dotting her face. "What does being your man entail?"

"Oh, hush," Retta whispered.

"You are blushing," he teased.

"I am not. It's hot out here," she protested.

"Weatherwise or otherwise?" he asked.

"Both," she answered honestly. "Now stop talking to me or they'll think we're flirting."

"We are." He chuckled again and moved over to help Alice try a second time.

\*     \*     \*

That evening after supper Retta was prepared to read a book while the girls talked to families, foster or otherwise. She took it with her to the living room but got so engrossed in Alice's actions that she didn't get past the first page.

The little girl had a towel wrapped around her wet hair and she talked to her sisters first and then her mother. She walked around the bunkhouse talking at warp speed trying to get every single detail in about her week at the ranch, but what she was most excited about was the fact that she'd thrown the football through the middle of the tire. When it was time to hang up, she told every one of them that she loved them.

Then it was Faith's turn, and she plopped down on the other end of the sofa and poked in the numbers to the foster care home. "Hello, Marsha. This is Faith and I'm calling from the ranch."

Retta was close enough that she could hear every word.

"Do you like it?"

"It's okay," Faith said. "I'm learning to cook so I can help when I get home."

"That's good. Mind what they tell you. Talk to you next week."

"Okay. Good-bye," Faith said.

The room was totally silent for a long, pregnant moment. "And that's the joy of living in a foster home," she said as she handed the phone back to Retta and headed up to her room.

"Don't leave." Retta hurried into the bedroom, grabbed her cell phone, and dialed the number on the bunkhouse phone. When it rang, she nodded toward Faith.

"I don't need your charity." Faith's chin shot up several inches.

"I need yours," Retta said.

Faith answered the phone. "Hello, Retta, this is crazy."

"Maybe so but I want to hear all about your week. What did you like best? Tell me about the other girls and all the boys." Retta went back to her room and closed the door. "You only used a minute of your time, which means you've got fourteen more and I like talking to you."

"Really?" Faith's voice quivered.

"Yes, ma'am, now start talking," Retta said.

"Well, I don't like Kirk much because he's so bossy, but Benjy is okay. I feel sorry for him because he's real smart but he's kind of weird like he don't know what to do with all them smarts. And I really like Alice because she's the youngest and she needs lookin' after." She rattled on for her full time with very little prodding from Retta.

"Time is up. Thank you for talking to me and I look forward to hearing from you again next Thursday night but you have to call you foster mother first and then me. Okay?"

"Yes, ma'am," Faith said and then whispered. "Thank you. The other girls were so busy they didn't even know I was talkin' to you."

"It can be our secret," Retta said. "Good night, Faith, and thanks for lookin' after Alice."

"I wish someone woulda looked after me when I was only ten," she said. "Good night. I'm hanging up and giving the phone to Gabby now."

When Retta crossed the living room floor on her way to the kitchen for a bottle of cold water, she could hear Gabby talking like a magpie to her mother. Part of the time she rattled on in Spanish and then she'd switch to English.

Retta sat down in a recliner and picked up her book. When Gabby's time was up, she pointed toward the clock on the wall and Gabby handed the phone off to Sasha, who was pacing the floor, waiting to make her call.

The minute her sister answered the phone, Sasha asked if the baby was there yet. When she found out it wasn't, she flopped down on the sofa. Evidently, her sister had put the phone on speaker mode because she talked to her mother and sister both every single minute that she had plus her five extra for being last in line.

"Now it's my turn," Retta said.

All four girls lined up in front of her.

"Who are you going to call?" Faith asked. "Your mama?"

"My mama and my daddy have both passed away," Retta said.

Gabby made the sign of the cross over her chest. "I'm so sorry."

"Your sister or brother?" Alice asked.

"Cade!" Sasha giggled.

Retta felt the blush rising from her neck. "I'm callin' my best friend, Tina, if you nosy little girls have to know. And I'm taking the phone into my bedroom."

"You got to listen to us when we talked," Faith argued.

"That was just this first time so that I knew you were talking to your parents and not a friend. The contract that was signed with your parents said that you would report in to them once a week. No one signed anything like that with me, so I'm going to my room and you girls can watch a movie, read a book, or play a board game. There's a bunch of them on the shelves," Retta informed them.

She went to her room amid moans about how that wasn't fair and shut the door behind her. Tina picked up on the first ring.

"I've been meanin' to call you all week but it's been so hectic around here that I barely know what day it is. Are you back in Dallas, yet? Tell me everything about the new job. I just know you got it with your credentials," Tina said without giving her a second to even speak.

"No job in Dallas but..." Retta went on to tell her the whole story of what she'd been doing the whole week.

"You are kidding me, right?" Tina said. "Four little girls? God bless your heart. I bet they're either arguing or wanting their mama all the time."

"Not really. They're pretty tough kids."

"Okay now tell me about the cowboys. Four of them if I got the whole thing right in my head."

Retta started with Skip and ended with Cade, describing each of them down to hair and eye color.

"Okay, now I want to know more about Cade," Tina said. "Why him?"

"Because when you talk about him, your voice changes. You're attracted to him, aren't you?"

"Yes, but oil and water do not mix. We'd have regrets if we started anything." Retta sighed.

"But you'd like to, wouldn't you?" Tina giggled.

"I'm not answering that question. Let's talk about you. How do you like being in Philadelphia?"

"Love it but then I've always been a city girl. Born and raised in Houston so it's what I know. You are torn between two worlds. Want to know what my granny told me once? She said that you can't ride two horses with one ass. You got to decide which horse you are going to ride. So does your heart want to be in the city or is it because of that silly life plan you made when you were just a kid? Don't answer me, Retta. Just figure it out and then plow forward without looking back or having regrets of any kind."

"But—" Retta started.

"There are no buts in the answer. You have to decide without any buts at all."

"You aren't a bit of help. You are supposed to be my friend," Retta said.

"I am and that's why I'm talking to you this straight. If I was you, I'd sample a little of that Cade…oh, my gosh, have you slept with him?"

"Good grief, Tina. It's only been a week," Retta gasped.

"Kissed him?"

Retta tried to figure out a way to beat around the bush.

"You have, haven't you?"

"Okay, I have, but that's as far as it went."

Tina laughed again. "I've got to go now. Got a meeting in five minutes with some clients but same time, same place next week?"

"Of course and you can call me, you know."

"And interrupt something with the cowboy. No thank you. You'd never forgive me. Bye now." Tina hung up with another burst of giggles.

When Retta laid the phone down she could hear more stifled laughter on the other side of the door. She tiptoed across the room and quickly slung it open to find four little girls all with their ears plastered to it. They tumbled over each other to keep from falling.

"You have what and how far did it go?" Faith asked.

"That darlin' girl is my business and none of yours."

"Was it Cade?" Gabby asked.

"Again, my business," Retta answered.

"She ain't goin' to tell us nothin'," Faith said. "Let's turn out the lights and tell ghost stories."

"Yes!" Gabby agreed.

"Lock the door first." Alice shivered.

Retta's phone pinged in her hands. She looked down and saw that the text was from Cade so she slipped back in her room.

*Phone calls go all right?*

Her thumbs flew over the tiny keyboard. *Went great.*

*Can you talk if I call?*

*Yes.*

The phone rang immediately and she answered on the first ring.

"You want to take the girls out with flashlights and hunt bugs? That's what Skip is doing tonight."

She stepped to the door. "You girls want to tell ghost stories or go outside with jars and flashlights to collect bugs with the boys?"

"That'd be like a real ghost night." Faith's eyes lit up.

"Need to take a vote on it?" Retta asked.

All four hands shot into the air.

"I guess they want to hunt bugs," Retta told him.

"See you on the porch in five minutes. I'll bring the jars and flashlights," Cade said.

The girls were waiting when Cade, Skip, and the boys arrived. Cade handed out fruit jars and flashlights. "Okay, here's the plan. One boy and one girl to each team. Don't touch the bugs but scoop them into the jar like this." He bent down to the ground and used a business card to flip a cricket inside the jar.

"I choose Benjy," Alice said. "And I need me one of them cards."

To Retta's surprise there wasn't a lot of arguing as the

kids chose partners, and then Skip gave them the area they could search in and carried a lawn chair with him to the backyard to keep an eye on them.

"So I choose you for my partner," Cade said when everyone had disappeared.

"What kind of bugs are we hunting?"

He drew her into his arms and bent slightly to whisper, "Kissin' crickets. Ever heard of them?"

She shook her head. "No, I haven't but I can take you on a snipe hunt."

"Kissin' crickets only come out when two people are kissin', like this." He tipped her head up with his thumb and lowered his lips to hers.

When the steamy kiss ended, she glanced all around. "I don't see any."

"It takes more than one kiss."

Retta tiptoed and wrapped her arms around his neck. "I wouldn't want to disappoint the kids, so we better give it another try."

His hands moved down her back to cup her butt and pull her even closer. The kisses got hotter and hotter until suddenly they heard a loud squeal and quickly stepped back from each other.

"Me and Benjy got two bugs," Alice screamed. "Right here in one spot. Benjy says they are crickets."

"See." Cade grinned. "I told you."

Retta slapped at his arm. "We'd better get around there with Skip to help watch the kids."

"Want to see if we can scare up a few kissin' prayin' mantises or maybe kissin' lightning bugs before we go?"

"Come on, cowboy." She pulled at his arm.

*Much more of that and there will be mating bugs not kissin' bugs out there,* she thought.

# Chapter Fourteen

The time was going too fast. It was already the second Sunday that Retta had sat on the church pew with all four of her girls beside her. She glanced down the pew and there was Mavis and Skip at the end. They sang a congregational song and the preacher must have been reading her mind because he spoke about time that morning. She tried to listen, but her thoughts flitted around from how the past week had sped by to counting the days until she'd have to leave the ranch. Finally her mind settled on her father, and she gave thanks for the privilege of getting to spend so much time with him the past three years. Then anger set in and she wanted to shake her fist at God for taking him from her.

"Are you okay?" Faith whispered.

"I'm fine," she said but her tone was ice cold.

"You look like you're about to jump over that pew and slap Cade. What did he do?"

"Shhhh…" Alice put a finger over her mouth.

Faith shot a look past Retta toward the little girl, but Alice didn't back down. "If you talk, he'll never stop preachin'. You have to be quiet so he knows you heard the message."

Retta leaned over slightly and whispered, "I'm not mad at Cade. I'm upset with God for not healing my dad."

Faith's nod and expression said that she understood.

Retta still couldn't make herself follow the preacher's sermon. Instead she let one of Miranda Lambert's older songs play through her head. "The House That Built Me" video had an old house in it that even looked like the one where she'd grown up. A tear hung on Retta's lashes as she thought about the tiny handprint on the sidewalk in the concrete leading up to the front porch back on her old farm.

*You can't be dead, Daddy. I can't let you go.* Tears threatened to roll down her cheeks. *I've been pretending that I'm at school and when I go home you'll be waiting for me on the front porch. It's the only way I can cope.*

*Let me go, Retta. You can't get on with your life unless you do,* her father's voice answered.

She shook her head. *Not yet. I don't want to, Daddy.*

\*       \*       \*

Cade caught a faint whiff of Retta's perfume when the breeze from the air-conditioning blew it over his shoulder. He couldn't turn around to look at her, but that didn't mean he couldn't close his eyes and see her dark hair flowing down to her shoulders. Or that he couldn't drown in those gorgeous brown eyes.

Benjy poked him in the ribs. "You don't sleep in church. That makes God cry."

"Wasn't sleeping. Was resting my eyes," Cade said softly.

Benjy kept his eyes straight ahead. "Kirk isn't an idiot no more. He helped me catch a camelback cricket for my jar last night because he already had one."

"That's good." Cade put his arm on the back of the pew and patted him on the shoulder. This time he didn't shy away, but then he didn't look Cade in the eye, either.

"Shhh…" Alice tapped Benjy and Cade both on the shoulder.

Benjy straightened up like he'd been caught with his hand in the cookie jar. Cade turned his head and caught a glimpse of Retta. She was a vision in a light blue sundress and the breeze from the air conditioner blowing across her hair.

*No talkin' in church,* she mouthed as she pointed toward Alice.

He nodded, turned back around, and whispered in Benjy's ear. "Alice says no talking."

Benjy nodded seriously. "I'd rather read the Bible as listen."

"Me, too." Cade nodded.

Since Benjy would be too old to come to the ranch next year, maybe Cade would ask if his grandmother would let him come for a week at spring break or maybe just before school started.

The preacher ended by asking Skip to deliver the benediction. Benjy's head was still bowed after the last amen and everyone else was standing up. Cade touched him on the shoulder and he looked up with a quizzical expression on his face.

"I was askin' God to tell my granny that I miss her," he said as he got to his feet. "What's for dinner?"

Cade laid a hand on his shoulder. "Kirk and Faith were putting a ham in the oven before we left. The kids are helpin' Mavis a lot."

"I'll be a good cook when it's my turn. I can peel potatoes and carrots and I can make green beans the same size when I break them," Benjy said.

"I peeled potatoes this mornin'," Kirk said. "It's not hard."

"That's because you aren't an idiot anymore." Benjy led the way through the pews until they could slip out a side door without going past the preacher.

Alice tugged on Retta's hand. "Can we do that, too?"

"If you promise you won't fight with the boys and you'll go straight to the truck," she answered.

"We promise," Sasha said.

Retta really was going to make a great mother—compassion and discipline in just the right amounts. Too bad her children would grow up in a big city without the freedom that ranch life would give them.

"You ever think about kids of your own?" he asked as they slowly made their way toward the doors.

"Sure, I do. I want two. But not for a long time yet."

"Only two?" he asked.

"I really like kids and would love to have a whole house full, but two is enough when you get a late start," she answered.

"Why not start earlier then?" he asked.

"First I have to find a husband." She looked around the church. "Where's Skip, Levi, and Justin?"

"Who do you think taught those boys about the side door?" So first she needed a husband and then she'd be ready for a whole house full of kids. A cold shiver shot down his back at the thought of a permanent relationship.

That would involve a lot of trust on both sides, and he still wasn't ready to go that far. Playing around with flirting and a few kisses and admitting that Retta would be a good wife and mother was one thing—acting on it was quite another.

*         *         *

The girls brought their letters to Retta that afternoon. After she'd put stamps on them, she put them in the basket on the kitchen counter. That evening she'd give them to Mavis, who would see to it they were put in the mail the next day.

"Okay, ladies, what do you want to do between now and supper?" she asked.

"Can we go outside and practice throwin' the football?" Faith asked. "I really, really want to beat them boys when we play a game with them and I need some practice."

"Gabby, will you catch for her?" Retta asked. "Pretend she's the quarterback and if it goes through the tire, you catch it and run with it. When we play the real game, you'll be the one who probably scores the touchdowns."

"I can do that." Gabby's dimples deepened when she smiled. "And I can run faster than any of them boys. You just get that ball in my hands and we'll have a touchdown for sure."

"But I won't be the quarterback," Faith said.

"If you get good enough at getting the ball through the tire, you can be," Retta told her.

Faith pushed a purple strand of hair back from her face. "For real?"

"For real. It wouldn't hardly be fair for me to play, since I've got more experience than any of those boys except maybe Cade." Retta pulled an elastic ponytail holder from the pocket of her sundress and whipped Faith's hair up into a ponytail. "There, now it won't get in the way of your spiral. Remember what Cade told you. Air in the palm. Two fingers on the laces and thumb down at the snap."

"Yes, ma'am." Faith beamed.

"And me and Sasha want to go see about Little Bit," Alice said. "I bet he's lonesome and needin' some pettin'."

Retta thought about going out to the barn but Alice and Sasha needed bonding time as much as Faith and Gabby did, so she picked up her book and carried it to the front porch. She propped her bare feet on the railing and Gussie jumped up in her lap. She took time to pet the cat before she opened the book. She hadn't even found her place when Beau flopped down on the top porch step. Cade was right behind him and he eased down into the other rocking chair with a loud sigh.

"We've got a problem, a big, big one," he said.

"Girls arguing with boys?"

"Bigger." He shook his head. "It's Benjy's grandmother, actually his great-grandmother. She died this morning. Dropped with a heart attack. Her sister called the social worker and she called me. They're willing to leave him here until the end of our time but then he'll have to go to a foster home."

"Oh, no!" Retta dropped the book on the porch. "Does he know?"

Cade removed his hat and toyed with it, nervously. "I'm going to tell him now. Can you come with me?"

"Of course," she said. "Can't her sister, the great-aunt or whatever she is to him, help?"

"She's ten years older than his great-grandma and isn't able. There's no other answer but foster care."

"We'll find another answer. Give me a minute to get my shoes on and we'll go...oh, Cade, there he is now, coming this way."

Benjy plopped down on the grass in front of the bunkhouse. "Skip said it would be all right for me to sketch Gussie and Beau again. They've gotten older since last year.

"If Beau will lay still, I want to draw him on the porch and then maybe I'll draw Gussie in your lap." Benjy laid his sketch pad to the side and sat down on the top step, beside Beau. He scratched the dog's ears and rubbed his head with his knuckles. "He likes me to pet him like this."

"Benjy, we need to talk." Cade's tone sounded as if he wanted to weep.

"We are talkin', Cade. Can't you hear me?"

"Yes, I can hear you, but I have bad news about your grandmother."

"Bad news?" He frowned. "What does that mean?"

Cade shook his head. "She had a heart attack last night and passed away. Her sister says that there will be a funeral on Tuesday and we'll be glad to take you to it."

"No…" The ragged gasp was followed by tears. Benjy jumped up and threw himself into Retta's arms, sobbing uncontrollably. The book went flying out into the yard and Gussie leaped over Beau's back and took off in a blur toward the barn.

Retta wrapped the child up in her arms and rocked him like a baby, weeping with him. Why did bad things happen to people who didn't deserve them? She hadn't been a terrible person and yet her father had been snatched from her before he could see his grandchildren. Benjy, God love his precious little broken heart, only had one person on earth to care for him, and she'd been taken.

Cade knelt down in front of the rocking chair and wrapped both of them in his strong arms. "I'm so so sorry but we'll get through this, and the social worker says that you can stay with us until the summer camp is over."

"No, no, no! No social worker. I don't like her." Benjy's wails were heartbreaking.

Retta wiped tears from Benjy's cheeks and then Cade's. "This is so hard."

"I know, but we've got him for three weeks," Cade whispered.

But then he'd have six more years until the system couldn't care for him anymore and he'd be out on the streets. And then what would happen to Benjy? Would he be able to function in society? Just thinking about that brought on more tears.

"I don't want to be a foster kid," Benjy sniffled as he moved from Retta's lap back to the porch step. He rolled forward until his head rested on his knees. "I want my granny back. She can't be dead. That means she will be put in a casket and put down in a grave."

Retta didn't even see Skip come out of the boys' bunkhouse but suddenly there he was on his knees right beside the rocking chair. "What's wrong, Benjy? Are you hurt, son?"

"My granny is dead and I'm scared."

"Shhh, now, we've got some time to figure this out, son." Skip patted him on the back and looked straight at Cade. "He gets to stay with us until..."

Cade rose to his feet. "Yes, he does."

"Come on with me, Benjy," Skip said. "We'll go tell the other boys."

"I don't want to. Kirk will tease me for being a crybaby. A grave is six feet deep and it's filled with dirt," he said.

"Kirk has lost family before so he'll understand." Skip took him by the hand and led him toward the other bunkhouse.

"Will you go to the funeral with me?" Benjy glanced over his shoulder at Cade and Retta.

"Of course we will," Retta said.

"All of us will go with you," Skip said. "Where and when?" He turned and asked Cade.

"Her sister is burying her beside other family members in Slidell," Cade answered. "On Tuesday afternoon at two o'clock."

"Will there be lots of people there?" Benjy pulled his hand from Skip's and stopped walking.

"Maybe not too many, but we'll be there with you," Skip said.

Together they walked across the lawn separating the two bunkhouses. Watching that little fellow square his shoulders and try to be brave, Retta lost it again. Cade scooped her up into his arms and carried her inside the cool house. She didn't even try to move when he sat down in a rocking chair with her in his lap.

"This is about your dad as much as it is Benjy's grandma, isn't it? You haven't really grieved yet, have you?"

She nodded and then shook her head. "It's not fair for Benjy. And my daddy was a good man. There are mean and ugly people who deserve to die but he didn't and neither did Benjy's grandma."

He brushed a soft kiss across her swollen eyelids. "I have no words."

She tucked her chin against his chest. "You are the strong cowboy. You are supposed to know everything."

"Hey, I couldn't even keep it together out there. I love that kid and I hate that he's going through this."

"We're both orphans," she whispered. "Only I'm an adult and I'm better equipped to handle it than he is."

The bunkhouse door opened but she didn't move, not until Sasha and Alice were standing right in front of her with big eyes and gaping mouths.

"What is goin' on?" Sasha glared at Cade. "Did you make Retta cry?"

Retta slowly got to her feet. "No, he didn't. He was trying to comfort me. Benjy's grandmother died and…" She sucked in a lungful of air and straightened her back. "It made me sad because Benjy was crying."

"We need to go see about him," Alice said stoically. "Is it okay for girls to go in the boys' bunkhouse?"

"I think it would be fine," Cade said. "Maybe we'll even go with you."

The two girls met Gabby and Faith coming back and after a brief huddle, they all four continued together toward the boys' bunkhouse with Cade and Retta not far behind. Her hand brushed against his and he laced his fingers with hers. She didn't even try to pull free when Justin and Levi came out of the ranch house and they all followed the girls into the boys' bunkhouse.

"Can we take him in as a foster child, Cade?" Levi asked.

"No way they'd ever let us bachelors have him, and it takes a lot of red tape to even get through the paperwork," Justin told him. "There are rules and regulations. It's not like bringing home a kitten or a dog."

"Well, hell!" Levi slapped the porch post. "What can we do?"

"We can get through the next couple of days and then the funeral and then we'll see what we can do," Cade said. "I'll bend over backward and do all I can to see to it that he's got a good home."

Nelson and Ivan were both sitting on the sofa with Benjy, who had a stiff upper lip but his eyes were swollen from crying. Kirk was sitting across on the floor in front of them.

"Are you okay?" Alice laid a hand on his knee.

"No," Benjy answered. "I'm never going to be okay. My

granny is gone and I don't have a home no more. She will be in a place with other dead people and I don't like cemeteries."

"You'll be okay in a foster home. You are very smart," Kirk said.

"I don't want that kind of home. I want my granny. She was my best friend. I told her everything." Benjy sighed.

"I wanted my mama when they took her away, but you just got to be a big boy and think like Cade and Skip and Levi and Justin. That way you'll be fine." Kirk stood up and headed toward the kitchen. "Anyone want a soda pop or a bottle of water?"

"Nothing for me," Skip said.

"Water, please. The body is made up of a high percentage of water and I cried out a lot of tears so I need water." Benjy sniffled.

"I'll help." Gabby jumped up. "Me and Faith could use some cold water too. It was hot out there throwin' that football."

"Can they all come with us to the funeral?" Benjy asked.

Levi had worked his way around behind the sofa. He laid a hand on the sofa beside Benjy's shoulder and said, "I'm so sorry about this and if you want all of us at the funeral with you then we'll be there."

Alice got to her feet and wiggled in between him and Ivan. She put both arms around him and pulled his head onto her shoulder. "You just cry until all them tears is gone. Sometimes that makes a kid feel better. When my granny died, I cried buckets full of tears and sometimes I still do when I think about her."

"Cowboys don't cry. Cade and Justin and Levi are big and strong cowboys and they don't cry." Benjy got the hiccups.

Sasha wedged in between him and Nelson on the other side. "Cowboys is just boys that chase cows and they do cry when their hearts hurt. We ain't none of us goin' to tease you or fuss at you about this, are we Kirk?" She shot him a dirty look.

"Not me, man. I carried on like a baby when my brother got killed." Kirk handed him a bottle of water and then he and Gabby passed out water and drinks to the rest of the kids.

"Y'all want something?" he asked Cade.

"I'm good," Cade said.

"Me too," Retta said around the lump in her throat. "I think I'll step out on the porch. If any of you need me, just yell."

Cade followed her outside. "You okay?"

"Those kids have been through so much. It breaks my heart."

He draped an arm around her shoulders. "That's why we bring them here and let them have a little bit of normal life for a few weeks. Sure, they learn to be teams and to work but they also learn self-respect and, like today, they learn to care for others. I'm proud of the way they're acting in there."

"Me too." She laid her head on his chest and listened to his steady heartbeat. Some woman, some day, was going to be very lucky to have him in her life.

\*       \*       \*

The girls were unusually quiet that evening, which was understandable. Retta went to each of their rooms and told them how proud she was of them for their actions that day, kissed them on the forehead, and then went to her room.

She slept poorly, waking every two hours and feeling like something was desperately wrong. It was the same feelings she'd had that last week that her father was alive. She'd come awake with a jerk and go check on him to be sure he was breathing. Convincing herself that it was empathy for what poor little Benjy must be feeling, she finally slept fitfully a few hours before she finally gave up. She crawled out of bed, checked each girl, and went to the kitchen to make coffee.

She'd just filled her cup and was on the way to the porch with it when Cade rapped on the door and called out her name. She opened it wide, and the expression on his face made cold chills run down her spine.

"What—" she started.

He held up both palms. "It's Benjy. He's gone."

# Chapter Fifteen

My God!" She dropped the coffee, splattering it all over her pajama bottoms. "What did he do?"

"Oh, honey." He wrapped her into his arms and pulled her close. "Not dead. Gone as in we don't have any idea where he is. Skip went to check on him a few times in the night and he was sleeping but half an hour ago he was missing."

"Do we put out an AMBER Alert?"

"No, we want to check the whole ranch first. He knows this place like the back of his hand and he probably just wandered off. Skip is going to stay with the other boys and we're going to take the four-wheelers out to scour the ranch. Could you please carry on as normal as possible?"

"I'd rather be out there hunting him, but you're right— they need normalcy right now." She nodded.

Cade put a finger over her lips. "I'll turn over every stone on this ranch. I really don't think he's run away."

Retta nodded. "You'll call me every half hour, right?"

"On the hour and the half, I promise, and if he shows up, you give me a call." He gave her a quick hug and then his phone rang.

"Hello, Levi, did you find him?"

"No, but I've got a pretty good idea what's going on. Little Bit has gotten out of the barn and I betcha that Benjy couldn't sleep so he came out here to draw the donkey and now he's out lookin' for him."

"We'll start there and go in different directions. He'll be on the ranch if you are right," Cade said and then turned to tell Retta what he'd learned.

"Just call us when you find him. Do you think maybe he went to the old cabin?"

"Maybe. We'll check there, first. If Skip could go help us it would be a big help. Think you can manage the whole crew until we find him?"

"I think we should wake all of them up and let them help find him. It will show him that they are all interested in him right now when he needs it most."

"Sounds like a plan to me. Let's everyone meet at the house in twenty minutes. That give you enough time?" Cade said.

"We'll be there in ten," she said as she hurried back in the bunkhouse.

Mavis put a full cup of coffee in Retta's hands when she made it to the kitchen. "Skip is scared out of his mind. Way he loves that boy, I'm surprised he hasn't had a heart attack. You girls grab a muffin and a glass of milk. I'm making Skip stay here and help me get breakfast ready for when y'all get back."

"Thank you." She took the full mug from Mavis's hand. The Longhorn was a big place and it could take hours and hours to search it. Maybe they should alert the preacher and the church members would come help out.

"Benjy knows this ranch and I bet Levi is right. He didn't think twice about goin' to hunt for the little donkey. He'll be all right, Retta. Oh, who am I kiddin'? I'm so worried I could cry. I swear if he's found safe, I'm going to have a long talk with Skip about fosterin' him." Mavis motioned toward the kitchen table.

Retta sipped her coffee. "That would be amazing."

Her phone pinged and she pulled it from her pocket in such a hurry that she dropped it. Mavis picked it up and handed it to her at the same time hers rang.

"Hello," they both said.

"He's not in the hay barn. Levi is going to check the two barns on the north side. Justin is coming back to the house in his truck to pick up the boys. Levi is bringing the ranch work truck to get the girls. They'll fan out and search by areas. You can get on the four-wheeler with me and we'll take it out to the old hunting cabin," Cade told Retta. "I was hoping that you'd have called by now to tell me that he'd showed up."

"Me, too," Retta said and started for the back door.

"I reckon you just got the same news I did. That was Levi." Mavis tucked her phone back into her apron pocket.

"I should go with them." Skip paced.

"No, you should not," Mavis declared. "These kids need to help with the rescue mission. Benjy knows this ranch. He won't go far. And I need help. We're going to make cookies until we get word that he's found and then we'll get breakfast started. With this arm in a sling, I need you to help me, Skip. Work will make the time go faster. And we can do our part right here and man the phones."

*A house needs laughter and kids.* Her father's voice was

back in her head with things he'd said so many times. *I miss you and your friends running in and out, slamming the back door and giggling.*

Skip nodded. "Retta, you tell Cade to call me every fifteen minutes and, Mavis, I'll get the stuff from the pantry. You can tell me how to go about makin' them and I'll do the work."

Mavis smiled. "Thank you, sweetheart." Then she turned to Retta. "I never could have kids of my own, but Levi stepped in and filled that void. Me and Skip are up in years but I believe we've got enough left in us to take Benjy in to finish raisin' him. And when he gets old enough, Cade can give him a job here on the ranch. He'd do fine at that," she said.

"That's a wonderful idea," Retta said.

"A word of advice from an old woman to a young one, darlin' girl. You don't wait until it's too late to have kids." Mavis shook an egg turner at her.

"Yes, ma'am," Retta said. "I can see Cade comin' this way. I'll make him call in every little while."

Her phone rang as she hopped over the yard fence. She answered on the second ring. "I see you and I'm ready to go."

The girls came out behind her and either climbed over the fence or slipped between the railings. Levi had hardly parked the truck when they all scrambled over the side like monkeys. "Don't worry," Alice yelled. "We'll find him, Retta."

"Oh, I forgot to mention that Beau is gone, too," Cade said as soon as she was on the back of the four-wheeler with her arms wrapped around him.

"Good. Maybe he'll protect Benjy."

"We're all callin' the house every fifteen minutes and

getting the updates from Skip rather than trying to call each other," he said.

"And it keeps Skip in the loop," she yelled as they headed toward the far side of the ranch. She'd figured that they'd go straight to the old hunting cabin, but Cade zigzagged across the land, stopping every few minutes to yell for Benjy.

Retta kept her eyes open for anything that might be a sign. A bit of cloth from his shirt, a torn page from his sketchbook, something that would say he'd gone in a certain direction.

*       *       *

Cade worried that Benjy might not have gone to the barn to sketch Little Bit but that he'd been so afraid of going into a foster home that he'd run away. He didn't voice his thoughts, but they were there at the back of his mind. When he'd been out for the better part of an hour and there was still no Benjy, he opened up to Retta, telling her his fears.

"I don't think he'd leave the ranch, Cade. I'm not just sayin' that to make you feel better either. I really believe he loves it here too much to run away," she said.

"I hope you're right." He stopped the four-wheeler, tipped his hat back, and yelled, "Benjy, can you hear me?"

The howl of a lone coyote off in the distance was his only answer. He checked the time. Ten more minutes until he had to call again and he dreaded hearing the sadness in Skip's voice.

He was about to start the engine when he heard a slight whimper, or maybe he only imagined it. He removed his cowboy hat and strained his ear. No, there it was again but he couldn't tell where it came from or if it was human. It could be nothing more than a baby coyote that had gotten lost from his mother.

"Benjy," he called out again.

This time the whine was a little louder and it came from his left. He turned his head that way and yelled again. "Benjamin!"

Beau came bounding out of the underbrush, jumped up on his knee, and wagged his tail. Then he dropped down on all fours, ran back toward the way he'd come and stopped to look over his shoulder.

"He wants us to follow him," Retta said.

Cade started up the engine again and drove slowly in that direction, but before they got to the old cabin, they could hear kids laughing and talking. He parked behind a big scrub oak tree and pointed.

"Would you look at that?"

"Looks like they found him first." She sighed. "I'm just happy he's okay."

He flipped around, drew her to him, and kissed her hard.

"What's that for?" she asked when the kiss ended.

"For going with me and keeping me from losing my mind," he said.

"You did the same for me, Cade. I'd have gone crazy back at that house," she said.

"So are you going to give me a thank-you kiss?" he asked.

Her arms snaked up around his neck and then her lips were on his in a long, lingering kiss that left him breathless.

"Thank you," she said.

They left the four-wheeler and walked the rest of the way. Benjy was surrounded by the kids, and Little Bit was tied to the porch post with a piece of rope.

"Mornin', Cade." Benjy grinned. "Guess what? I tracked

Little Bit to right here with my flashlight. I found him and then I got some rope from the cabin and tied him up. I knew you'd come find us. Donkeys are not idiots, but they don't have a big brain. Is breakfast ready? We don't go to the funeral today, do we?" Benjy asked.

"Not today but Mavis and Skip have been worried about you. Think you could ride in the truck with Justin and hold on to Little Bit so he don't jump out the back?"

"I'll help him," Kirk said. "It might take two of us."

"Or three," Faith said.

"How are you getting back?" Benjy asked.

"Retta and I'll go the way we came, on the four-wheeler," Cade said.

Benjy nodded. "A four-wheeler is really called an ATV, which means 'all terrain vehicle.' They used to make three-wheelers but they rolled over easier than one with four wheels."

"That's right." Cade smiled.

"I went to the barn to sketch Little Bit and I left my drawing things there," Benjy said.

"We'll get them when we get the donkey back in the barn," Levi said.

"You can sketch what you want," Cade said. "But how about we make you a picture album of our time together and all the kids? Then you can take it with you to look at whenever you want. And I'll do everything I can do to see to it you visit us for a little while every year on the ranch."

Benjy nodded and looked Kirk in the eye. "I will need a picture of you to put in my book."

"And I want one of you. You ain't so weird after all," Kirk said.

"A picture book will help you to remember and be smarter," Benjy told Kirk.

Kirk shot a look toward Benjy, but he didn't comment.

Cade's hand brushed against Retta's on the way back to the four-wheeler and she quickly tucked hers into it. He hated to let go but at least she'd have her arms around him when she got on behind him.

## Chapter Sixteen

The kids all gathered around Benjy when Skip and Mavis came from the house to meet the truck. Cade parked the four-wheeler a few feet from the yard gate, and he and Retta both hung back, just staring at him. Cade finally turned around and brought both her hands to his lips where he kissed the palms.

"I worry about him so much in a foster home. They might not understand that he's a borderline genius but so socially limited," she said. "Mavis said that she and Skip are going to talk to the social worker about fostering him, but their age might throw a wrench in the works."

"I still belive in miracles." He gave her shoulder a gentle squeeze and then snapped several pictures of the kids with his phone. "These can be the pictures that help them remember the day they all pulled together to find him."

"It was so cute when he wanted everyone, even Kirk, to have one, too. That boy's got a big heart," she answered.

"Okay, kids, let's go put the food on the table," Mavis called out.

"Coffee still hot?" Cade asked.

"Pot is full and ready," Retta answered.

His eyes met hers and held for several seconds. "Thanks for everything."

"No thanks necessary. I love that kid," she said.

"You are going to be a fantastic mother someday," he said.

"Thank you for that. I had some fine role models so I hope so."

He wanted to really kiss her but there were too many people watching for that.

*          *          *

"That was definitely flirting." Justin followed him into the house.

"You're just cranky because you're hungry," Cade said. "We have had a good day. We found Benjy and he's not hurt. We'll discuss whatever is between me and Retta another day."

"So you admit something is there?"

"Hey, I fell head over heels in love with Macy Simmons in the third grade, but I got over it. I'm not in love with Retta but if I was, I could get over her just like I did Macy when she moved away and Julie when she walked out on me," he said.

"I don't like you much when you are in the 'gettin' over it' stage," Justin said.

"Well, I don't like you much when you meddle in my business or when you are cranky because you are hungry."

"The new word is *hangry*."

"And you've got a double dose of it." Cade headed toward the dining room, where the kids were already gathered around the table.

After grace, Kirk leaned around Skip and asked, "Wasn't you afraid of the dark, Benjy?"

"No. Dark don't hurt a person. It's just the absence of light. Only what is in the dark will hurt somebody and the ranch don't have them kinds of people on it," he answered.

"Well, I don't like the dark," Kirk said. "If I go out in it, you should go with me since you aren't afraid of it."

"I'll do that and we'll learn things," Benjy said.

"Listen up everyone," Skip said. "From now on you have to clear it with me or Retta before you leave the bunkhouse and the new rule is that you must always take someone with you."

Kirk raised his hand. "I call Benjy."

The pancake platter emptied quickly, so Retta carried it back to the kitchen to make more. Cade followed her with the excuse that he needed to refill the milk pitchers. She looked downright cute with her hair up in a ponytail, shirt-tail untucked, and those tight fittin' jeans. Would she ever figure out that she was a ranch woman or would she find a high-powered executive to share her life with?

The idea of another man holding her in his arms and kissing her shot a blast of jealousy through him. He moved closer to her. "Can I help?"

"Sure you can." She nodded. "You can get that milk back to the table and come back to take back what pancakes are finished cookin' in to them. I'll finish up and bring in the rest."

"Yes, ma'am." Cade dropped a kiss on her forehead.

Benjy was telling the other kids about the picture books they were going to make when Cade set the milk on the table. "And we all get a picture book to take home with us when we leave so we can remember all the good times we had here. But I won't be goin' home because my granny is dead."

"Really?" Alice passed the plate on to Gabby. "But where will we get the pictures?"

"Cade and I will take them with our phones," Retta answered from the kitchen.

"A couple of times a week, maybe starting Friday," Cade said. "We'll get out the craft supplies and each of you can make a scrapbook. You can put pictures or write in it whatever you want."

"All of us together?" Benjy asked.

"Yes," Cade answered quickly. "All eight of you right here at this table. I'll be taking pictures all week and I'll have a bunch printed and ready for you to put into your books on Friday evening after supper."

Retta carried in a platter full of pancakes and set them on the table.

"I thought I was supposed to bring those," Cade said.

She sat down beside him. "Got them done faster than I thought."

Cade hurried to the kitchen and returned with another platter stacked high.

"I can help take the pictures." Levi took the platter from him, piled three onto his plate, and handed them off to Benjy, who did the same thing and gave them to Justin.

"Me too," Justin said.

"Will Kirk say I'm weird if my book isn't like his?" Benjy kept his eyes on his plate.

"No, I won't. We'll all make our books like we want to. You ain't weird, Benjy. You're just too smart for the rest of us," Kirk answered.

"Amazin' progress this mornin', wouldn't you say?" Cade laid a hand on Retta's knee under the table and gave it a gentle squeeze. "You were wise to say that we needed to let the kids go help hunt for him."

She covered his hand with hers. "It turned out better than I would have ever figured possible."

\*        \*        \*

It didn't take long for the kids to start bickering again that afternoon when they headed out to the corral to practice their roping skills. Retta followed behind them and listened to Kirk brag about how he could outdo any of them and Faith telling him that he better be ready to back up all that big talk with some action.

"Is this keepin' it normal?" she muttered.

"That's what's best for Benjy right now," Cade said and then jogged on ahead to get the ropes out of the barn.

"Kid really needs a mama and a daddy a lot younger than me and Mavis. Why don't you and Cade adopt him?" Skip asked as he walked up behind her.

Retta stammered and stuttered and finally got out part of a coherent sentence. "Because we are not...and because I'm leaving...and because..."

Skip's laughter rang out over the pasture. "Didn't know anything would rile you that much. You got a thing for Cade, don't you?"

"I don't really know what I've got for Cade," she told him.

"Well, you got to figure that out before you can go forward."

"But I think it's amazing that you and Mavis are thinking of taking Benjy. He'd be happy with y'all."

Skip nodded. "I hope that they let us have him. We took in Levi and raised him from a baby. I figure we got enough years in us that would be good enough to raise another kid, but don't say nothing to the kids until we're sure. I'd hate to get Benjy's hopes up and then shatter them," he said.

"My lips are sealed." She grinned.

Levi pulled his truck into the barn with a load of feed in the back at the same time Retta and Skip arrived at the corral.

"Hey, if you'll come out here and show them some of your fancy work, I'll unload the feed," Cade called out.

"You got a deal." Levi hopped out of the vehicle and then jogged over to the corral fence.

"Retta, you can go help Cade while me and Levi work with the ropin' business," Skip said.

Cade hefted a bag up on each shoulder and carried them into the barn with only a nod toward Retta when she followed him into the barn and rolled a wheelbarrow out to the truck, dragged three bags out onto it, and pushed it into the area of the barn where he'd put the other two. When she turned around to go for more, their paths crossed and her breath caught in her chest at that gorgeous display of strength and sheer masculinity.

When the job was done, she sat down on a hay bale and fanned herself with her straw hat. Trying to keep her eyes off him as he leaned on a support post, she said, "So I've been wondering—" She took a deep breath and banished the real thoughts in her head about how it would be to fall back on the hay with him and make out like a couple of teenagers. "I've been thinking about—" Mercy! She couldn't tell him what was really on her mind and yet, she couldn't remember what she was about to ask. "About how we're goin' to get all these kids to the funeral. It'll take a caravan of vehicles," she finally blurted out.

"I talked to the preacher and he's letting us borrow the church van. He'll deliver it this evening sometime and we'll take it back tomorrow when we get home."

*Home!*

She'd heard that word several times from the kids and Benjy throughout the day. Her home had always been the farm in southern Oklahoma. Even in the college dorm and in the apartment she'd rented after she got her first job, home was where she was raised, where her father lived, and where she went back to on holidays and summer vacation time.

Now she had no home.

"What are you thinkin' about?" he asked.

"Home. It just now hit me that my home is gone," she said honestly. "I'm in that limbo state between when one door has closed and another hasn't opened yet. I can sympathize with these kids in foster care, not knowing if it's permanent and knowing that it probably isn't. I'll be okay once I get a job and an apartment of my own."

Cade wiped sweat from his forehead with a red bandanna. "I can't imagine not having a permanent home. Longhorn Canyon has always been that for me."

"It's not a good feelin'." She got up and settled her hat back on her head.

"Thanks for helpin'," he said.

"You're welcome. I don't hear kids arguing anymore out there in the corral, so we'd better check on them. They may have poor old Skip roped and tied to a fence post," she said.

He reached out a hand and tipped up her chin. "Mavis says that home is where the heart is. Find your heart, Retta, and you'll find your home."

He lowered his lips to hers and brushed a sweet kiss on her. It didn't last long because four little girls dashed into the barn saying that they were finished with roping posts and now they were going to throw the football through the tire.

"Benjy is going to help me," Alice whispered before she took off in a dead run.

"Wouldn't you just love to have that much energy?" Cade laughed.

*Oh, honey, I would have even more than that if we were in the right place, like tangled up in sheets under an air-conditioning vent. Or even in a hayloft on an old quilt with our sweaty bodies . . .* she shook her head to clear it and pulled her phone from her hip pocket to catch a picture of her girls, hand in hand, headed out of the barn.

*       *       *

With hair fixed and wearing their Sunday best, the girls were ready fifteen minutes early that Tuesday morning. Retta had laid out a simple black suit—the very one that she planned to wear to her job interview—but when she saw that the girls were wearing the same little sundresses that they'd worn to church the past two Sundays, she hung it back up. Choosing a long denim skirt and a pearl snap shirt, she hoped that Cade wasn't disappointed in her, but she couldn't make those children feel like they weren't dressed fancy enough.

The white bus emblazoned with the church logo was parked in between the two bunkhouses. At the right time, they all marched outside and Levi opened the doors for them.

"Don't you ladies all look nice," he said.

"Thank you," all four chorused.

Retta was glad to see that all the cowboys were wearing jeans and nice shirts, but no ties or suits, when they got into the bus. Once they were all inside, Cade sat down beside Retta, leaving the seat across from them for Mavis and Skip.

Skip leaned across the aisle and said, "It was pretty quiet on my home front this morning when we got back from breakfast."

"Mine, too," she whispered.

"Mavis got a call as we were leavin' the house. The social worker says we got a good chance," Skip said.

"I really don't like funerals," Cade whispered.

"Me, either, and—" She paused.

"Been too soon since your dad died, right?"

She nodded. "I thought I was ready for him to go and I wouldn't wish him back in that kind of pain, but I had no idea how long this whole grieving process would take. I grabbed my phone last night to call him and tell him all about our day with Benjy."

"They say you have to go through the five steps of grieving," he said.

"And every one of them is tough," she said. "Are we going to a church?"

"No, just a graveside service. The sister who was the executor of her will is frail and isn't able for much more than that. I hope that it brings closure to Benjy. He's so different that I don't know what to expect."

*He's a good man,* came her father's voice.

She looked out the side window at a couple of miles of mesquite bushes, Angus cattle, and cow tongue cacti. She felt a movement and turned to find that Cade had leaned his head back, pulled his hat down over his chest, and crossed his arms over his broad chest.

Half an hour later, Levi pulled the bus through the open gates into the cemetery. An arched sign above the entry announced that it was the Slidell Cemetery. It was smaller than the Waurika Cemetery, where she'd laid her dad to rest, and had fewer trees. Retta spotted only a few offering shade in the hot morning sun. A barrel at the side of the gate held lantana plants and a sweet potato vine that crept down the sides.

Levi quickly spotted the green awning that had been set up with the casket underneath it and drove down the gravel pathway toward it. When he parked, Skip left the bus first with Benjy at his side.

Faith nudged Retta and whispered, "I ain't never been to one of these things. What am I supposed to do?"

"Not a thing but listen and maybe sing if they want us to," Retta answered softly. "And afterward, maybe be nice to Benjy while he adjusts to the idea."

Faith nodded and grabbed Alice's hand.

Benjy went right to a woman who was sitting in a wheelchair at the end of a row of seats. "Aunt Rosie, my granny is dead."

She put up her arms, but he took a step back. "Yes, she's gone but she didn't suffer. One minute she was reading your letter to me over the phone and then she was gone."

Benjy wiped tears from his cheeks with his shirtsleeve. "I'm scared to go where people don't know me."

"I would let you live with me, Benjy, but I'm going to a nursing home, sweetheart. I'll be checkin' in next week but I've rented a storage unit near here and I'm having all your granny's things moved into it. When you get settled you can come visit me in the nursing home and I'll give you the key so you can get whatever you want from it," she said.

Cade walked up and extended a hand. "I'm Cade and we'll take good care of him on the ranch until..."

Aunt Rosie grabbed his hand and held it to her face. "I know you will. My sister spoke highly of what you are doing for these kids. Will you keep me informed about him?"

"I promise," Cade said.

Aunt Rosie pointed to a chair. "You sit right here, Benjy, beside me."

They all moved forward to sit down and then Rosie nodded at the preacher, an old guy with bushy eyebrows that matched his snow-white hair and a long, wrinkled face.

"Maudie Green was born Maud Charlotte Anderson on July tenth, 1943, and passed from this earth..." he started.

When he finished, he said, "Let us pray."

He could have recited a chapter from Job or Exodus instead of asking God to deliver Benjy's grandmother into the angel's hands. Retta could never be sure what he'd said because she was feeling every emotion that Benjy did. Denial, sorrow, and anger all mixed up into one ball of fear.

When he finished praying, he nodded toward the funeral director, who opened the casket, being careful to lay back the satin so that Benjy's grandmother, Maudie, was visible. She wore a pink dress with a little corsage of silk blue bonnets pinned to the pocket.

"She liked them flowers, bein' from Texas and all." Rosie sniffled.

"Anyone that would like to pay last respects will have a few minutes," the preacher said.

"Will y'all go with me, Mavis and Retta?" Benjy whispered.

They stood up at the same time. He put one hand in Mavis's and the other one in Retta's. Together they took a couple of steps and he gazed inside the casket for a long time.

"Good-bye, Granny," he whispered. "You are really dead and I have to live with someone else. Cade will fix it though. I know he will."

Retta had to swallow half a dozen times to get the lump

down that closed off her throat. Then she felt Cade's strong arm slip around her shoulders and noticed that Skip was on the other side of Mavis.

Benjy inhaled deeply, let it out slowly and motioned to the other kids. "This is my granny. If you want to see her, you can."

One by one they circled around the front and ends of the casket.

"Now we're goin' to sing 'I'll Fly Away,'" he said. "Because that was her favorite church song." He started it in a little boy's voice and the others sang along on the parts that they knew. Cade, Justin, Levi, and Skip carried the words all the way through. Retta knew every word but she couldn't make a peep through some of it.

*It's time to let me go now, Retta Jo. I'm ready to go be with your mother and I can't until you say the words.* Her father's words the day before he died came back to her.

"Oh, Daddy, I can't," she'd said around the pain in her heart.

"Please, baby girl," he'd gasped.

"I can't imagine living without you in my life," she'd said.

He gripped her hand as tight as he could and slipped off into a coma. The next morning he took his last breath.

*I won't be at peace until you are.* She could hear his voice in her head.

*Okay, Daddy, I'll try harder,* she promised.

After they finished singing, the preacher stepped up beside Benjy. "We'll wait to close this until everyone is gone."

"Thank you." Cade shook hands with him.

Benjy tucked his hand into Skip's and without looking back headed toward the bus with all the kids behind them.

"I hope this works out with Mavis and Skip." Cade's

voice was deeper than ever and his eyes so filled with sadness that Retta wanted to hug him right there in front of everyone.

"I hope so. And if it doesn't, then we'll both have to b-be...," she stammered.

"Brave?"

"That's right," she said.

"Nothing has ever brought me to my knees like thinking of that boy in a foster home with people that don't understand him," Cade said.

She wanted to ask if Julie hadn't done a pretty good job of bringing him to his knees too, but she kept her mouth shut.

# Chapter Seventeen

On the way home, Levi stopped in Sunset at a little barbecue place and Cade treated everyone to lunch. The kids sat together at a long table and whispered to each other the whole time they ate.

"What do you think they're talkin' about?" Skip asked.

"Who knows? Maybe they're just trying to help Benjy," Cade answered.

"Or they're plotting against the adults and they're all going to run off together to keep him from going to a foster home." Justin chuckled. "Remember when you and I ran away from home?"

"I think that's a story worth tellin'," Retta said.

"I was eight and Justin was six and we decided we'd join the circus after we'd seen a show on television. We snuck out one night and we were walkin' down the road about midnight," Cade said.

"I was terrified of the dark and we couldn't really remember how to get to Skip's house so we could talk Levi into going with us." Justin laughed.

"I wouldn't have gone, believe me." Levi shook his head. "I was even more afraid of the dark than Justin, and besides I'd just rescued a puppy from getting killed on the road about then and I wouldn't have left it."

"But we never made it to Skip and Mavis's house. A neighbor came by and offered us a ride and he turned his truck around and took us right back home," Cade said. "We were grounded to the yard for a whole week and then we had to wash dishes for the whole next week."

"And that was the biggest punishment of all," Justin said. "I hated it because Cade always washed and I had to dry them. He was slow as molasses and it seemed like he was trying to wipe the roses right off Mama's dishes instead of just getting the food cleaned off."

"If they weren't clean, then Mama added another week to our punishment," Cade explained. "But back to the kids. We might want to keep an eye on them this afternoon just in case they've got something crazy up their sleeves."

"I agree," Skip said.

"Me too," Retta said. "They're bonding together since all this happened and they very easily could be planning to try to whisk Benjy away to the city and take care of him themselves."

"Tell you what. Why don't we put them all busy tomorrow at the cabin? Y'all said the porch railing could use a coat of paint. If they're having fun, maybe they'll forget about doing something stupid," Skip offered.

"Great idea," Retta said.

\*       \*       \*

It only took fifteen minutes to go from the café to the ranch and the minute Levi opened the bus doors, the kids scattered to their bunkhouses. They'd changed from their good clothes into shorts and T-shirts and were circling around Skip when he got off the bus.

"Can we all go to the barn and check on Little Bit? We've been talkin' about it and we don't want a contest. We want that to be his real name. And will you go with us, Skip, because we need to practice our ropin' and after that we want to get in some football practice," Kirk asked.

"Please, please, please," Benjy begged.

"Let me get changed and I'll go with you," Retta said.

Faith quickly whispered something into Skip's ear, and he nodded.

"I was wonderin'"—he rubbed his chin—"if you'd like to drive to Bowie and pick up groceries. It's been a couple of weeks and Mavis has a grocery list made, but she's too tired to shop today, especially with that hurt arm. And she needs a rest, both physically and emotionally. If you don't want to go, one of the guys can."

Skip grinned and the children all beamed. It didn't take a rocket scientist to know that they were up to something when Faith grabbed Alice's hand and they skipped together toward the barn with everyone else following after them.

"Don't you have to go into Bowie this afternoon to the vet's office so we can work some calves tomorrow?" Levi asked Cade.

"I don't mind doing the shopping at all but I can go by myself," Retta said.

Cade tossed his pickup keys to her. "I've got to take this bus back to the preacher. You can follow behind me, and then we'll get whatever Mavis or you and Skip need for the bunkhouses."

"Give me five minutes to talk to the girls," she said.

"Sure thing." He nodded and headed into the ranch house. He went straight to his room and opened the bottom drawer where the wedding rings were still stored. He flipped it open and there wasn't the usual pain attached to the memories they created—they were just rings. Still, there was something not quite settled because he wasn't ready to let them go completely. He slipped them back in the drawer and picked up Mavis's list from the kitchen table on his way out.

\*       \*       \*

Retta drove up beside him when he parked the van at the church. By the time he got out, she'd changed from the driver's to the passenger's seat.

"You could've driven. I'm not so macho that I can't ride with a woman driver." He grinned as he strapped the seat belt across his broad chest.

"Your truck," she said.

He turned north on the highway toward Bowie and she tried to think of something—anything—that would start a conversation. She didn't want to bring up the funeral because that reminded her of the last one she'd gone to, and thinking of her father made her sad. They'd already discussed how great the kids were behaving when it came to taking care of Benjy.

"Okay," she finally said.

"Let's," he said at the exact same time.

"I'll go first," she said. "I think we should talk about the elephant sitting in the truck between us."

"I'm attracted to you," he blurted out. "And have been since you walked into that first interview."

Well, now that was bold enough, she thought.

"Me, too, but—" she started again.

He butted in for the second time. "But why start something that has no finish line?"

"Exactly." She took a deep breath and let it out slowly. "Unless we agree that it's only a fling and there'll be no regrets or tears when I leave." Before he could speak she said, "But I'm really not..."

He laid a hand on her shoulder. "Me either."

"So you treat every date like she could be your soul mate?" she asked.

"Do you?" he shot back, as if he was avoiding the question.

"Haven't had much time for dating." She fidgeted with her hands. "I was so busy with my job and then taking care of my dad."

"Which leaves very little time for fun, right?" he asked.

"Something like that. I've had dates and I had one serious relationship in college, but we wanted different things so it didn't last," she said. "Now your turn. How many relationships have you had since Julie?"

"Nothing serious. Just a few dates here and there," he answered.

Well, that was honest enough, but that would essentially make Retta the rebound woman. The one who'd finally gotten him past his heartbreak over Julie. Maybe kind of like a new puppy after one had died—loved but not the same or as deep as that first little guy who'd stolen a little boy's heart.

"It's strange to be talkin' about this instead of just letting it go wherever it goes," Cade said after a few moments of silence.

"Yep." She nodded.

He snagged a good parking place in the Walmart lot and

she quickly unfastened her seat belt and got out of the truck. She was halfway to the doors when she glanced back to see him still sitting in the truck with a phone to his ear. She lengthened her stride, grabbed a basket someone had left in the middle of the lot, and got a blast of wonderfully cold air when she pushed it inside the store.

She pulled the grocery list out of her hip pocket and started checking off the first one when she got in line at the deli to get three pounds of smoked ham. Before it was her turn to order, Cade was right beside her.

"Sorry about that. Skip called to report in about Benjy."

"Is he all right? We can go back right now and do this later if he needs us." Retta started to turn the cart around.

"He's fine, real good in fact. The social worker called and said that they were pushing the foster papers through fast since Mavis and Skip had done this before and that Benjy can definitely go home with them when camp is over. It'll take a while for the adoption, but now we know. But Mavis has decided to quit work when camp is over. I don't know what we're going to do without her." Cade groaned.

"So you'll hire someone else," she said. "Unless you guys are going to do all the cooking."

"You think I could ever replace Mavis?" His voice had a slight edge to it.

"That's not at all what I said," she bit back at him.

*You are fighting because you don't want to face your feelings for him and you are disappointed in him and in yourself,* her father said so distinctly in her head that he could have been right in front of her.

*I won't be a rebound toy,* she argued.

She waited for her father to say something else but he didn't.

"While you get that list filled, I'm going back to the

sports area. I need to get a couple more rods and reels so we can take the kids fishin' this week." Cade was gone before she could comment.

Her cart needed sideboards by the time she made it to the checkout lines. She'd already started to put items on the conveyor belt when he showed up again and added what he'd picked up to her things.

"Looks like you've found everything you needed," he said.

"Did you?"

"Oh, yeah. We'll be caught up enough after today that the guys and I can take the kids fishin' sometime in the next couple of days. Did you get enough sandwich supplies so Mavis can pack a little picnic lunch for them?"

With a curt nod, she kept putting items on the belt as the cashier moved it forward and bagged the groceries. "Where do you fish?"

"Canyon Creek," he answered as he pulled out the ranch credit card and stuck it into the chip reader. "It's too far for them to walk. We'll pile them into the back of a truck."

"Is everything always spur-of-the-minute planning?" she asked.

He pushed the loaded cart toward the door. "Pretty much. We're a working ranch, so if there's time, we gladly give it to the kids. If not, then they can go with us and learn something new. And besides all that, we have to depend on the weather. Why are you so cranky?"

"Me? You're the one who's acting like it's the end of the world because Mavis is quitting to take care of Benjy. I just stated the obvious and you got snippy." It was well over a hundred degrees, but the weather wasn't nearly as hot as Retta's anger.

*This is ridiculous. He's done nothing to make you this*

*mad.* This time it was Tina's voice in her head. *You are just fighting against your own feelings. He doesn't want a summer fling and neither do you. You want more and he's not willin' to give it, so back off, girlfriend, and settle down.*

"What makes you think I was snippy?" Cade asked as they finished loading the truck and climbed into the cab.

"Didn't you just walk away without finishing our conversation?" She didn't even glance his way.

"Because I needed rods and reels and I've been to the store with Mavis before. It takes a while to fill the list."

"Did you get bait for the fishin' trip?" she asked.

"We dig worms."

"Well, good luck with that."

He stopped what he was doing and took a step forward. "And that means?"

"Not a drop of rain in several days. Worms are all down deep in the ground except maybe out in the shade of the barn. Grasshoppers would be better, and we're still avoiding this chemistry between us," she said.

"What do you know about fishin'?"

"I know enough about fishing to bait a hook."

"Oh, well, you're baitin' this hook real well, darlin'," Cade snapped back. "I thought we had this chemistry thing settled because neither of us wanted to start something we couldn't finish. After all, you'll be leavin' in a few weeks."

"I'm not baiting anything just because I think something needs a little more discussion!" She turned and her gaze locked with his.

"Well, I don't see the point in talking things to death and then resurrecting them and talking about them some more."

Retta huffed. "You ever go fishing with Julie?"

"No, Julie didn't like to do anything that might make her sweat or get her hands dirty. She sunburned easily, so we usually did what she wanted, which didn't involve being outside," he answered.

"I can't imagine you with a woman like that," she said. "Sounds like a one-sided relationship to me for sure." She took a deep breath and caught a whiff of what was left of his shaving lotion from that morning.

"Why are we talkin' about her anyway? That chapter of my life is finished and done with."

"Are you sure about that?"

"You want proof?"

Retta didn't have time to wipe the sweat from her upper lip before his mouth landed on hers in a kiss that was far hotter than the weather. He flipped the console up and moved closer to her, wrapping her in his arms and deepening each kiss until she was on the verge of begging to get a motel room. When they came up for air, she was panting and blushing so fiery red that she felt blistered.

He nodded toward the van parked right next to them. "Guess we've got an audience."

"What?" she asked.

"That would be the preacher's wife right next to us with her eyes bugged out and her jaw draggin' down to her chest," he said.

"So? We're both a good bit over twenty-one and neither of us are married." She waved at their audience.

"If that's what makin' up is like, maybe we should fight more often," Cade said as he put the console back down. "Imagine what will happen after a real argument." He glanced over and waggled his eyebrows at her.

"What makes you think that will ever happen?"

"A cowboy can dream, can't he? And besides I might just start an argument to see where it goes."

"Did you start that spat in the store so that—"

He cupped her chin in his hand and planted a kiss so full of tenderness and passion mixed that it made her head swim. "No, darlin' Retta, I did not start that fight but I think I did a fine job of finishing it."

"That's pretty cocky," she whispered.

"Yep, it is." He started the engine and drove out of the parking lot.

# Chapter Eighteen

The girls and boys both came running out to the truck to help carry food inside when Cade and Retta got home. They were all talking at once about the little donkey and how he was walking all over the corral even if he did still limp a little.

"And Benjy roped the post twice," Ivan said.

"And I beat Kirk," Faith bragged. "And Little Bit likes me better than him."

"You did not," Kirk protested. "It was a tie and I would've got that last throw if you hadn't poked me with a stick. And Little Bit don't like you better. Benjy is the one that he really likes best because Benjy found him when he was lost."

Cade picked up four heavy bags to carry inside. Justin leaned on a porch post and shook his head at his brother when he passed by him.

"Mavis is quittin'," he said.

"I know," Cade said.

"Here, let me take those on inside for you." Skip took the bags from Cade and held the door for Retta who brought in boxes with the new fishing equipment.

"What are we goin' to do?" Justin asked.

Cade clamped a hand on Justin's shoulder. "We'll get through it."

"The preacher's wife called her," Justin said. "She said that you and Retta were actin' like teenagers, makin' out right there in public."

"Yep, we were. We had a little spat and then we made up," Cade said.

"Mavis thought it was great," Justin said. "Faith has told the kids that you like Retta so they're plotting all kinds of things to throw y'all together."

"Smart little devils, ain't they?" Cade opened the screen door and held it for Justin. "We might as well get on in the house. Don't mind the heat when I'm working but to just stand out here in it when there's cool air in the house seems kind of crazy."

The kids had helped put away the food, except what Mavis and Retta needed for supper, and now they were all asking what they could do to help get it ready to eat. They clustered around Mavis like baby chickens around a mama hen, and she gave each one a job.

"Sweet tea?" Cade asked.

Mavis pointed over the tops of Benjy's and Kirk's heads. "In the refrigerator. There should be enough for you guys to have a glass and we'll make more for supper. I want to tell Benjy the news tonight at the supper table so everyone will hear at once." She turned her finger around to Cade.

"Sounds great to me." Cade poured two glasses of tea and started out of the busy kitchen.

"And Cade," Mavis said, "next time don't get caught."

Heat filled Retta's cheeks in a deep blush.

Mavis whipped around toward Retta. "And that goes for you too."

"Yes, ma'am," they said in unison.

*        *        *

Faith grinned and winked at Retta, causing high spots of color on her cheeks again. Dammit, what was it with this place? She hadn't blushed so much since she was in junior high school.

With lots of help, supper was on the table at exactly six o'clock, and Retta was emotionally and physically drained. She wanted a hot bath, maybe a call to Tina, and a good night's sleep, in that order. Usually fried chicken was her favorite supper too, but she couldn't even finish off one drumstick.

"Boy, your plate looks like a bone yard for dead chickens." Skip teased Kirk when everyone had pushed back their plates.

"Chickens have only two legs but Mavis buys extra legs. So did my granny but she is dead now and I will never see her again because that's what *dead* means," Benjy said.

"I ate eight," Kirk bragged. "One more than Faith did."

"Look at my plate," Ivan bragged. "I did good. I ate four."

"Beat you." Faith brought two bones from her lap that had been folded into a paper napkin. "Finally, we don't tie and I ate one more than you."

Kirk picked up the last wing on the platter and quickly ate it. "Tie!"

"Yay for the boys." Nelson pumped his fist in the air.

"Who wants ice cream for dessert?" Mavis asked. "There are four flavors or you can make sundaes or banana splits."

Eight hands shot up in the air.

Skip shook his head. "I've had enough. But I thought the kids could start making their scrapbooks after supper. Then they'll be ready to put the pictures in when the guys get them printed. What do you think, Retta?"

There went the nice long bath, the visit with Tina, and an early night in bed. But this was her job, so Retta nodded. "We can get that bin of construction paper and art supplies out of our bunkhouse after we help Mavis clean up the kitchen."

"We already did, and the boys are going to help with cleanup tonight," Skip said.

"Do we have to?" Ivan groaned.

"Yes, you do." Skip's tone didn't leave room for even a little negotiating. "And after we get the scrapbooks made, we're going to watch a movie together. You get the night off, Miz Retta. I'll take care of these hooligans."

"I owe you," she said without argument. "Any night you want to have some free time, I'll take them all."

"I'll hold you to that. Like maybe Friday afternoon and evening both, so me and Mavis can have us a date night?" Skip asked.

"You got it." Retta nodded.

"And I've got something to say before y'all all get involved with the scrapbook business," Mavis said. "This is mainly for Benjy, but we want all of you to know so you won't worry. Skip and I've been in touch with the social worker, and she's agreed for Benjy to come and live with us when camp is over. How do you feel about that, Benjy?"

"Oh, man." Kirk reached around and patted him on the back. "That's the best news ever."

Benjy pushed back his chair and slowly rounded the

table. When he reached Mavis, he wrapped his arms around her and hugged her tightly. "I will be a good boy."

Uncontrollable tears ran down Retta's cheeks. Cade turned her face toward him and dabbed them away with a napkin.

"Did Cade make you sad?" Faith asked.

"No, these are happy tears. I'm glad that Benjy is going to have a great home," Retta answered.

"Me too," Faith said.

Benjy calmly walked back around the table and picked up his plate. "It's time to clean up so we can work on scrapbooks. We will need paper, glue, and scissors and a ruler to get things right. Justin, you or Levi want to make scrapbooks?"

"I've got work out in the barn," Levi said in a hurry.

"And I've got to help him," Justin came in right behind him.

"Not much into scrapbook making?" Retta swiped the napkin across her cheeks once more and managed a weak smile.

Levi shook his head emphatically. "Anytime I get around glue and paper, I get it all over me. I'd rather go stack hay or hang out with Little Bit."

Justin laughed. "Don't let him fool you into believing that. He used to eat glue when we were in kindergarten."

"Okay, okay." Levi held up a hand when the kids couldn't contain their laughter by covering their mouths with their hands. "I really did until I got real sick one night and Mavis told me that it was from glue stickin' my guts together."

"That's impossible. The glue went to your stomach and the acid there would have destroyed it," Benjy said.

"It wasn't true but it sure enough broke him from eating

it." Skip chuckled. "Why don't you let us take it from here, Retta."

"Thank you," Retta said with a yawn. "You girls bring your scrapbooks home with you so I can see them."

Faith and Sasha gave her a thumbs-up sign and went back to eating.

Gabby whispered, "I'll make sure everyone remembers. If you're asleep, we'll be quiet when we come home."

There was that word again—*home*.

Retta pushed it to the back of her mind and left the dining room and kitchen to them. Another day, she'd do something with all the kids and give Skip a rest, but that night she was very grateful for a little time to think about those steamy hot kisses in the parking lot.

She went straight to the bedroom, stripped out of her clothing and padded barefoot and naked to the bathroom. She found the bath salts that Tina had sent her for her last birthday and poured them under the running water and then crawled into the tub, leaned her head back and shut her eyes.

"Now about those kisses," she muttered. "They didn't mean anything, nothing at all. They were just kisses because we each thought the other one was angry and wanted to make it right."

*Sure they were,* Tina's voice in her head taunted her. *Don't give me that load of bull crap.*

"I'm not having this conversation with you. That's why I didn't call you, yet. You always figure out a way to get me to tell you everything and I've got to figure this thing out before I talk to you." She leaned her head back and shut her eyes.

When she awoke the water was cold and the air conditioner was on, making goose bumps on her arms and neck. She quickly got out of the tub and wrapped up in her white terry-cloth robe. Now she was hungry, so she went to the kitchen, grabbed a bag of chocolate mint cookies and a glass of milk, and carried them to the living room, where she sat down on the sofa and stretched out her legs to the other end.

She had a mouthful of cookies when the back door to the bunkhouse opened. Figuring it was one of the girls who'd remembered something she wanted for her scrapbook project, she didn't even get up. But she almost choked when Cade's deep voice asked, "You decent, Retta?"

She quickly folded her robe over her naked body and yelled, "I am and I'm in the living area."

"I brought contraband. Can I come inside?"

"What kind of contraband?"

"Two icy cold beers," he answered.

"Then enter, and lock the door behind you so we don't get caught. We don't want Mavis mad at us twice in one day." She giggled.

His eyebrows shot up when he saw her. "You look like a goddess."

Another one of those damned blushes started but she warded it off. "Flattery and a beer. This is a good evening."

He put a longneck bottle of Coors into her hand, sat down on the other end of the sofa, and put her feet into his lap. "It's the truth, not flattery."

She took a sip. "I'd forgotten how good a cold beer could be at the end of a day."

He picked up her right foot and began to massage it.

"That's wonderful. You can have my summer salary if you'll do that every night from now to the end of the job."

He took a long draw of his beer and began to work on the other foot. When he finished, he kissed each toe, then the sole of her foot and made his way to her knee, one slow hot kiss at a time.

"Tell me to quit," he said.

"I can't. I don't want to," she said.

He opened her robe and the kisses continued up her thigh, across her belly, and she thought she'd die before he ever made it to her lips.

"Sweet lord," she muttered when he spent extra time and kisses on her breasts. Then suddenly he was sitting up and she was in his lap. Her robe was open and his big hands were gently rubbing her back as the kisses on her mouth got more and more passionate.

"Tell me to quit. Tell me we have no business doing this. Tell me now because in ten minutes it'll be too difficult to stop." He pushed her dark hair back with his hands and cupped her cheeks, staring into her eyes.

"This sofa is too short and too narrow for us." She reached between their bodies to unbuckle his belt.

He stood up and she wrapped her long legs around his waist. "To the bedroom?" he asked.

"That's softer than the floor." She nibbled on his ear.

*Just a summer fling, that's all this is. And when it's done I'll wave good-bye and only remember him when I see a sexy cowboy in boots and a hat.*

He laid her on the bed, robe gaping open, and quickly undressed without taking his eyes from hers. "You are stunning, Retta."

"You are all muscle and…" Her breath caught in her chest.

"I've ached for you," he said as he entered her and they began to work together with a perfect rhythm.

He certainly was not a novice at the game. Bringing her right up to the edge of a climax until she panted so hard that she could scarcely breathe and then slowing down, kissing her neck, her ears, her eyelids all the while.

"Tell me what you like." His warm breath caressed her ear as he shifted from low into high gear again.

"Everything. Don't stop any of it." She swung her legs up to wrap around his body.

"Protection?" He groaned suddenly. "I forgot about that."

"I'm on the pill," she told him.

"Thank God."

She dug her fingernails into his back and put a huge hickey on his neck as she reached the clouds of the most amazing climax she'd ever experienced.

"Sweet Jesus," she gasped.

"Feel the need to pray? That's a first." Cade rolled to the side but kept her in his arms. Somehow the robe was now on the floor and they were both slick with sweat. The air conditioner kicked on and a steady stream of cold air flowed down onto their bodies.

"I'm hot and cold at the same time." Retta felt as if she were floating above her body, that things that amazing didn't happen to her and she wanted to spend the rest of her life in the bedroom with Cade Maguire. Something this emotional could never be just a summer fling.

"That was . . . no words." He panted.

"I know." She cuddled up closer to his side.

How was she ever going to wave good-bye without regrets after what she'd just experienced?

# *Chapter Nineteen*

The next morning should have been awkward, and it might have been, if there hadn't been eight excited children bouncing around, all eager to get a paintbrush in their hands. The noise level as they all sat down to breakfast would have put a busy airport to shame. Then suddenly it was so quiet that they could've heard a kitten breathing in the other room as Skip said grace.

While Retta's head was bowed and her eyes were closed, Cade's hand closed over hers under the table and squeezed gently. She opened one eyelid and he mouthed, *Amazing.*

"Amen!" Skip said.

"Yes," she said.

"Hungry are you?" Levi asked.

"I am and I'm grateful to be sitting here at this table with this awesome bunch of kids and family this morning. Now let's eat so we can go spruce up the cabin," Retta said.

"Amen to that," Skip agreed.

Cade squeezed her hand one more time and then picked up a basket of biscuits and passed them to her. "Are you going with us, Mavis?"

She shook her head. "Wild horses couldn't drag me out there. If there's a single leaf of poison ivy anywhere within ten miles, I'll be broken out so bad I'd have to leave the ranch for a week."

"Oh, no!" Gabby's hands flew to her cheeks. "That would be awful."

"Besides the social worker is comin' by this mornin' with some paperwork that Skip and I need to look over so that Benjy can come and live with us," Mavis told them. "I've put a bunch of raggedy shirts in a basket. Each of you put one on over your clothes so you don't get paint all over you."

"Yes, ma'am." Benjy nodded. "I'm glad that I get to live with you and Skip, so why am I sad—" He stopped and covered his face with his hands.

Levi put his fork down and patted the boy on the shoulder. "It's okay, little man. It takes a long time to get over losing someone that you love."

"But cowboys don't cry, and someday I will be a cowboy and work on a ranch," Benjy muttered and then straightened his back.

Justin clamped a hand on Benjy's shoulder. "It's okay to be sad sometimes. We all know you'll miss her."

Cade's hand rested on Retta's knee under the table. When she looked up at him, his slight smile and the kindness in his blue eyes said volumes—he understood that Benjy's sadness went even deeper for her as she tried to get closure for her dad's death.

"Well," Alice piped up from across the table. "I bet that

painting the porch today and getting to have a picnic in the
woods will make you happy, Benjy."

The corners of his mouth turned up in a sad little smile.
"They used to make paint with lead in it but now they
make it like a layer of plastic. It's called latex paint and the
brushes clean up with water. I don't like the smell of gaso-
line or paint thinner like they used to clean up the old kind.
I will be happy to paint the porch. I will show Kirk how to
do it right."

"How about you?" Cade whispered from the corner of
his mouth. "Does anything on the ranch make you happy?"

"Some things more than others." Retta ran her hand from
his knee halfway up his thigh.

He quickly clamped his hand over hers. "Y'all want to
ride in the back of a pickup or do you want to get out the
hay wagon?"

"Pickup!" Kirk shouted. "That'll get us there faster."

"Then pickup it is." Cade nodded.

She moved her hand and went back to finishing breakfast.

"That was mean," he said softly.

"Two people can play the flirting game, cowboy," she
said softly with a wink of her own.

*       *       *

After breakfast, Cade drove one truck with the kids in the
back and Retta riding shotgun beside him. Skip drove a second one with food and drinks, along with paintbrushes and
two gallons of paint in the bed of the truck.

"I dreamed of you last night." He deliberately drove
slowly so he could spend more time alone with Retta.

"And what happened in the dream?" she asked.

"I didn't wake up in my bed alone."

"And what lucky woman was sleeping with you?"

"Oh, this brown-eyed brunette that I'm getting to know. She's an awesome lady. Real ranch savvy and is great with kids," he answered.

"Imagine that."

"Want to know what happened before we went to sleep?" His heart threw in an extra beat just thinking about the dream.

There was that heat rising in her cheeks again. "I think I know."

"It was fantastic." He started to reach over and lay a hand on her knee but caught a glimpse of three faces in the rearview mirror. Alice, Gabby, and Sasha all had their faces pressed against the back window.

"Looks like we have an audience. Justin said they were inventing things to do to throw us together and that Skip is in on it." Cade adjusted the mirror so she could see.

"The little imps. I wonder if Mavis put them up to it." Retta giggled. "Are the boys in on it too?"

"Yep. That and the funeral is what's bonded them all together. Think we could play along so they'll think they've done something really great?"

"Looks like we did a pretty good job of playing along last night, doesn't it?" she whispered.

"Honey, that was not playing. That was as real as it gets," he told her. "And here we are. I wish now that this cabin was ten or maybe even a hundred miles away so I could spend hours in the cab of this truck with you."

"That's about the most romantic thing anyone's ever said to me."

"Then you've been dating idiots and you know what Benjy says about the stats on them. They have an IQ of twenty-five." He parked the truck under the shade of a big gnarly scrub oak tree and the kids looked like monkeys as they scrambled over the sides to the ground.

Before she could respond, Skip pulled his truck in beside them, got out, and whistled loudly.

"Hey, kids, gather round for your directions. I've got a paintbrush for each of you and paint in two buckets. The girls will take the left side of the porch and the boys the right side. The trick is to paint the railings and the posts, not to paint the porch or yourselves." He chuckled.

Cade slid out of his seat and propped his elbows on the bed of his truck. "This is not a race or a competition. Fast does not win a prize. Work together and make it look really nice."

"When we get done, can we explore?" Ivan asked.

"Like go inside the cabin?" Nelson asked.

"We thought maybe y'all would like to take the picnic lunch inside to keep from sharing it with the ants," Retta said.

"Yay!!" Benjy raised his hand to high-five with the other boys. "This is going to be a fun day. Come on boys' team. Let's get this job started."

Cade kept his eyes on Retta as she followed her girls to the porch. Tight jeans hugged her curves and that chambray shirt tied in a knot at her waist accentuated her slim figure.

"She's a keeper," Skip said as he passed by him with a bucket of paint in each hand.

"Yep." Cade put down the tailgate and sat down on it. "Too bad she won't let us keep her on the ranch."

"Sometimes when it comes to a woman, you got to be patient and let 'em think it was all their idea," Skip said seriously.

Watching her designate certain spots for each girl and

then show them how to paint, Cade was again amazed by her patience and kindness with them. They'd remember that for years after they left the ranch.

"And after she leaves, I may never be able to forget her after last night," he muttered. "Or the way it felt so right in my dream to have her lying beside me when I woke up."

\*          \*          \*

The small porch was crowded with eight kids so Retta and Skip both backed away several feet and kept watch until the kids got the hang of painting. When she was satisfied that the girls could finish without supervision, she joined Cade on the tailgate.

"They'll have a lot to report home about tonight," she said and then slapped a hand over her mouth. "Benjy won't have anyone to call."

"I already thought of that and got it covered. Scoot over a little, Cade, and give me some room," Skip said.

Cade slid over close enough that his hip was right against Retta's and Skip eased down beside him. "He's goin' to call Mavis, and when it's time to write his letter, he can write one to me."

"Great!" Retta sighed. "That makes him like Faith."

"And that is?" Cade asked.

Retta told them about her calls only lasting a few minutes. "So I go into the bedroom and she calls me after she talks to her foster mom. She rattles on just like the other girls do when they make their calls. I think it helps her and I know it does me. So I'm glad Benjy will be talking to Mavis."

"You think you could come back next year?" Skip asked. "This has been the easiest year since we started this program and I think you are the key to the success."

"Thanks but I don't think my new job will let me have a five-week vacation the first year I'm working." She laughed.

"Let's just say for the sake of conversation, would you if they did?" Skip asked.

"In a heartbeat," Retta answered without hesitation.

# Chapter Twenty

I've been expecting your call all evening," Tina said when she answered the phone that night. "So how's this week been?"

"Awesome," Retta answered and gave her a play-by-play of what all had happened.

"And you slept with the sexy cowboy?" Tina asked when Retta finally wound down.

"What makes you think that?" Retta asked.

"Remember, I've been your best friend since freshman year in college. We lived together in the dorm for four years. I know you, Retta Palmer," Tina said.

"You told me to go for it. To have a summer fling," Retta shot back at her.

"That's right, but I'm thinking maybe I told you wrong."

"Why?"

Tina sighed. "There's something in your voice. You've

fallen in love with those kids and it wouldn't take a hard shove for you to do the same with that cowboy."

"Your hearing is off." Retta laughed. "You've got love on the brain since you got engaged at Easter. I'm not nearly ready to take that step."

"What if you listened to your heart rather than your mind?" Tina asked.

"Enough about me. Let's talk about your Christmas wedding. You still having a destination wedding or has that changed?"

"Keep your bikini ready. We're going to Florida's Laguna Beach for the wedding. That's about the middle distance for both families to have to travel and I don't have to wear shoes. I'm picking out bridesmaids' dresses in a few weeks. I'll send you pictures."

Retta groaned. "Not anything pink or with bows on the butt."

Tina giggled. "I was thinking a floral sarong around a lime-green bikini."

"You wouldn't!" Retta gasped.

"Now that pink taffeta with a big bow on the fanny don't sound so bad, does it? Got a beep from my future mother-in-law. Got to go, since she's also my boss. Talk to you next week and I'll expect a full report on the first sex by then." Tina didn't even say good-bye.

Retta tucked her phone in her hip pocket and wandered out of her bedroom. Restless and feeling cooped up, she stood at the back door and looked through the window for several minutes.

Everything seemed to be under control in the living room. The girls were sprawled out reading books. Gabby and Sasha took up the whole sofa. Alice and Faith were on the floor with a couple of throw pillows under their elbows.

"I'm going for a walk but I won't be far," Retta said.

Faith gave her a thumbs-up. "I'll call you if they get rowdy."

"And I'll call you if Faith gets bossy," Gabby said.

She'd only gone three steps out into the darkness when Cade slipped his arms around her waist from behind and kissed her on the neck. "This is a sweet surprise."

She covered his hands with hers. "What are you doing out here?"

"I was restless. Couldn't keep my mind on anything so I came out for a walk. You?" he whispered, his warm breath sending delicious little shivers down her spine.

"Same," she said.

"Let's take a short walk out to the barn."

"That's where I was headed. Thought maybe I'd check on Little Bit."

He slipped his arm around her waist and kept pace with her stride. "Levi turned him out into the corral today. He's a happy critter with all that room to run around in but now Levi says that he's lonely and needs a girlfriend so he's looking for a miniature jenny to bring to the ranch."

"Daddy used to say that all animals need a mate. It's the order of things," she said.

"That's what my dad says too. I talked to them a while ago and told them about Benjy and"—he paused a moment—"and you."

"Oh, really? What did you tell them about me?"

"That you were amazing with the kids and that I'd hire you in a minute to help me run this ranch. That you were business savvy so you could take care of the office stuff, which would leave me more time to work outside. And that you could cook and that Mavis loves you," he said.

"Cade Maguire, are you offering me a permanent job?"

she asked as they crossed the pasture from the yard to the barn.

"I would but I don't take well to rejection. But if you decide that the big city business life doesn't make you happy, then yes, ma'am, I'd gladly give you a job."

"You aren't teasing are you?" she asked.

"You can't even imagine how serious I am." They both entered the big open barn doors together.

"I appreciate it." She didn't even get the whole sentence out before his lips closed on hers. She tiptoed slightly and locked her arms around his neck.

He teased her mouth open with his tongue and with a little hop, she wrapped her legs around his waist. He backed up and sat down on a bale of hay with her still in his lap. His hand slipped up under her cotton shirt and closed around her ribs, drawing her so close that she could feel every beat of his heart.

The kisses got hotter and hotter and he'd undone the first hook on her bra when her phone rang, startling her so badly that she jumped up out of his lap. She quickly dug it out of her hip pocket.

"Hello," she said.

"Gabby is trying to boss us. She says we can't watch another movie and that we have to get to bed because we're getting up early for fishin' in the morning and I told them that ten o'clock is not late," Faith said.

"Has every one of you had a shower or bath, brushed your teeth, and gotten your clothes out for tomorrow morning?" Retta hoped the kid couldn't hear the breathlessness in her voice.

"No," Faith answered.

"I'm on my way back to the bunkhouse right now. Be there in less than five minutes and there won't be another movie tonight," Retta said.

"I hate it when she wins," Faith huffed.

"It's not a win. It's just a fact. I'm on my way."

"Okay," Faith dragged out the word into three syllables.

"Dammit!" Cade said behind her.

She bent forward slightly and patted him on the cheek. "Job comes first."

"But I don't have to like it." He stood up and kissed her on the forehead.

"Give me four or five minutes before you leave," she said. "I'm sure at least one of them will be at the kitchen window watching, and we don't want to fuel this meddling they're doing."

"Why not? I'll stand on the top of this barn and tell everyone that I was making out with you." The moonlight lit up his smile.

"And what kind of example would that be to a twelve-year-old who is planning to wait until she's thirteen to have sex? She might change her mind and hook up with the nearest boy when she gets home." Retta reached around and fastened her bra.

"She said that?" Cade stammered.

"Oh, yes. See you tomorrow. I'll be the one with the most fish at the end of the morning," she said.

"You wish." He spun her around for one more tantalizing kiss.

Since she'd wasted time flirting and sinking into that last steamy kiss, she jogged back to the bunkhouse where she found Faith slumped on the sofa.

"You're out of breath. You been kissing Cade?" Faith asked bluntly.

"I'm out of breath from running, young lady," Retta told her.

"Gabby is in the shower. Alice and Sasha will be next

and I'm going last. Since I sleep on the sofa, I can watch television all night if I want to at my foster house. I thought I'd miss television here in the bunkhouse but it ain't been too bad," she said.

"This is not your foster house. Ten o'clock is bedtime and you girls are going to have to hustle to get there by ten tonight," Retta said. "Tell you what, so that we don't break rules, why don't you go run a bath in my tub."

Faith's eyes popped wide open. "For real? Can I put some bubble bath from my basket in it?"

"Yes, you can, but you've got to be out in twenty minutes." Retta sat down on a recliner and popped up the footrest.

"Thank you, Retta. Thank you, thank you!" Faith wasted no time getting from the living room to her bedroom to gather up her nightshirt and the basket of bath things that Retta had given her.

Retta put her fingers to her lips, and surprisingly enough they were cool, not hot and bee stung like they felt. Every single kiss or touch was going to make it that much harder to leave the ranch behind but—

*Think long and hard before you shut a door and regret it a year down the road,* her mother's advice came back to her mind.

"Mama, I miss you and Daddy so much. I need you right now to help me." She covered her eyes with her hands.

*I'm always in your heart, Retta. Just listen to what it tells you and you'll have my advice every time.*

\*          \*          \*

She was still thinking of the memory of her mother the next morning when she and the girls made it to the kitchen. A pot of oatmeal was brewing on the back burner of the stove and Mavis was frying sausage links to go with it.

"Good mornin', ladies," Mavis said cheerfully.

The four girls and Retta went to the apron hooks and either tied one around their waist or slipped a bibbed one over their heads.

"All four of you girls go on and work together getting the table set. We need plates and bowls this morning," Mavis said. "And when the boys get here, send them in here and I'll give them some jobs."

They went straight to the dining room and started removing dishes from the cupboard without fussing or even moaning.

"You can take those muffins from the pans, Retta." Mavis pointed.

"Everything smells amazing," Retta said.

"What do you eat for breakfast when you're workin' in the city?" Mavis asked.

"I usually grab a mocha latte from Starbucks and maybe a biscotti or a muffin but they'd never compare to these," she said.

"Hmmmph." Mavis snorted. "That ain't a fit breakfast. You might not know it, young lady, but you were born to be a rancher and you ain't never goin' to be satisfied with anything else. Just like Cade was born to do the same thing."

"Mavis, darlin'." Retta slung her arm around the short woman's shoulders. "I love this place and I love the kids and my job here, but if I don't do what I set out to do, then I'll always have regrets."

"That all depends on how you study the situation," Mavis said. "Cade's a good boss and a good man and you fit in well here."

"What does 'study the situation' mean?" Retta asked.

"It means to think hard about things. Now I ain't one to meddle, but that cowboy's eyes light up when you are around. Either step back or dive in but don't break his heart. Ain't a one of us forgot the way Julie did him and we ain't never forgivin' or forgettin' no matter what the good book says. But you need to think about the possibility that's right in front of your nose right now. Maybe God put you here to take the job that Cade offered you, just like he's let me and Skip live to help out with Benjy," Mavis whispered.

"I'll think long and hard, but..." The front door opened and Kirk led the boys toward the kitchen.

Mavis motioned with her good hand. "Y'all got here just in time to help get the food on the table."

When they'd all taken something and disappeared out of the kitchen, Mavis turned back to Retta. "No buts. Make up your mind and never look back. Now let's get breakfast over with. These kids are probably antsy to get a fishin' pole in their hands. I've got a picnic lunch all ready again. Me and Skip will be leavin' right after breakfast. We've read the papers and signed them and we're takin' them back to the social worker today," she said.

"Don't you worry about a thing, Mavis. We'll take care of everything." Retta was glad to change the subject.

"I know you will. You could probably run this place with one hand tied behind your back," Mavis declared.

\*　　\*　　\*

"I hope you aren't disappointed," Cade said as the kids piled out of the back of the truck.

"About what?" Retta asked.

"This is only a small stream. Most of the time it's dried up by this time of year but Levi was down here when we were looking for Benjy and he said that it's running pretty good. Nice and clear right now so if the kids go wading after they get bored with fishing, it's okay. I just hope you weren't planning on reeling in a catfish the size of Moby Dick." He grinned.

"It'll be exciting to watch them. Not one of my girls has ever been fishing," she said.

"Skip says it's the same with the boys, except Benjy. Did Mavis tell you that they are signing the final papers today? Since they'd been foster parents before, it could be rushed through."

She hugged herself and a smile covered her face. "He couldn't have better parents than they will be, and they'll watch after him even after he's eighteen."

"We all will." Cade nodded. "I'm so glad he doesn't have to go to another home before he moves in with them."

"Me, too." She opened the door the minute that Cade parked in a small spot that had been cleared from trees and underbrush. All eight kids beat a path straight for the water and stood there mesmerized, watching it move slowly with barely a ripple.

With a good running leap, Retta could have jumped over the stream. Cade was right—it could hardly be called a creek. But it would be a fun place to spend the morning outdoors with the kids.

"Okay, first thing is that you line up so I can spray you with bug repellent," Cade called out. "Don't want the whole lot of you whining from chiggers or mosquito bites."

Retta stepped in behind them and when it was her turn, he asked, "You remember that old country song about checking you for ticks?"

She nodded. "Maybe I'd like to do the same for you."

"Anytime, sweetheart," he said under his breath as he sprayed her arms and neck. "Just name the place and time." And then he started singing the chorus of the Brad Paisley tune. The lyrics said that he'd like to see her in the moonlight and kiss her back in the sticks and that he'd like to check her for ticks.

"Shhh... the kids will hear you." She giggled.

He whispered the lyrics that said the only thing that would be able to crawl all over her would be him. Her cheeks turned bright red when he sang that there were lots of places that might be hard to reach.

"Cade Maguire, that is enough," she said.

Benjy ran back from the edge of the water. "When can we have a rod and reel?"

"Right now. You remember how to bait a hook with a worm?" Cade handed him the first one from the backseat.

Benjy nodded his head slowly. "Yes, you put a wiggly worm or a grasshopper on the hook so that it can't get away and then you push down on the reel button and throw the line out into the water."

"Okay, you carry this can of worms and Retta and I'll bring the rest of the equipment," he said. "Tell the kids to line up but not too close."

When they'd given each of the kids a rod and reel, Cade brought out the worms. The boys watched him lace the first one on Benjy's hook and then watched carefully as Cade showed them how to release the button on the reel to get the line out into the stream.

"Bet you can't touch that worm," Kirk said to Faith as he managed to get his hook baited.

"Boy, I could eat that worm and not bat an eye but I ain't wastin' good bait." She picked up a worm, and twirled it around the hook, tossed the rod over her shoulder, released the button and the bobber danced out there about halfway. "You got anything else to say to me, Kirk?"

He executed a fine throw and his line landed downstream from hers by about eight feet. "I bet you can't clean a fish if you catch it."

"Be careful. Your motorcycle mouth is about to bite off more than your bicycle butt can back up," she taunted.

"What's that mean?" he asked.

"I think it means that you're talkin' bigger than you really are," Alice said. "Retta, I can't put a worm on my hook. I'm afraid I'll hurt it. Will you do it for me?"

"Of course I will." Retta picked up a worm and then helped Alice get the line into the water.

"Me too." Sasha blushed. "It's wiggling and it's squishy."

"That's what draws the fish to it," Benjy said. "It sits down there in the water and wiggles and I think it sings. Then the fish comes along and has a little nibble and we reel it in."

"You are full of bull," Nelson said.

"Nope, just muffins and oatmeal," Benjy said, seriously. "It would be impossible to eat a whole bull. An Angus like Cade raises weighs over a thousand pounds. How could I be full of bull?"

Ivan looked into the can of worms and shivered. "I need help, Retta."

Cade had spread out the quilts and put the cooler with the food in the middle of one of them. Then he set up a couple of chairs for himself and Retta and handed her a rod. "Still think you can catch more fish than me?"

"Unless one of those minnows has a mouth big enough to latch onto a hook, I don't think any of us are catching fish," she whispered as she sat down and leaned the rod next to her chair. "But watching them is more fun than really working on catching supper, which by the way is catfish that Mavis brought out of the freezer."

He sat down beside her and did the same. "So what's your secret to frying catfish?"

"Red cayenne pepper," she said without pausing.

"Really?" he drawled.

"I won't use too much since it's kids but when..." She grinned.

"When what?"

"Daddy liked to fish and we always had a freezer full by the end of summer so my best friend, Tina, and I always did a fish fry at the boys' dorm in the fall," she said.

"You had different dorms?" he asked.

"Some of us. There was one girls' dorm left when I was there. The others were coed," she said. "But the boys had a bigger kitchen than ours, so we had a fish fry and they could have all they wanted for free, but we made them buy the beer that we brought in. So we laced the cornmeal pretty good with pepper. We made enough money to do our laundry all fall."

"That's evil," he said.

"No, honey, that's business." She laughed. "Tonight I'll just put a dash in to give it flavor. And we'll have hush puppies and fried potatoes. Mavis left two big pans of sheet cake for dessert and told me to bring out the ice cream to go with it."

"Sounds like we don't even need to catch supper."

She nodded. "But the kids do need this experience. With this and getting to put the first pictures in their scrapbooks, they'll have a lot to talk about Sunday night when they write home."

Cade stretched his long legs out toward the water and

crossed his cowboy boots at the ankle. He tipped his hat to the back of his head and focused on the kids for a few seconds as Benjy warned them about watching their bobber. But Cade's eyes kept wandering back to Retta. Dressed in skinny jeans, boots, and a knit shirt that hugged her body, she sure didn't look anything like a high-powered businesswoman.

"Mavis talk to you?" she asked.

"Yep," he answered. "She have something to say to you?"

"Oh, yes, and she didn't beat around the bush. She sounded a lot like my mother." She grinned. "But I'm not complainin'. It just means she loves me. You going to stick around this afternoon for the scrapbooking process?"

"You bet. After I got back to the house last night, I printed over a hundred pictures. And that reminds me." He pulled his phone out of his pocket and began to snap away. "I need to take more pictures of the great fishin' expedition. It's hard to believe that half their time is already done, isn't it?"

"Time flies when you're havin' fun," she said, but he thought he heard a bit of wistfulness in her voice and hoped he was right.

\*      \*      \*

*And half of my time here is over too. I would have never believed that a simple little babysitting job would turn my world upside down.*

The kids were "starving" a half an hour before lunchtime, so she and Cade got out the sandwiches, chips, and cold drinks.

"Okay, kids, time to load up now that you've had lunch

in the wild. I think that you're supposed to put pictures in your scrapbook this afternoon," he said.

"But, Cade, can't we just take off our shoes and wade in that water?" Ivan asked.

"Please," Benjy begged.

"One hour and no fussin' when I say it's time to go home?" Cade asked.

"No fussin'." Kirk crossed his heart with his finger.

"We'll have to put off the scrapbook until evening," Retta whispered.

"I think they'll enjoy this experience enough to warrant that and I'm thinking of all the pictures I can take," he said.

"Yay!" Nelson pumped his fist in the air.

All four boys dropped to the ground and yanked their shoes off but the girls were hesitant until Kirk goaded Faith. "Afraid a shark will come up out of the water and eat you?"

"No, I'm afraid that I'll get your germs on my feet," she retorted with a dirty look his way.

"Water will wash all of them away," Benjy told her. "And Kirk takes a shower every night so there shouldn't be germs on his feet."

"There could be," Faith argued.

While they argued Cade leaned close to Retta's ear and whispered. "You want to wade?"

"Of course I do," she answered as she kicked off her boots. "You joinin' us?"

"Wouldn't miss it for the world, but I haven't had my toes in this stream since me and Levi and Justin were kids so I can't tell you how deep it really is." He sat down on the grass, pulled off his boots and socks, and rolled up the legs of his jeans.

The water was warm when Retta stepped off the grassy

bank into it. She took a couple of steps and it was only ankle deep so she took a couple more and looked back over her shoulder at the kids who were gingerly making their way to the middle of the narrow stream.

"This feels great," Faith said. "Like a warm bath but—" Her feet went out from under her and she sat down with a splash, throwing water all over Kirk.

He started to laugh and she grabbed his leg, pulling him down beside her.

"I can't swim," he yelled.

"You don't need to, dummy." She laughed. "It's only up to your waist when you are sitting down."

"Oops, I'm slipping!" Alice eased down beside Faith. "Oh, this feels good. Look! There's a minnow nibbling on my toenail polish."

"Does it hurt?" Gabby joined them.

Retta walked back to the bank and sat down on the grass. Cade laughed the whole time he snapped pictures. She'd be willing to bet that he knew all along that one of them would slip and fall and the others would join. Well, that was something else they could talk about when they wrote home on Sunday for sure.

*That man would make a great father.* Her mother's voice was in her head again. *You need to take the job he's offered you and see where this relationship goes.*

"I'm afraid to, Mama," she said softly.

\*       \*       \*

Cade switched the phone around and took several shots of Retta without her knowing. She was a beautiful woman, even sitting there with all her makeup gone, her jeans rolled up to her knees, barefoot, and her cowboy hat tilted back on her head so she could see the kids splashing around in the water.

He scrolled through the photos and took a couple more, catching her expression of pure joy when Sasha finally sat down in the water and splashed Kirk and Benjy both. Then he got one of her giggling when Benjy sent a wave over Faith's head, getting her face and hair both wet.

He didn't even hear the four-wheeler coming down the path until Justin was already in the clearing.

"Hey, come join us." He waved.

"I thought this was a fishing expedition not a swimming trip." Justin grinned as he squatted down on the grassy area beside his brother. "Looks like y'all been wadin' too. Can't remember the last time we got in this stream."

"Oh, come on," Cade teased. "It was the summer you and Levi was fifteen and you talked those two girlfriends of yours into skinny-dippin' with y'all."

"How'd you know about that?" Justin chuckled. "Hello, Retta. Did you get your feet wet?"

"Yes, I did and don't try to change the subject. I want to hear about this skinny-dippin' business," she answered.

"I'll tell you what happened," Cade said. "Mama sent me to hunt for Justin and Levi when they didn't come home in time for supper. Guess the two of them had better things to do than come in for fried chicken."

Retta giggled. "I'm glad these kids' hormones haven't kicked into high gear."

"That's part of the reason why we ask for this age," Justin said with a sigh. "And now I am changing the subject. What are we going to do about Mavis retiring?"

"Hire Retta," Cade answered simply.

"Whoa!" She threw up both palms. "That ain't happenin'."

Cade winked at Justin. "Help me out, brother. She knows

the computer system and she's lived and worked on a small spread in Oklahoma."

"And she can cook," Justin said. "At least she could stay through the summer until we slow down enough to interview some folks."

"I'm sitting right here," she said.

"Yes, you are," Cade said with a smile.

# Chapter Twenty-One

Saturday had been one of those days when everything went smoothly, which meant that the other shoe was dangling and waiting to fall. When darkness came she decided that maybe she was borrowing trouble from tomorrow as her mother used to tell her when she was in high school. It was one of those perfect nights when the humidity and weather were just right for the lightning bugs to be out in abundance.

"Look at all them," Mavis said when the whole family had gathered on the ranch house porch that evening. "We used to catch them in fruit jars and pretend they were lanterns."

"Can we do that?" Alice asked.

"You sure can. Justin, you come help me bring out some fruit jars." When they brought them out, holes had been poked in the lids where the kids' names were written in permanent ink. "Okay, here you go and when the evening is over and you set them free, you can keep the flat part of the lid for your scrapbooks."

"You ever done this before?" Kirk asked Benjy.

"Nope. Lightning bugs taste awful. I never ate one but the book I read said that it was their protection so other things won't eat them." He removed the lid and went running out across the yard.

"I'm surprised they aren't making bets as to who'll catch the most," Justin said.

"I'm just hoping they don't damage a wing or snap off a tail or Levi will want to adopt the thing and nurse it back to health." Cade chuckled.

"Oh, come on now," Levi argued. "I'm not that bad."

"Yep, you are," Skip said.

"But we still love you," Mavis told him. "Think y'all ought to help—never mind. Alice has got the hang of it and they'll follow her lead."

She'd captured a firefly in her hands then gently put it into the jar. The boys were running around with open jars, trying to scoop them up like butterflies in a net until they saw what she was doing. Then boys and girls alike stopped and followed Alice's lead.

"Smart little critters." Mavis laughed. "They'd never catch them by waving the jar around. I got to tell y'all, I feel younger just knowin' that Benjy is comin' to live with us. It's been mighty quiet around the place since Levi left. Benjy's aunt, the lady we met at the funeral, put in a good word for us. We'll probably foster him for a year because the adoption stuff takes a while."

Justin sucked in a lungful of air and let it out slowly. "Best news ever. None of you can imagine how happy that makes me. I was already trying to figure out ways that I could get him back here for a week maybe at

Christmas. Now he'll be in and out with Skip all the time," he said.

"I got five and they're all flashing," Alice called out.

"Mine is the lights on a police car." Ivan made the noise of a siren and ran around the yard, holding the jar on top of his head.

"Well, mine is a night-light," Faith said. "Look, I can find my way to the kitchen for a midnight snack with it."

"They'll remember this night forever," Mavis said.

"I wonder if they'll catch them when they get home," Cade asked.

"I doubt it," Retta said. "I remember flies and definitely mosquitoes in Dallas, but I never saw a lightning bug in the city. Maybe I wasn't in the right spot but—" She shrugged.

"I wouldn't want to live there, then," Cade said. "It can't be a good place to live if there's no lightning bugs. You should stay on here until we find someone to take on Mavis's job." Cade gazed right into her eyes.

"That would be a great idea," Mavis said. "I won't feel so bad about leavin' if you'd stay on for a while, Retta. One of the reasons the social worker was agreeable was that we were both retired and we'd be home with him, since he's a special needs child."

"I can't stay, Mavis. I've got that interview in Dallas and…" She paused. "It's complicated."

Justin glanced over at Skip and sighed. "And she already said no, but that don't mean we can't keep askin', does it?"

"Who knows?" Skip said. "She might say yes if we let her know how much we want her to stay."

"I'm right here," Retta said.

"Yep, you are." Cade nodded. "Right where we'd like for you to stay."

"Okay, changing the subject," she said. "The way Benjy

loves animals, I can see him getting interested in the Future Farmers of America program."

Skip nodded. "I'm glad we've got a few acres so the boy can have some animals for his school projects. Levi, you need to help me find a couple of good show sheep for this next year."

"Will do." Levi stood up from the porch step where he'd been sitting. "I'm turning in. It's past ten o'clock and tomorrow is church."

"Good grief. I had no idea it was that late," Retta said. "Girls, it's time to let your fireflies go free. We've got to get back to our bunkhouse."

"Awww, man, I just got a dozen and it's makin' a good night-light," Faith groaned. "Can I take it in with me and turn them loose in the morning?"

"Afraid not. They might not survive," Mavis answered. "What y'all need to do is set the jars on the porch and remove the lids. That way they can find their way out and back to their homes."

"Ahhh," Sasha said. "I can just see them flying back to their little houses in the trees and tellin' their brothers and sisters all about this adventure."

"Yep, mine are going to tell how they saved lives because they were the lights on police cars." Ivan was the first one to set his on the porch, twist the lid off, and pocket the flat part.

"Maybe a few minutes on the porch after the kids are in bed?" Cade asked while everyone was talking at once.

"Sure," she said. "Meet you there in an hour."

"I'll be the one in the rocking chair." He grinned.

"I'll be the one with my wet hair wrapped in a towel," she said.

"Now that's a sexy picture," he said, flirting.

She air-slapped him on the arm. "Don't make fun of me."

"Honey, any way I picture you is sexy."

Faith grabbed her hand. "That was so much fun. Can we do it again?"

"Anytime they're out, but right now it's bedtime," she said loud enough for all the girls to hear. *See you later,* she mouthed at Cade.

When the girls were all tucked into bed, she hurriedly took a quick shower and washed her hair. She dressed in Minnie Mouse pajama bottoms and a bright red knit tank top, wrapped a white fluffy towel around her hair, and eased out the door onto the porch.

Sure enough Cade was sitting in the rocking chair back in the shadows. She plopped down in the one right next to him and he reached over to touch her bare shoulder. As usual, shock waves of desire, swept through her and she almost got up and moved to his lap.

"Please," he said.

"Please what?" she asked.

"Please stay with us on the ranch, Retta. We've got this connection and chemistry and . . ."

"How do we know this isn't just a flash in the pan?" she asked.

"We don't. I guess it would be a leap of faith for you even more than me. But there are always jobs in the big cities," he said.

"You wouldn't want me to beg you to sell the ranch and move to Dallas just so we could enjoy this chemistry, would you?"

He cut those blue eyes around at her and they were not one bit happy. "I have a life here. Roots that go so deep they can't be moved."

"Then I guess we're at a standstill. This job will put me

right back where I was when I left. I won't have to start at
the bottom again." An emptiness filled her chest as if her
heart had been removed leaving a hole. When did she begin
to have such deep feelings for him?

"I want you to stay here and I want to hire you to work
for us, plain and simple," he answered. "Everyone here
loves you. You won't be starting at the bottom here either. I
don't think you're as ready to give up ranch life as you say
you are."

"But I'm not ready to give up on my own goals either,"
Retta said. "You have to respect that."

"Of course I do. But dammit, Retta. You've got me
twisted up in knots."

She stood up. "I think maybe it's best if we keep to a professional relationship from now on and just nip this thing
between us in the bud, don't you?"

He set his mouth in a firm line. "If that's the way you
want it, but if you change your mind . . ."

"I won't. Good night, Cade." She flipped the towel from
her head, shook out her long dark hair, and left him sitting
on the porch.

Before she even shut the door, she could hear her
mother's voice in her head, scolding her. *You don't get
dozens of chances to meet your soul mate. What if you are
blowing your one chance?*

"Whoever my soul mate is will accept me as I am and
not try to change me into something I don't want to be."

Faith came out of the bathroom rubbing her eyes. "Is it
mornin'? Who were you talkin' to? I'm hungry."

"I was talkin' to myself and it's not mornin' but if you
are hungry, how about some cookies and milk?"

Faith yawned and made her way across the floor to the
tiny kitchen area. "What did Cade do to make you mad?"

"How do you know that I'm mad or that it has anything to do with Cade?" She opened a package of chocolate chip cookies and poured two glasses of milk.

"I've had lots of foster sisters, remember? And most of the time they were all older than me." Faith took a cookie from the package and dipped it in the milk.

"Do you have any goals, Faith?"

"Sure. I'm going to get through school, go to college, and be a teacher."

"I thought you were going to have sex when you were thirteen."

"Naw, I was just mad and tryin' to rile you up." She giggled. "I know all about that stuff though because of those older sisters."

Retta took a sip of her milk. "What if someone told you that you had to change those goals and be something you don't want to be? Like maybe a waitress in a diner the rest of your life?"

"I'd tell 'em to go to hell," she said bluntly and then cut her eyes around at the demerit board.

"It's okay. I won't give you a black mark tonight," Retta said. "Now tell me about your plans."

"I make good grades in school. I'm not popular and the kids call me a nerd because I like doin' computer stuff. My last foster mother told me that there were scholarships for kids who do good in school so I study hard. I'll be in seventh grade when school starts and I like learnin' so maybe I'll get me one of them scholarships. But if I don't, then I'll work my butt off at however many jobs I have to so I can be smart like you." She yawned again.

Retta gave Faith a quick hug. "I have confidence in you, girl. And when you graduate from high school and from college, I want to know so I can be there for you. Now we'd better get these cookies and milk finished and get to bed or we'll be snoring in church tomorrow morning."

Faith giggled. "Alice will fuss at us if that happens. And would you really come to my graduations?"

"I sure will," Retta told her. "Now finish up that milk and go get some sleep."

"Yes, ma'am." Faith beamed.

Retta made sure the girl was back in her bed before she went to her own room. She brushed out her damp hair and crawled into bed. Lacing her hands behind her head, she stared at the ceiling and didn't try to keep the tears at bay. So Faith wanted to be smart like her and Cade wanted to put her in a mold she'd been running away from for years.

\* \* \*

Cade stormed back to the house only to find Justin sitting on the porch with a cold beer in his hands.

"That one's for you." He pointed to the porch railing where another one sat, sweat covering the outside.

"We're breaking the rules." Cade picked it up, twisted the top off, and took a long drink before he sat down with a thud on the porch step.

"After the wonderful news about Benjy, we should celebrate. I wish Retta would stay with us and we could celebrate that too," Justin said.

"Me too, but she's leavin' soon as the camp is over."

"Come on," Justin said. "You got a way with women. Sweet talk her. Hell, promise her a salary bigger than what any company could pay her. We need her here even if you two can't get along past the job. None of us can cook worth a damn. We all hate housecleaning and she's good with the business end of the ranch. She's perfect for the job."

"Then you go sweet talk her or both you and Levi go give it a try. She's got her mind set. I don't think God could change it," Cade said. "I'm going to bed. See you tomorrow mornin' and thanks for the beer. I needed it."

"Hey, bro, just remember what Mama always said. It ain't over 'til it's over. If you really have a thing for her, you got almost three weeks left to change her mind. You might not be God, but you are a Maguire. Don't forget that," Justin said.

"What made you change your mind about her? You were against me havin' anything to do with her in the beginning." Cade got up and opened the door.

"I been watchin' her with the kids and in the kitchen with Mavis and most of all with you. There's not a fake bone in her body. She's up front and honest and there aren't many women in the world like that anymore. I can see her growin' up to be like Mavis or Mama, and that's a good thing," Justin said. "It wasn't an overnight thing but something I figured out over the past couple of weeks."

"Good night, Justin," Cade said.

"I'm comin' in too," Justin said. "Mavis will have my hide if I fall asleep in church."

"Or she'll tell Mama and she'll threaten to move back to the ranch." Cade tried to smile but it didn't work.

"At least Mama can cook and clean. We've got to get a housekeeper in addition to a cook, you know." Justin said.

"We could ask Mama to come back to the ranch until we find someone," Cade said.

"Sweet lord, no! She's so bossy that we'd all be crazy. Can't you just see her if one of us stayed out until daybreak because we picked up a woman in a bar? The lectures would drive us to drinkin' and cussin'," Justin replied.

"Amen!" Cade nodded.

He went to his room, kicked off his boots, and slumped

down in the recliner. He only sat there for a few seconds and then popped up, went to the drawer, and brought out the ring box. This time when he opened it, there was nothing there. No pain, no memories. It was just a ring. He carried it to the living room and tossed it in Justin's lap.

"Take that thing and sell it on eBay. Whatever it brings, put it in the bank to use to buy show sheep for Benjy."

"You sure about this?" Justin asked.

"Absolutely." Cade turned around and started back down the hall.

"Well, it's about damn time," Justin called out.

Cade dreamed of Retta again that night and awoke the next morning with his arms wrapped tightly around his pillow. When he figured out it wasn't her, he threw the pillow against the wall.

He dressed in work clothes, went through the kitchen, and told Mavis that he wouldn't be going to church that morning or sitting down to breakfast. His excuse was that he had a heifer due to give birth and she was going to need lots of help.

"What're you runnin' from?" Mavis asked.

"Nothing." He picked up a couple of muffins from the day before and filled his coffee thermos from the pot.

"You plannin' on bein' here for Sunday dinner?" she asked.

"We'll see what's going on with the heifer," he answered.

\*     \*     \*

Retta came into the kitchen with four little girls behind her just as Cade was closing the back door. "Are we the first ones here this mornin'?"

"Nope." Mavis shook her head. "You just missed Cade.

He grabbed some muffins and coffee and headed out some-where on the ranch to see about a heifer that's about to deliver. Said he probably won't even be back for church."

"Well, God ain't goin' to be real happy about that," Alice said seriously.

"Don't reckon he is," Mavis told her. "But that's between Him and Cade."

Sure enough, a few hours later when everyone was scrambling to get seated before the song leader led the con-gregation in a hymn, Cade Maguire's seat right in front of Retta was empty.

"If you'll turn to hymn number three eighty-two," the song leader said, "we'll all sing together this glorious Sun-day morning."

What's so glorious about it? Retta wanted to know. Cade was pouting.

When the song ended, the preacher started his sermon by reading a psalm about not fretting or worrying but trusting in God to help a person get through the tough times. She didn't even try to pay attention but let her mind wander back to the night before and the argument that ended any relation-ship that she and Cade might have. He could have at least suggested a long-distance relationship. It wasn't that far to Dallas—she clamped a hand over her mouth.

"What?" Faith asked.

"Nothing." She dropped her hand.

He'd had that kind of situation with Julie and it had ended in disaster. No wonder he didn't want to even think in those terms. He'd said that she had him all twisted up. Well, he sure didn't leave her singing happy songs, either.

*       *       *

Cade wasn't in the house when they got home but boys and girls alike must have been hungry because they all wanted jobs so that they could get dinner on the table. When they were seated, Mavis asked if one of the kids would like to say grace and Kirk raised his hand. It wasn't a long prayer but it was a sincere one and they all said "Amen" when he finished.

Faith squeezed Retta's hand when the food started around the table. "I don't like Cade's chair bein' empty. It don't seem right."

"I know." Retta glanced over that way and more than just his chair was empty—so was Retta's heart and soul. Suddenly, she lost her appetite. "Girls, y'all do what Mavis says. I'm going to the bunkhouse. I'm not feelin' too good."

"I'll go with you," Alice said.

Retta laid her napkin to the side of her plate. "That's so sweet, but I'll be fine."

She'd almost made it out of the house when Justin called out her name. "Hey, before you leave, I want to talk to you just a minute." He laid a hand on her shoulder. "I just want you to know that I was against the flirting between you and my brother at first because I thought you might be a gold digger out to take him to the cleaners. But I can see that you are honest and sincere, and we are serious in wanting you to stay on the ranch as a hired hand—that didn't come out right. You'd be more than a hired hand."

"I appreciate your honesty, but no thanks," she said.

"If you change your mind, the offer still stands." He removed his hand. "And I hope you get to feeling better." He turned around and headed back to the dinner table before Retta could answer.

As she was leaving the ranch house, Cade parked his truck, got out, and started up the three porch steps as Retta was going down. Her breath caught in her chest at the simple sight of him, and when his arm brushed against hers, a tingle shot down her back bone.

"Retta?" He tipped his hat.

"How'd the heifer do?"

"Didn't deliver yet. We may have to pull the calf because she's so small," he answered and kept walking.

"I'm pretty good at that business. Call me if you need help," she said.

He nodded but didn't answer.

# *Chapter Twenty-Two*

Cade was at the breakfast table the next morning and he was the same old cowboy with the kids. Coolly professional was the way that Retta described the way he treated her. When he passed food or took it from her hands, he made sure there was no touching. He didn't lock gazes with her and when the meal was over, he sure didn't linger in the kitchen.

"You and Cade had a fight, didn't you?" Mavis asked when they were loading the dishwasher.

"Not a fight, an understanding," Retta answered.

"If it looks like a fight, walks like a fight, acts like a fight, it's not an understanding," Mavis argued.

"You know that he wants to hire me to do office work and cook."

"Be a fantastic job. You'd get room and board with it, probably your own place in the girls' bunkhouse, and he'd include a nice benefits package. You won't get a better deal in the big city," Mavis said.

Gabby set an empty bowl on the counter. "Sounds like a great job to me, and you could be around Cade all year. Man, if I was old like you, I'd jump at that."

"Ouch!" Retta grinned.

"It's all relative." Mavis patted her on the back. "To me you are just a young kid."

"Well, that at least puts a bandage on the pain." Retta gave her a quick hug. "I told him no."

"So that's why he's—" Mavis started.

"Actin' like a jack—I mean like he don't even see Retta," Sasha finished for her. "I didn't say a bad word so I don't get black marks."

Mavis closed the dishwasher and poked a few buttons. "It'll pass like all things do and you'll be stronger on the other side for it but don't completely shut the door, Retta. You are cut out for this job and if you think about it, you would be shooting straight to the top of the company."

"How's that?" Retta asked.

"You'd be the CEO of the office from day one. Cade hates the work and puts it off until it takes him a week inside the house to get it done and he also hates to interview folks, so you'd be in charge of hiring and firing a new housekeeper and a cook," Mavis answered. "And I bet no company that you'd find in Dallas would cover more than two square miles of territory and have many more employees than the Longhorn Canyon Ranch."

"You've got a very good point," Retta agreed. "But—"

Mavis put a finger over Retta's lips. "No buts."

Alice giggled. "That sounded funny. We all got butts."

"They hear everything," Mavis said.

"Yep, they sure do."

"I get it that you have a degree and are capable of a big

bank job, but that don't mean jack squat if you ain't happy," Mavis said.

"What makes you so smart, Mavis? What do you have a degree in?" Faith asked.

"Tellin' kids what to do." Mavis stopped and hugged her tightly. "Now you girls get on out of here and go check on Little Bit. I bet he's lonely. And you go with them, Retta. Give Cade all the space he needs. He has to mull over things for days before he comes to grips with them. That's the Maguire in him. His daddy is cut from the same bolt of denim."

"Yes, ma'am," Retta said.

\*          \*          \*

On Tuesday evening Cade started home from an all-day trip to Muenster where he'd gone to a ranch sale to look at cattle. He was in a pissy mood because the bull he wanted had already been sold when he got there and the lot of cows he'd thought he might buy had been a negotiating point with the sale of the ranch, so he'd missed out on those too. He'd come home with nothing in his trailer but a miniature jenny, which would make Levi and the kids happy, but it was a total waste of time as far as he was concerned.

He turned on the radio to his favorite country station to catch the last song in an hour-long session from the 1990s. Conway Twitty was singing, "I'd Love to Lay You Down," and he kept time with the beat with his thumbs on the steering wheel. The lyrics said that she had a way of doing things that turned him on and that he'd love to lay her down and tell her all the things a woman loved to hear.

He slapped the steering wheel near the end of the song and glared at his eyes in the rearview mirror. Of course he'd love to do just what Conway sang about, but it wasn't happening, and that added fuel to his pissy mood.

"And now let's move up to something that's almost vintage but not quite. Let's shove off this hour with 'Home' by Blake Shelton," the DJ said. The lyrics said that he understood why she couldn't come with him because it wasn't her dream.

Cade sang the last chorus and every single word hit a spot in his heart. He did want to go home. He wanted to see Retta. He imagined her with that dark hair up in a ponytail, her cowboy hat set just right on her head, and a shirt tied up at waist level.

That song ended and the DJ announced that they were moving forward and Jon Langston would be singing, "Right Girl, Wrong Time."

"Ain't that the truth?" Cade said when the words said that they weren't good at being long-distance lovers. But he was thinking of Julie.

And you're judging Retta by Julie and that's not fair, that aggravating voice said in his head. *It could work between y'all if you'd give it a chance. And eventually she might decide on her own that she wants to be on the ranch rather than in the city.*

The last song playing was "H.O.L.Y" by Florida Georgia Line when he drove up into the driveway at the house and eight little kids ran out to the trailer to see what he'd brought home. Retta stood on the porch just as he'd imagined her—tight jeans, shirt tied up, boots, and a ponytail. The only thing missing was her hat, and she was holding it beside her. Through his sunglasses he drank in his fill of her and admitted that it wouldn't take a very hard shove for him to fall in love with her. The end of the song said that he was healing where it used to hurt. That was the gospel truth, because for the first time, he felt as if he was truly over Julie.

She didn't leave the porch when he slid out of the pickup but he could feel her eyes on him when the kids circled around him, squealing about the little donkey in the trailer. Justin and Levi rounded the end of the house and stopped when they saw that the trailer wasn't loaded with cattle or even a single bull.

"Not much luck?" Justin asked.

"Bull sold before the sale even started and that lot of heifers we wanted went with the ranch," he said.

"That's what you get for not going to church," Benjy said. "God ain't happy with you."

"I reckon you're probably right." Cade ruffled the boy's hair. "But I'll be sure to be there next Sunday."

"Little Bit is going to be so proud of his new friend," Nelson said. "Can we go out to the corral and see how much he loves her?"

"Sure you can," Levi said. "All y'all pile in the back of the pickup. Here, Alice, let me give you a boost. You go on inside, Cade, and fix you a plate. Mavis left it all ready for you to pop in the microwave. She drove into town for some more stuff for the kids' scrapbooks."

"Thanks," Cade said.

"We'll unhook the trailer and have the kids back in less than an hour." Justin crawled into the passenger-side seat.

With another nod, Cade started across the lawn toward the house, but Retta was gone. Had she ever been there or was it his imagination? Then he caught a glimpse of her headed toward the bunkhouse, so he changed direction and caught up with her in front of the boys' quarters.

"We need to talk," he said.

"What about? Am I doing my job all right?"

"Of course." He took her by the shoulders and looked into her brown eyes.

"Then what, Mr. Maguire?"

"You are driving me crazy," he said.

"Me? I thought I was doing everything that the contract said for me to do and even beyond that." She shrugged off his hands and started up the steps.

"You are doing a fantastic job with the girls. I couldn't ask for more."

"Good. If that's all, I'm going inside for a cold drink. Would you like one?"

"No, Retta, I want to talk about us."

"Nothing to talk about. Will you be at breakfast?"

"Probably."

"Then I'll see you there. Good night, Cade."

"We will talk before you leave here."

"I'm sure we will. Lots of times," she said.

*         *         *

Retta went inside and slid down the back side of the door. With every nerve in her body tingling, she put her head in her hands and sighed loudly. Pride was a dangerous thing. The discontent in her heart said she wanted to be on the ranch—if not daily, then at least coming for visits on week-ends. But she'd set her heels so strongly that now she felt like she couldn't back out. She was sitting there when the girls came running in the back door telling her all about the new donkey that they'd named Jasmine for a Disney princess. They gathered round her on the floor as if that were the most natural place in the world to sit and said that Little Bit had sniffed her nose, rubbed his neck on hers, and then walked away.

"He's playin' hard to get," Faith said. "Kind of like you're doin' with Cade."

"I. Am. Not," Retta declared.

"Yeah, you are," Sasha said.

"Then why didn't you come out to the trailer and see Jasmine and talk to him when he came back? He looked right at you and you just walked away," Gabby said.

Alice held up a hand. "We might be young but we ain't stupid. He likes you a lot and you like him but y'all are more stubborn than my sister, and that's sayin' a lot."

"I'm not having this conversation." Retta got to her feet.

"Okay, then, we'll put it off until later," Faith said. "Will you take pictures of all four of us for the scrapbook after we get our showers? We got lots of pictures but we ain't got any of just us girls in our own bunkhouse."

"And I want a picture with you," Alice said. "Because I'm going to grow up and be just like you but if I ever meet someone as pretty as Cade, I'm not going to be mean to him like you are."

"I said I'm not talking about it anymore," Retta said. "And yes, get into your pajamas and we'll take funny pictures of all four of you. Or we can have a dress-up evening and fix hair and do nails and have a photo session like you were models."

"Yes!" Faith said. "Will you do all of our hair? Do you have polish for our nails?"

"I've got maybe three colors but no black or blue. I've got a shade of pink and plain old red and we'll have to get into my stuff to see if there's another color," she said, glad that they'd gotten away from talking about Cade. "And Alice, you can have a bath in the tub tonight."

"Yay!" She pumped her fist in the air. "And I want pink fingernails and I want my hair fixed all pretty for my pictures."

With all the to-do with hair and nails and getting into their different outfits for pictures, they were up past their bedtime that evening. When Retta went into each of their rooms to tell them good night, she noticed that Faith's tattoo was gone.

She reached out and touched the girl's shoulder. "Where did the heart go?"

"It flew away in the shower a couple of days ago. It wasn't real, Retta. It was a fake one, and I just didn't get water on it, but I got tired of it and washed it away." Faith grinned. "You don't have one, do you?"

"No, ma'am. I'm terrified of needles, but don't tell Cade," she whispered.

"I won't." Faith grinned. "Good night Retta. Tomorrow we get to talk on the phone."

"Yes, we do." She eased out of the room and sent the whole huge file of pictures to Cade with a note asking if he could print them by Friday, when the girls would be working on their scrapbooks again.

She got a message back a few minutes later with one word: Yes.

\*     \*     \*

Cade's phone awoke him on Thursday morning. Groggily, he answered it without even checking to see who was calling.

"Cade Maguire, I'm not one to meddle, but I don't like this iceberg between you and Retta." Like always, Mavis dived right into the problem without an ounce of sweetness beforehand.

"Yep," he said. "And why are you callin' on the phone? Aren't you in the kitchen?"

"Because it's hard to talk to you when the house is full

of kids or even when Justin and Levi are around," she answered. "So are you going to melt it or just let it sit there and freeze you to death?"

"Not much I can do. What's for breakfast?"

"Don't you try to change the subject. And there is something you can do if you want this to work," Mavis said.

He slung his legs over the side of the bed and sat up. "And that would be?"

"Women don't like to be told what to do, Cade. They like to be in control of their own lives and follow their own dreams. So she'll live in Dallas. That's only sixty miles from the ranch. You can go visit her through the week and she can come to the ranch on weekends."

"But—" he started.

"She's not Julie!" Mavis said emphatically. "And y'all have more in common than you and Julie did. Retta loves the ranch. Give her wings, Cade. She'll fly away, but pretty soon she'll come back and light on the ranch and never leave."

He started to pace around the room. "That's not a guarantee."

"Life don't come with guarantees, cowboy, but it's a start," she said. "Go down to that bunkhouse and get this iceberg melted today or else I'm goin' home to stay after breakfast."

"Mavis, are you blackmailing me?" he asked.

"Call it whatever you like but I mean it." Mavis hung up on him.

"Melt an iceberg with one conversation," he muttered. "Impossible."

"What's impossible?" Justin rapped on the door and then poked his head inside the room.

Cade got to his feet. "I just talked to Mavis or rather she talked—but she wasn't meddling."

Justin leaned against the doorjamb. "She was fussin' at you about Retta, right? I was actually comin' in to do the same thing, but since she beat me, I'll just add an amen and leave."

"Why?" Cade asked.

"Because you're in love with that woman and she makes you happy," Justin told him bluntly.

"I like her, admire her, appreciate her, but love? I'm not sure about that." Cade started to pace again.

"Yep, you are and it's deeper than what you had with Julie. Levi is out of the bathroom so it's my turn. Good luck, brother, but I've got faith in you." Justin hurried off for his turn in the bathroom.

*You got to let a woman think it was her idea,* Skip's words came back to him.

A smile started as a twitch and then spread over his face. He could hire someone to do Mavis's job. It wouldn't be a surrogate grandmother like Mavis had been all those years, but there would be food on the table. Someone could come in once or twice a week and keep the ranch house clean and he could continue to do the book work. What he really wanted in his life was a solid relationship—with Retta. And dammit! Justin was right. He had begun to fall in love with her.

Melt the iceberg? That could be simply bringing back the heat between them.

Her idea? Pray that Skip was right.

# Chapter Twenty-Three

Retta picked up her pen and paper on Sunday night while the girls were writing home. How to start, what to say—finally she wrote:

Dear Mama,

It seems strange to write to you and yet something seems right about it tonight. I wish you were here to give me some advice about my life. Sometimes things that you said in the past come back to me when I need them. I wish it happened more often and I sure wish that you could appear before me right now and tell me what to do.

I've got a complicated dilemma going on in my heart. Cade offered me a job right here on the ranch. I turned him down but now I'm having second thoughts about it. There's such peace here and it's the first place I've been that I can almost feel you and daddy with me. But then you both loved the ranching life so I shouldn't be surprised.

There's a connection between me and Cade that I can't explain. I could so easily fall in love with him. He's everything you told me to look for in a man when I was ready to settle down and start a family. But I'm not sure I'm ready to settle just yet. I need a sign to help me, Mama.

She put the end of the pen in her mouth and chewed on the cap for a full minute before her phone rang. Cade's picture showed up on the screen and she hesitated before she answered it. Could this be her sign?

"Hello," she said cautiously.

"We really need to talk, Retta. I've got some things I want to say but not on the phone."

"My girls are writing letters. Meet me on the porch at ten?"

"Mavis is on her way to the bunkhouse with a platter of fresh cookies to share with the girls and to baby-sit. Would you please meet me in the barn right now?"

"Okay, but—"

A knock on the door interrupted her sentence and then Mavis was in the room with a huge plate of warm cookies. "Thought the girls might like some cookies right out of the oven."

"Hey, Mavis!" Faith was the first one out of her bedroom. "Those look so good."

"All of y'all take a break and come on in here. I'll pour up some milk and we'll have a visit. I try to get to each bunkhouse during the time y'all are here. Haven't been to the boys' yet but maybe next week I'll find time to do that."

Mavis talked as she made her way to the refrigerator and poured five glasses of milk.

"There's six of us," Alice said.

"Nope, just me and you girls. This is my time with you and it gives Retta time to take a little walk and get away for an hour or so. She'll be back by bedtime. Now tell me, Faith, has your opinion of this place changed since you first got here?" Mavis asked.

"Bunches and bunches," Faith said. "I wish I wasn't already twelve so I could come back next year but Retta and all the girls say that we can keep in touch. Will you write letters to me and call me too, Miz Mavis?"

"Of course I will." Mavis pointed toward the door. "Get your boots on and get hustlin', Retta."

"I'll be back in an hour or less," Retta said.

"Don't rush." Mavis shooed her out the door with a wave of the hand.

The walk from the bunkhouse to the barn wasn't much more than a couple of football fields long, but that night it seemed like twenty miles. At times she took long strides and then she'd realize that she needed to think about what she'd say when she got there and slow down.

"Is this your sign, Mama?" she asked.

That old Mark Chesnutt song, "Old Country," started playing in her head again. Seemed like every time she and Cade got together she thought of the lyrics again.

"Okay, Mama, I get it." She lengthened her stride.

She was listening to the part of the song that said they kissed and held each other tight when she walked into the barn. A beam of light shot down from the loft so she climbed the ladder. When she reached the top, Cade was standing between her and the moonlight coming through the wide open doors at the end. She stopped and stared at his silhouette, so tall, so strong, so bold—and then he turned around and whispered her name.

She took a step forward and he did the same. He opened his arms and she walked into them. "Dallas is only sixty miles away and I'm not Julie," she said.

"I realize that." He buried his face in her hair.

"I love the ranch but..."

"It's okay." He tipped up her chin and she barely had time to moisten her lips before his closed on hers.

When the kiss ended, she took a step back. "I hated the way things were this week."

"Me too." He hugged her so tight that their hearts seemed to be beating in unison.

"I'm torn between two worlds. I want to get my old job back but I love the peace on the ranch," she admitted.

He pulled her down to sit beside him in the scattered hay. "I would love to hire you to help me with books and give this thing between us a chance to see where it might go. But I realize that's not your dream and you'd always have regrets. So I'll support you in whatever you decide, but please give us a chance, Retta."

"How will we know if this is just a flash in the pan or if it's real and enduring?" she asked.

"Time, darlin'," he answered. "You can go get that fancy job and I'll be right here on weekends. You can have the best of both worlds and I'll never stand in your way."

"I thought this talk would take a lot longer. What changed your mind?" she asked.

"I realized that I don't want you to be strapped to something that you hate. That you mean enough to me to support you in your dreams, and this chemistry between us is something that I've never felt before—before you ask, not even with Julie. And I don't want to lose it, because it makes me happy," he said.

She moved over to sit in his lap. "I could so easily fall in love with you even if you are a Texas fan."

"And I'd think maybe that I've already fallen for you, but that's crazy." He leaned back and grinned. "We come from two worlds that can never meet in the middle—you yell for the Sooners and I'm a Longhorn to the death."

"You got that right." She was glad that the mood had lightened.

"And besides we've only known each other a little more than three weeks."

Her arms snaked up around his neck. "So you don't believe in love at first sight?"

"No, I don't."

She brought his lips to hers for another steamy kiss and then whispered, "Neither do I, but we might both be wrong."

"I'll be the first to admit it if we are. God, you feel good in my arms, Retta."

She moved her arms and leaned back to look at him. "I missed you, Cade. You were right there but you weren't."

"I know exactly what you're sayin'," he said.

They sat like that in comfortable silence, his arms around her, her head on his chest for several minutes. It was enough for one night, enough that they'd both made peace with the issue that had been between them.

"I'm a mess right now, Cade. I thought I was over my dad's death but I'm not. I'm not even over my mom being gone. I just put it all in a box and sealed it shut and immersed myself first in college and then work and then taking care of Daddy," she admitted. "And now the box is falling apart and I have to deal with it before I can move forward."

"Let me help you heal. I've never had that experience but I'm here for you. And in some ways, I guess I'm still a mess too. Because I was judging you by Julie. And that's not fair to you." He rested his chin on the top of her head.

"If either of us isn't happy in this new relationship or the distance thing, then we'll be honest and up front about it from the beginning." She reached up and touched his cheek.

His hand covered hers and held it there. "Do you have any idea what your touch does to me? How it affects me for your fingertips just to brush against mine at the dinner table?" He ran his forefinger down her arm to her wrist and brought her hand to his lips to kiss each knuckle. "Or for your knee to touch mine under the table?"

Shivers chased down her spine in spite of the heat. "Oh, honey, I know exactly what you are talking about because you affect me the same way."

"It's too intense to just throw away, Retta. We've got to give it time," he whispered seductively in her ear.

She opened her mouth to say something and her phone rang. "Damn cell phones," she muttered as she fished it from her hip pocket.

His lips brushed against hers in a sweet kiss. "We should have turned them off."

She touched the screen. "Bad timing, Tina."

"Amen, darlin'. The wedding is off."

"What happened?" Retta gasped.

"The wedding is off. The marriage is on. We got married to-day at the courthouse. I'm pregnant and we didn't want to wait. So start thinkin' of baby names. Now get back in bed with that sexy cowboy you've been talking about. Love you, girl."

"Don't you dare drop this bombshell on me and then hang up," Retta said.

"Okay, okay." Tina giggled. "We were shocked by the

pregnancy test but then we figured what the hell, we want a family so we're gettin' a head start. I want a daughter so bad, but that's only because I don't know anything about boys. All I had was sisters growing up."

"Just don't name her Retta. No one can spell it right, and she'll be called Rita most of her life," Retta said. "I'm so happy for you and jealous as hell."

"Hey, it don't take a genius to know how to make a baby so go get busy with that sexy cowboy," Tina said. "And now I am hanging up because we have to tell our mothers that we are married. Love you."

"Right back atcha."

"Cousin?" Cade asked.

"Friend." She told him about Tina and why she'd called.

"Lucky guy." Cade chuckled. "Come on, I'll walk you back to the bunkhouse. It's about bedtime for your kids."

"I wish we could stay here forever." She sighed.

"Me, too, darlin'." He got up and pulled her up with him. "But for tonight I'm just happy with this much."

"I feel like I've been on a date," she said when he walked her all the way to the door and kissed her good night.

"Me too," he said. "See you in the morning."

"I'll be the one to your left with dark hair and brown eyes," she teased.

"The sexy one on the way to stealin' my heart." He dropped another kiss on her forehead and was gone before she could reply.

The girls were gathered around Mavis when Retta went inside. All of them were in pajamas and their hair was still damp. She looked up and winked at Retta. "We've had a lovely time. We started with each one of them telling me their favorite color and went from there. But now it's time for bed and for you to get them tucked in."

Alice giggled. "We're too old to get tucked in but Retta comes in and tells us good night. We like that."

Mavis didn't ask questions, which was good because Retta wasn't sure if she could explain what had happened in the hayloft. For sure, the turmoil in her heart had disappeared, but to put into words the feelings that she'd shared with Cade—impossible. Mavis just gathered up an empty plate and, with a wave, she left.

Retta made sure all the girls were in bed and then went back to her bedroom to find her half-finished letter lying on the bed. She picked up the pen and continued to write:

Thank you, Mama, for the sign.

It's now more than an hour later and I spent that time with Cade in a hayloft. I'm wondering if, when you and Daddy argued, if you ever took the fight to the hayloft. I never heard you have a disagreement but you weren't angels, not then anyway, so there had to have been times when you didn't get along.

Tonight Cade and I took our fight to that peaceful place that smelled like hay. The moon and stars were right out the window. I felt like I could have reached out and touched them and now as I write this, I'm realizing that maybe that's why we went there so that I could realize that some things never change. And it's in those places that I can and will find happiness. I think that when we fight from now on, I'll make him meet me in the hayloft.

Good night, Mama, and thanks again for the sign. I love you so much—

Retta

Cade whistled all the way to the ranch house. He'd thought he'd sneak inside and go straight to his bedroom where he'd let the events of the last hour play through his mind over and over again.

But Mavis followed him into the house, where Justin and Levi were grinning like a couple of possums trying to eat grapes through a barbed wire fence. He nodded at the bunch of them and started down the hallway.

Mavis grabbed him by the arm. "Not so fast, Cade Maguire. I did my part and now you owe me the story of what happened."

"Didn't Retta tell you?" he asked.

"Not in front of those little girls. They thought she was out there petting those two donkeys."

"Nope, she was out there fussin' with a full-grown jackass," Justin said.

"Hey, now." Levi laughed. "With a miracle he might grow another inch or two. With that bein' said, he might just be a jackass, but not a full-grown one."

"Okay, okay, we settled our cold war," Cade said.

"And?" Justin raised a dark brow.

"And she's still not staying, so we have to interview a cook or two and get a housekeeper," Cade said.

"But?" Levi tucked his head to his chest and looked up at Cade from the recliner where he was kicked back.

"But we aren't going to let whatever we've got between us die in its sleep. We're going to try to work with a relationship that will involve some traveling. But she did say that she loved the ranch and felt at peace here," Cade said. "Now is the interrogation over? Is it all right if I go to bed?"

"Alone? Damn brother, I'm disappointed in you," Justin teased.

"Justin Franklin Maguire!" Mavis scolded.

"Well, I am," Justin said. "I thought he could sweet talk the jeans off any woman out there."

"Retta isn't any woman." Cade grinned. "Good night guys. And remember, when it's your turn to be in my boots, I intend to give you hell."

"I can't wear your boots." Levi pointed at his feet. "These are size twelves. They'd get lost in those fourteens that you have to have special made."

Cade could hear the low tones of conversation as he left but he didn't really care what they said or talked about. He just wanted to lie down on his bed and think about Retta until he fell asleep.

# Chapter Twenty-Four

There was not a single moment from Sunday night until Wednesday morning for Retta and Cade to even sneak a quick kiss. The guys had to work from daylight until after dark to get all the ranch work done so they could be away all day Wednesday and Thursday on a campout trip with the kids.

Excitement abounded in the yard that morning like a sugared-up six-year-old who'd spent the whole day at grandma's house. They were each allowed one small tote bag, provided by the ranch and personalized with each kid's name. In it they were to put what toiletries they'd need and a change of clothing.

The covered wagon was parked in front of the house that morning. Two mules were hitched to it and looked docile enough that Retta didn't think she'd have a problem driving the wagon. At breakfast, Retta could feel as much enthusiasm in the four cowboys as she could in the kids.

The last time she'd camped out was back when she was a kid. For her tenth birthday her parents had let her and six friends set up a tent out by the barn. They'd stayed up all night telling scary stories, but the thing she remembered the most was all the mosquito bites she'd taken with her to the breakfast table the next morning. Remembering the way they itched had kept her from ever asking for a party like that again and had reminded her to tuck a can of bug repellent in her bag that morning.

"Okay, kids, we've got two extra horses. That means two of you get to ride and then we switch off about a fourth of the way to the campsite, which this year is going to be out on the edge of Canyon Creek. I figured we'd start with the two youngest and in half an hour, we'll switch off and keep working our way up the list until we get to Benjy and Faith. That seem fair?"

Alice eyed the two big roan-colored horses and shook her head. "Not me. Someone else can have my turn and I'll ride up by Retta."

"Me too." Ivan scrambled up the side of the wagon right behind Alice and sat down on the buckboard with Retta.

"Anyone else want to give up their turn?" Cade asked. No one raised their hand or spoke up, so he went on. "Okay then, I guess Gabby and Nelson are first."

"Wagons ho!" Cade shouted after Skip and Justin helped the two kids get mounted.

Retta snapped the reins against the mules and they moved forward at an easy pace. Mavis waved from the porch and yelled, "Y'all write me when you get to California to the gold mines."

"Gold mines?" Ivan asked.

"Never know what we might find," Retta said as the bumpy ride out across the pastures continued.

Cade rode up beside the wagon and tipped his hat back on his head. "Y'all gettin' along okay here?"

"Yes, wagon master, we're doin' fine," Retta said. "Are we going the whole ten miles this first day?"

"Ten miles?" Cade asked.

"That's what wagon trains tried to do each day from Saint Jo, Missouri, to the gold mines in California," Benjy said. "It took many months for them to go all the way to the gold mines on the West Coast."

"Man, I would have loved to have been the wagon master for one of those journeys." Cade tipped his hat at Retta. "But I reckon two and a half miles will about be our limit. We got to toughen up these cowboys and cowgirls. We'll go easy on 'em today and tomorrow."

"You were born a couple of hundred years too late," she told him.

"Or maybe at the exact right time." He flirted as he dropped back to follow the wagon and keep an eye on the kids.

Going was slow in an authentic covered wagon with wood wheels and two old mules that acted like they had nowhere to go and all day to get there. According to Skip they'd get to Canyon Creek right before noon. Levi would serve as the scout and ride on ahead to get the campfire started so they could roast hot dogs for lunch. Then he'd put a pot of beans on the fire for supper while the kids panned for gold in Canyon Creek.

"Man, this ain't like ridin' in a car," Ivan said.

"You can always get in the back," Retta said. "Just crawl back there and stretch out on the top of all those sleeping bags for a nap."

Ivan shook his head. "No, thank you. I might miss something. Like right there, did you see them two rabbits?"

"I missed them," Retta answered. "What color were they?"

"Gray with white tails."

"Oh! Oh!" Alice pointed. "Look at that dog that Beau is chasing away."

"That's a coyote," Retta told her.

"Really? I thought a coyote was a person who helped folks get into the country from Mexico," Alice said.

"Me too," Gabby said as she rode up beside the wagon. "Look, Retta, I can hold the reins all by myself. Justin showed me how to keep the horse goin' straight or to make it turn."

"Doin' good there." Retta grinned.

By noon the kids had all had a turn and Retta's two kids were eager to get off the buckboard bench of the wagon. They weren't the only ones—she rubbed her fanny when she hopped down and handed the reins to Cade.

"The guys and I will take care of the mules and get them staked out by the edge of the water. You did a fine job." He brushed a strand of hair back behind her ear.

His gentle touch on her sweaty face created all kinds of vibes. She glanced over at the clear water bubbling over a gravel bottom and wished they were alone so she could strip down to nothing and go skinny-dipping with him.

"Penny for your thoughts," he whispered.

"Oh, honey, they'd cost you far more than that but they had something to do with cold water and hot skin." She laid a hand on his arm.

"Whew!" He took off his hat and fanned with it. "It is gettin' hotter by the minute out here."

"I told you that a fire wasn't a good idea." Levi threw another stick of wood on the blaze.

"After we eat can we wade in the water again?" Nelson asked.

"Where's the bathroom?" Kirk looked around frantically.

"How do you think the folks who rode on a real wagon train took care of that?" Levi asked.

Kirk's hazel eyes got wider and wider. "Are you serious?"

"Naw, I was just jokin' with you, son. There used to be an old house about twenty yards that way." He pointed to the left. "It burned years ago, but the outdoor toilet is still standing. I made sure the spiders were all gone and there weren't any snakes in it so it's safe."

"Don't tease me," Faith gasped.

"He's not," Benjy said. "There's real toilet paper in there but it does get hot and there ain't no lights so if you got to go at night then you have to take a flashlight or a lantern. Y'all follow me and I'll show you where it is. It's even got a moon in the door to let a little bit of light in it."

"For real?" Gabby asked.

"Aww, come on. At least it's got a door on it and we don't have to squat behind a tree," Benjy said. "And just think about the stories you get to tell tomorrow when you call home."

Retta was having a hard time keeping the giggles down. There was an old toilet just like they were describing on the back side of the farm where she grew up. Her dad had left it there when he'd torn down the rest of an old dilapidated house, and it had sure come in handy a lot of times.

Benjy waved a hand in the air and they all followed him, as if he were the Pied Piper and they were little mice. Retta sat down on a fallen tree trunk as far away from the fire as she could get, removed her hat, and fanned with it.

The grass was unbelievably green for the latter part of June in north-central Texas, and the creek was running really well, but then they'd had more rain than usual. She instinctively checked the sky. Not a black cloud in sight, which was good since she didn't want to sleep with twelve other people crowded into the wagon all together.

She took her hair down from the ponytail, shook it loose, and then bent forward to gather it all up again on top of her head, bringing in all the strays that had gotten loose on the ride.

*     *     *

Cade sat down on the tree trunk beside her and fanned her with his hat. "I'd rather be out there in the water with you, letting it wash over our bodies. That would cool us down."

"No, honey, that would boil the water."

"Anyone ever tell you that you are downright cute in jeans and boots?"

"No one that I would believe," she answered. "How far is it to the outside two-holer?"

"Who said anything about two holes? It's not far, maybe half a city block, and it's only slightly better than the bushes." He laughed. "I imagine the health department would have a fit if they knew."

"Probably, but it's only for an afternoon and night and I'm not tellin'." She took his hat from him and fanned him for a few minutes. "I hear them coming. Good thing they aren't trackin' game for supper. We'd all starve to death."

"You ever been huntin'?" Cade asked.

"Every fall with my dad until he was too sick to go anymore. Nothing better than venison made up into summer sausage," she answered.

"You got a gun then?"

"A rifle for hunting, a pistol for protection and a license to carry it, and a BB gun because Daddy got it for me when

I was five so I could target practice on tin cans," she answered.

"Ever shoot anything?"

"Every year if I was lucky."

The kids came runnin' back through the underbrush like the devil was chasing them. Out of breath and panting, all eight of them fell down in front of Cade and Retta on the grass. Seeing all their little sweating, red faces and their hair plastered to their heads, put a smile on Cade's face.

"So who's hungry? I think our cooks for the trip have got the fire hot enough to make hot dogs, but if any of y'all want to go rabbit huntin' for something better..." He let the sentence hang.

"No!" Sasha said emphatically. "Don't kill a little bunny. I could never eat that. We'll have hot dogs and be happy with them."

"And canned beans and potato chips. That's what people ate on the trail except they fried the potatoes instead of buyin' potato chips," Benjy said.

"My sister makes fried potatoes and pork'n'beans sometimes when my mama don't get home in time to fix supper," Alice said. "Sounds good."

Justin came up from behind the log and said, "Okay, go find yourself each a stick to use to roast your hot dogs."

They scrambled like ants off into the nearby trees looking for long sticks, and Justin sat down on the other side of Retta. "Don't you wish you had that much energy?"

"For just an hour a day would be wonderful," Retta answered.

"Think what we could do with it if we could harness it and use it for power, like they do those wind things out in western Texas. Between the eight of them, they could probably keep the whole ranch in electricity for a year." Cade nudged Retta on the shoulder and took back his hat. "Look at those kids. They've all found a stick and we don't have one."

"Skip done took care of half a dozen just in case." Justin stood to his feet and the three of them headed back toward the infernally hot blaze.

"So how do you like your hot dog? Burned?" Cade asked as he took two sticks from Skip and handed one to her.

"Toasted nice and brown and with lots of relish and mustard," she answered. "And I hope you brought lots because I love bonfire hot dogs."

Dammit! She fished. She hunted. She knew the difference between a bull and a heifer, and a computer worked for her like it knew her personally, Cade thought.

"Man this is fun," Faith said. "If we had a real bathroom out here, I could just stay here forever."

Benjy squirted ketchup down his hot dog in a long line and took a bite. "Mmmm," he said. "This is even better than the wagon where me and Granny used to get one on payday."

"We got one of them wagons that come to our school for lunchtime but I ain't never got to buy nothing from it. I eat in the cafeteria for free. Now I won't even want one of theirs cause I done had one that is better." Kirk's face lit up in a brilliant smile that looked so much better than his usual scowl.

"Me thinks the kid is comin' around," Retta whispered.

Cade had just stuffed a huge bite of food into his mouth so he just nodded and hoped that maybe Retta would come around someday too!

# Chapter Twenty-Five

It seemed as if Retta could reach out with a cup and fill it up with twinkling stars that night as she lay on her back on top of the sleeping bag not far from the wagon. She could hear the girls whispering and giggling inside the wagon, where they were lined up on the floor like sardines in a tiny little can. It would be an evening they'd remember forever and maybe even tell their kids and grandkids about it someday.

The boys had chosen a spot under a big scrub oak tree not far from the wagon. Four of them were with Skip and Levi. Justin and Cade had chosen places a few feet away where they could keep watch on both boys and girls.

Outside, with no walls and no boundaries, Retta felt safer than she had in ages. She closed her eyes and went right to sleep only to dream of another time and era when she and Cade were traveling on a wagon train from Texas to California to the gold mines.

She awoke to the aroma of strong coffee and opened her

eyes to see Cade propped up on an elbow right beside her. He held out a blue granite mug of coffee and smiled even brighter than the stars had been the night before. She sat up, and he put the mug in her hand.

"Mmmm," she said when she took a sip. For a split second she was still in the dream and they were a married couple going on an adventure to discover gold. But then Skip clanged a triangular dinner bell and reality jerked her back to the present. After another couple sips of the coffee, she handed it back to Cade.

"Great way to wake up. Thank you." She inhaled the morning air and tried to shake off the disappointment that surrounded her the moment she realized she hadn't stepped into a time-travel machine that transported her back over a hundred years.

"You are beautiful with the morning light shining in your eyes," Cade said softly.

"And in the heat of the day when I'm hot and sweaty and beginning to smell like I've been drivin' mules all day?" she teased.

"Then, and in a hayloft, or playing football with the kids. Which reminds me, I thought maybe we'd have a game this afternoon. It'll run some of the energy out of them after sitting all the way back to the ranch." He tossed the coffee grounds from the bottom of his cup out onto the grass.

She stood up and worked her sleeping bag into a tight roll. "It's been years since I've slept out under the stars. It's so peaceful."

"Have to admit that I enjoy it sometimes, but I miss air-conditioning and a nice hot shower at the end of the day."

Retta stretched the kinks out of her back and neck. "Not much beats the smell of morning air, listening to water bubbling over rocks, and hot coffee brought right to a woman's bed. But that sleeping bag is not made of feathers or memory foam."

"Did Cade bring you breakfast in bed?" Faith asked from the back of the wagon. "What did you do to deserve that? We didn't get breakfast in bed."

"Coffee, not breakfast," Retta said, quickly changing the subject. "And we're playing football this afternoon when we get back to the ranch house. Tell Cade who's going to win."

"Girl power!" Sasha said as she hopped out of the wagon and ran off toward the outdoor toilet.

"See." Retta tapped him on the chest. "My girls are a mean fightin' machine."

He grabbed her hand and kissed the palm. "Don't get your hopes up too high, darlin'. My boys have a Longhorn coach."

"And my girls have a Sooner coach." Her voice was only slightly higher than normal, which was a surprise after the way the touch of his lips on her hand made her knees go weak.

"Mornin', Cade. How you doin', Retta?" Levi said as he tucked his sleeping bag inside the wagon. "Y'all ready to go home and take a nap in a real bed?"

"We're goin' home to play football and you are the referee," Cade said.

"That ought to be a hoot," he said flatly. "I'd rather go for a root canal as get in the middle of you two. You are coaching, right?"

"We are," they said in unison.

He walked away, muttering under his breath.

"Breakfast in ten minutes," Skip yelled.

Cade got to his feet and offered a hand. She took it and he pulled her up to her feet. Suddenly she remembered a television show that she'd watched with her dad. The character on the show told her partner that she felt like she was standing in the middle of a frozen lake. What she wanted in life was right there in front of her and all she had to do was reach out and take it, but the ice was cracking all around her. That's the way Retta felt that morning. For more than half her life she'd been on a mission to get what she wanted and she'd gone after it with the gusto of a hound dog chasing a squirrel. But now the ice was cracking under her feet and nothing was as sure as it had been a few months or even weeks ago.

# Chapter Twenty-Six

Six-man football in some of the small Texas schools wasn't unusual. A few in the really small schools even played three-man ball, but Retta had never watched four-man ball with girls on one side and boys on the other until that afternoon. Faith and Kirk went at it with a passion, both determined to win. When Gabby ran in the first touchdown, Retta wanted to chase down to the end of the pasture and do the happy dance with her. Sasha kicked for the extra point and missed.

Then Sasha kicked off to the boys and Nelson ran the ball all the way back to the twenty-yard line. The girls held them right there for two plays, but on the fourth down, instead of punting, Nelson flipped the ball over to Kirk, who scored. It was the boys' turn to do their wiggly dance, but the girls stopped the run for two points, so the score was tied.

They played hard, back and forth, getting more serious and dirtier with every play. When Skip's clock said they had one minute left in the game and the score was tied, the boys had the ball thirty yards from the end zone. Kirk snapped it and tossed it off to Benjy, who tucked it under his arm, put his head down, and headed for the goal at the end of the pasture. The other three boys surrounded him, giving him support and protection. Sasha took down Nelson and Gabby managed to knock Kirk flat on his back. Benjy was still running hell-bent for leather straight toward the goal when Alice grabbed Ivan around the ankles and he landed on his butt. Now there were only two kids on the playing field and Benjy was huffing for air. Faith was right behind him, her long pigtails flapping in the wind. She reached out to tackle him at the five-yard line and missed.

Benjy ran the final five yards, spiked the football, and dropped down on his knees with both hands raised to heaven. The boys surrounded him, jumping up and down like windup toys, Cade right in the middle of the mix. With her head down, Faith jogged back to the girls' side of the pasture.

It wasn't until she raised her head and Retta saw the smile and twinkle in her eyes that she realized what the girl had done. The other girls patted her on the back, and to all outsiders it would look as if they were all commiserating with her but the whispers said otherwise. They'd let the boys win on purpose so that Benjy could have a final moment of glory.

"What just happened?" Retta asked, as if she didn't have a clue.

"They whooped us." Alice sighed. Her cute little face had smudges of dirt, and grass stains were probably permanently ground into the knees of her faded jeans.

"Fair and square?" Retta asked.

"In Benjy's eyes." Faith grinned. "What happens in the

huddle, stays in the huddle, right girls?" She held up her palm, and they high-fived with her.

"You worked awfully hard for that trophy," Retta whispered.

"Yep, we did. We outplayed them," Gabby said.

"And we ain't got no regrets." Alice wiped her forehead, smearing the dirt as much as getting rid of the sweat.

Sasha shrugged. "It's an ugly trophy anyway, ain't it girls?"

Another high five and they ran across the pasture to congratulate the boys.

Retta was proud of her girls and what they'd accomplished in the time they'd been at Longhorn Canyon. When Cade brought out the trophy and gave it to the boys, Benjy held it high for a picture. Faith and Kirk exchanged a long, sly look, and Retta had to wipe away a tear, hoping that the camera caught that precious moment.

"We won." Cade grinned. "But I've got a feeling that—"

She put a finger on his lips. "Shhh. Don't say it out loud and it won't be true. I'm proud of the whole bunch of them for coming together for this moment."

\*　　　\*　　　\*

Cade could hardly wait to get to the house on Friday evening. Five more days and the kids would be gone...but so would Retta. "Everything is changing," he told the dog sitting beside him on the passenger seat. "Mavis will be gone. We have to have a cook and a housekeeper."

Beau whined.

"I know, old boy." Cade rubbed the dog's head with his knuckles. "At least this way I get to spend time with her every day until she leaves. And to be honest, I'm still worried about this long distance, even if it is only from the ranch to Dallas. I'm in love with her, Beau. I don't know how it happened or when and I know it's way too soon, but my heart hurts at the thought of her not being here."

Beau barked as if he understood.

Cade parked the tractor and started toward the house in long strides with the dog right behind him. Gussie met them halfway, nosed Beau, and joined in the parade. When Cade put a hand on the fence and jumped over it, he noticed that Hopalong and Hard Times were both up against a pecan tree, enjoying the shade.

"So you've all come to spend some time with them before they leave, have you? Maybe we should get Little Bit from the corral and turn him loose in the yard so we'd have the whole bunch of you." Cade bent down and rubbed the bunny's ears.

"I kind of like that idea," Retta said as she rounded the corner of the house. "And the kids would love it right up until the time they stepped in fresh donkey droppin's."

Cade rose to his full height, slipped an arm around her shoulders, and brushed a sweet kiss across her lips. "I missed you today. What did y'all do?"

"We made a list for shopping on Monday. They're really excited about that and we all worked in the garden. Before you ask, it was a competition for sure. The boys picked more beans than the girls but the girls beat them on numbers when it came to the cucumbers and the tomatoes."

"So working as a team for Benjy on the football pasture is over?"

"Honey, that was a one-time deal."

"I won our bet, no matter whether it was thrown or not." He pulled her tighter against his side.

"How do you figure that?"

"Let's see. I think you have to sit on the Longhorn side of the stadium in October when we play Oklahoma, right?"

"And I'll be yelling 'Boomer Sooner' so you can get ready for it." She smiled up at him.

"Think either of us will ever change our football minds?"

"Hell, no!" She giggled. "What would be the fun in that and what would we have to bet on other than paper wads and trash cans?"

"Oh, honey, I bet we could find something." He lingered back, hating to go inside, where he'd have to share her with the kids and Mavis.

"Seems like the time has gone so fast." She sighed. "That first day I wasn't sure that Faith or Gabby would ever come around, but I'm so proud of them. And..." She sniffed. "Cade, how do you tell them good-bye every year? I feel like they're family and I'm probably never going to see them again."

He stopped on the porch and put his hands on her shoulders. "You can have their addresses and there's nothing in your contract that says you can't call them or even drop by their houses to see them. You'll be living right there in Dallas so..." He shrugged.

"It won't be like having them right in the house with you, though," she told him.

"Confession." He raised a palm. "I hate the first week that they're all gone because I miss having them underfoot. We were both made for a family, Retta."

"Yep, at least two kids are on my plan." She nodded.

"Only two?"

"I'd like more but it's not in the books," she said.

"Then throw the books out in the yard and let it rain on them."

She stopped at the door and turned to put her hands on

his chest. "Cade, this plan of mine is what has held me and kept me through everything. To throw it away would…" She paused. "I can't describe it."

"It would be something like when I had my whole life planned out with Julie and then suddenly it was gone. I felt like a fish floundering around in shallow water."

She nodded and then laid her head on his chest. "Yes, that's right. It's something I have to do or I know I'll look back with regrets."

"Then let's do it together. You go get into big bankin' business and I'll be right here waiting every weekend. Like the song 'Old Country.'"

She started humming the tune to the song by Mark Chesnutt and he wrapped his arms around her and two-stepped with her on the porch. The lyrics said that the country boy had plowed until noon but that every now and then he and the city girl got together. Cade could feel every one of the words and he'd take what he could get for sure, but he wanted so much more with her.

*     *     *

The kids had worked on their scrapbooks on Friday but they hadn't finished them, so on Saturday evening, they gathered round the table and argued over the football pictures that had been printed. Retta slipped a picture of each girl into her purse that evening as she glanced through the scattered photos on the dining room table. There was one of Sasha with Gussie slung over her shoulder, Alice having a staring contest with Hard Times, Gabby giving Hopalong a carrot on the back porch, and her favorite was a photo of Faith sitting on the porch after the big football game with her arm thrown around Beau.

She'd pulled her phone from her hip pocket and snapped several shots of a gorgeous Texas sunset that left trails of bright orange, pink, and yellow streaks across the sky but when she flipped through the pictures, not a one of them did justice to what was out there on the horizon.

"Not any more than the photos of the girls," she muttered.

"What's that about photos?" Cade asked from the deep shadows.

She turned quickly to see his silhouette leaning against the post at the far end of the porch. "Where did you come from? You were in the house when I slipped out."

"Went out the back door and hopped over the porch rail. Are you okay? You looked like you were going to cry just before you left the dining room."

She walked up to him and looped her arms around his neck. "I hate good-byes."

He folded his big arms around her and rested his chin on her head. "Me too, darlin'."

"Hey, Retta, guess what?" Alice poked her head out the door.

Retta took a step back. "You finished your scrapbook?"

"Yes, I did but not really. Skip and Mavis say that after church they're takin' us to get hamburgers tomorrow and then we're going to a movie all together and then we're going to get ice cream after that."

"Well, that sure sounds like fun."

"But it's just for us and them," Gabby yelled as she bounded out on the porch.

"I'm not invited?" Retta stuck her lower lip out in a pout.

"Nope, you have to stay home." Sasha joined the party. "I'd bring you ice cream but it would melt."

"That's sweet of you, darlin'."

"I'll stay home with you," Faith offered.

"No, you won't. I was pretending to be upset. I'm glad that y'all are going with Skip and Mavis and you can tell me all about your afternoon when you get home."

"I wish it was home," Alice said. "But I'd want to bring my sisters and my mama and all my friends with me."

"Betcha I can beat all of you back to the bunkhouse," Gabby said.

"Not with them short legs." Faith hopped off the porch. "Line up and we'll see who's the fastest."

The girls got in position like they were about to set off on a marathon. "You call it, Cade," Gabby said. "And I'll show her just how fast these legs can go."

"Ready, set…" Cade paused a second and then shouted, "Go!"

After they'd taken off in a blur, Cade drew Retta back into his arms. "I was about to tell you about the Sunday evening movie business. It's not on the regular agenda, but Mavis and Skip wanted to take the kids to their house to see where Benjy would live. We decided this would be the best way to handle it."

"I thought they were doing burgers, movie, and ice cream," she said.

"Burgers and movie in Wichita Falls. Ice cream is going to be at their house near Sunset. They'll be home at supper time and we're ordering pizza for their last Sunday on the ranch," he said.

"Kids' description of heaven. Burgers, ice cream, and pizza."

Cade kissed her on the forehead. "And the added bonus is that we get an afternoon to ourselves. Want to go out for lunch after church and then take in a movie?"

She leaned back. "Are you askin' me out on a date?"

"Yes, ma'am." He tipped up her chin and kissed her on the lips this time.

"Then the answer is yes but I can watch movies anytime. I vote that we take a picnic out to the cabin. I'd rather spend my time with you here on the ranch."

"Retta!" Sasha's angry voice floated across the yard. "Faith is being bossy again."

"Maybe I don't want a yard full of kids after all." Cade laughed.

"Kind of puts things into perspective, doesn't it." She tangled her hands into his hair and pulled his lips down to hers for another kiss. "Good night, Cade."

"Night, Retta. I'm lookin' forward to tomorrow."

"Not as much as I am. I have a date—the first one in a very long time."

# Chapter Twenty-Seven

Retta tossed her cute little red-and-white-polka-dotted sundress on the bed and kicked off her sandals. She flipped her dark hair up into a ponytail and then dressed in jeans, a tank top, and boots. She started to reapply a touch of makeup but decided that would take too long. She still needed to pack a picnic lunch to take to the cabin before she and Cade could slip away for what would probably be their final time alone.

She heard the four-wheeler engine coming toward the bunkhouse. Starting toward the door, she remembered her hat and grabbed it from the back of the sofa, crammed it on her head, and had her hand on the doorknob when someone on the other side rapped three times.

She settled the hat onto her head and opened the door to find Cade standing there with a gorgeous yellow rose in his hand. "Why did you knock and is that for me?"

"Because this is a date and yes, it is. I picked it from a

rosebush at the church this morning as we were leaving," he answered.

"Stealin' from the Lord?" she teased.

"God understands the heart of a man who's infatuated by a lovely woman." He put the rose in her hand. "Are you ready?"

"As soon as I put this in water. Come on in and give me a minute. I need to go up to the house before we leave and pack our lunch. Where are Levi and Justin today?" She talked as she found a glass, put water into it, and slipped the rose into it.

"They both went different ways, but I think there's a woman involved for each of them. It was a don't ask, don't tell. I didn't ask them what they were doing and they returned the favor. Not that I wouldn't have said anything. I'll stand in the middle of the street in Sunset or Bowie either one and tell the whole world I'm going on a date today with you if you want me to," he said. "And I've already got a cooler of food strapped down to the four-wheeler so we're ready to go now."

"Roses and food. You are a romantic, Cade Maguire," she said.

He held out an arm for her and she lopped hers into it. "Ahh, shucks, ma'am, it's just a yard rose and some cold fried chicken and a bottle of wine."

She leaned in closer to him. "Don't you get all shy with me. I know how bold you are."

"And I know how stubborn you are, so we make a pretty good match," he teased.

\*      \*      \*

Cade had always thought of himself as a risk taker but not necessarily a bold cowboy, but hey, if she wanted to give him that quality, he'd take it. He helped her onto the four-wheeler before he settled into the driver's seat. Then he reached around, picked up her arms, and brought them around so he could kiss each palm before he tucked them against his chest.

When they reached the cabin, he hopped off, scooped her up like a bride, and carried her across the lawn and onto the porch.

"You're going to break your back," she protested.

He shut her up with a long, hot kiss but didn't miss a single step across the porch.

"Honest, Cade, you should put me down," she managed to get out when he threw the door open and carried her over the threshold.

"Food or dessert first," he asked as he laid her or the bottom bunk.

"I've always been partial to sweets." She pulled her shirt up over her shoulders and tossed it at the sofa.

"And you think I'm bold?" He kicked off his boots.

"We've only got this one afternoon before this party ends and I'm not wasting a minute of it," she said.

"We're going to make every minute count, though, darlin'." He pulled her up into his arms and removed the ponytail holder, then combed her hair with his fingers. "Soft as silk." He bent forward and nibbled on her earlobe.

She turned her head and captured his lips with a searing kiss that made the whole room spin. "It's hot in here. If we don't get this show on the road, we're going to be playing slip and slide all over each other's bodies." During the next kiss, she undid his belt buckle and unzipped his jeans. Then she tugged them down over his feet, taking socks with them and threw them in the general direction of her discarded shirt.

He stood up and whipped off his shirt and then hurriedly

crossed the room, pulled back a curtain, and turned a dial on a window air conditioner. "A little cool air will keep us from setting the cabin on fire."

She propped up on an elbow. "I wondered if you might have a fire extinguisher in here."

"Nope but maybe we won't need it with the A/C unit."

Retta looked like one of those statues of a woman lying on a long chaise lounge, only instead of a sheet draped over one breast, she was totally naked from the waist up and wearing jeans and boots on the bottom. A cowboy's dream lying right there waiting for him. He wouldn't think about this being the ending party for them, but he'd make it a day that she couldn't walk away from.

He strung kisses down her body and removed her jeans and underpants an inch at a time. She was panting by the time he worked his way back up those beautiful long legs, across her belly, and to her lips once again.

"Oh, darlin', I don't know that I can take much more," she said. "Please make love to me."

If she'd asked for the moon at that point he would have tried to lasso it for her, so making love, not merely having sex with her was an easy thing to do. Not wanting it to end, he did all he could to make it last for a long time, and when it was over, he collapsed beside her on the narrow bunk bed and held her close.

"I've fallen in love with you, Retta. I know it's crazy and it's too soon to say the words but I have and I can't hold it in any longer," he said.

She rolled even closer to him and raised up so that their noses were practically touching. "I love you, Cade. I didn't believe in love at first sight and I've fought it but I'm tired of fighting now. I love you and we'll make this distance between us work. I promise."

"And I give you the same promise," he said.

Retta yawned and her stomach growled. "Nap or food?"

"Better have some food first, sweetheart. We got to have fuel for round two and three."

"With a short nap between each one. What time did you say we have to go home?"

"Mavis said they'd be home at six," he answered.

If hearts ever smiled, his was grinning really big right then. She probably didn't even realize that she'd begun to think of the Longhorn Canyon Ranch as home.

# Chapter Twenty-Eight

The girls rattled on and on about their Sunday afternoon until bedtime that night. They didn't write letters home that evening. But after they went to sleep Retta took out her stationery and a pen.

Dear Daddy,

I wish you were here tonight. I'm in love and I actually said the words out loud. You'd like Cade. He's a hardworking, kind man but I tease him about being a bold cowboy. He takes charge and

She laid the pen down and relived the feelings she had when he took charge of her body that afternoon. She'd felt as if they were the only two people left on Earth and it didn't matter if they ever saw family or friends again. If they could have stayed in that cabin forever she would have died a happy woman.

Picking the pen up again, she thought for a few minutes and continued.

Daddy, I don't want to leave, but I've got to. It's a driving force inside me that has to continue down this path. I appreciate Cade for letting me be myself and not demanding that I change. We're going to have a long-distance, well, not really such a long distance since it's only a little more than an hour to Dallas, relationship. I'll come to the ranch every weekend I can and he'll try to get down to the city once a week to see me. It'll work because we are determined. You told me once that love conquers everything. I wish now I'd asked you exactly what you meant. Did Mama have dreams of something other than being a farmer's wife? Did you have dreams that you had to lay aside? Even if I could talk to you, I know that you'd tell me to follow my heart and not just to listen to it. Right?

I've enjoyed writing letters to you these past weeks. I wish we'd done more of this when you were still alive so that I'd have them to read over and over.

Missing you,
Retta

On Monday morning they were still talking about it when the whole bunch of them plus the boys, Mavis, Skip, Cade, and Retta got into the borrowed church van again to go to the shopping mall in Wichita Falls to buy school supplies and clothing.

"It's getting them used to being away from the ranch in small doses," Mavis told Retta as she sat down on the same seat with her.

"How did yesterday really go?" Retta asked.

"Benjy was a delight. He loved our little place and asked a thousand questions about why Levi moved away when he had his own room and could even have sheep or steers to show at the county fair. This is going to be good for me and Skip both," she answered. "How'd your afternoon go with Cade?"

"What makes you think we had an afternoon?" Retta blushed.

"You've got the glow of a woman either in love or pregnant," Mavis said bluntly.

"Well, I'm not pregnant." Retta's cheeks turned even brighter red.

"Hmmph," Mavis snorted. "I'll keep prayin' for you then."

"Mavis!" Retta exclaimed.

"Well, I will. Woman gets to a certain age, they need children. I ain't blind. I see the way you are with those girls. You'll make a great mama," she said. "But changing the subject here. I'm gettin' antsy to be back home and have Benjy there with me and Skip."

"He's goin' to love it." Retta was glad for the change of subject matter.

"Benjy will have the best of two worlds, since he'll get to come to the ranch pretty often. I just can't tell you how much I'm lookin' forward to having him. Skip is already talkin' about how he'll take him to school and go get him in the evenings. It'll give that old guy something to do every day," Mavis rattled on.

Retta listened with one ear but she couldn't keep her

mind or her eyes off Cade, who was sitting right across the narrow aisle from her. More than once while they were in the cabin, he'd said that he loved her. Emotion, passion, fire, heat—they'd all been wound up together in one amazingly wonderful afternoon. She'd replayed every nuance and every word until well after midnight the night before.

"Okay, kids." Cade stood up in the front of the van when Skip parked it in the mall lot. "Here's the deal. I figure you've each worked extra hard these past five weeks, so your bunk parent, either Skip or Retta, has been given an envelope with your money in it. The envelope has one half of that money you've earned and must be spent on school clothes and supplies. The rest will be given to you on Thursday morning when you get in the vans with your social workers to go home. Promise me it won't be used for drugs or alcohol."

"Promise," eight voices singsonged.

When they filed out of the bus, Retta handed her four girls their envelopes. "You don't have to compare notes. You each get the same amount, and it all has to be spent like Cade said, but whether you want to shop for sales and get more for your money or spend it on high-dollar items is totally up to you."

"I want more," Alice said.

"Let's hit the sales," Faith declared.

Gabby opened her envelope and gasped. "This is a lot of money. I ain't never been shoppin' with this much. I want five new pairs of skinny jeans and new shirts so I can wear something different every day the first week of school."

"I want new shoes, not used ones," Sasha whispered. "And then new things to wear too."

They started in one end of the mall and made their way through store after store until they reached the other end.

Alice spent the last five dollars of her money on a package of socks with kittens on them. Faith probably had the most in her bag but she'd hit a fantastic end-of-season sale on jeans and shirts.

At exactly five o'clock they crawled back into the van—tired, more than a little irritable, and hungry. The boys had been waiting for nearly an hour so they weren't happy campers either. Cade rolled his eyes at Retta who shot him a look that said he'd better not say a word.

"We thought we'd have to send out the army to get y'all. What'd you do? Buy out every store in the whole place?" Kirk asked.

"Cade said we could go to the buffet if y'all got here on time and I ain't never been to a place like that so if you done ruined it, I'm going to have to kick your butts," Nelson said.

"Well, bring it on, big boy!" Faith did a head wiggle.

"They're here on time and the buffet is only two blocks from here." Skip ended the argument before it got off the ground. "So sit down and get ready for takeoff."

"Is it really all you can eat?" Nelson asked. "Like you can go back as much as you want? And they have desserts too?"

"Yep," Benjy answered. "It's like eatin' at home on the ranch only there's lots more of it. My granny used to take me to one for my birthday and sometimes we'd go on Thanksgiving. I like the mashed potatoes and the hot rolls. They're almost as good as the ones Mavis makes us."

There was that word again...*home*!

Retta liked it because she'd begun to feel the same way Benjy did about the ranch. It was home and might be permanently someday when she was ready to start a family.

"Thank you, son," Mavis beamed. "But you have to all

mind your manners while we are in the restaurant. Show everyone around you that you are little ladies and gentlemen."

"Yes, ma'am," Faith agreed. "But hungry as I am right now, I hope they've got a whole helluva—" She covered her mouth with her hand. "I mean heck of a lot of food in that place."

"How about you? You going to have dessert or real food first today?" Cade leaned across the aisle and whispered softly in Retta's ears.

"Dessert if I had my way but we should set the example for the children, right?" she answered.

"I suppose so but I'd rather have a ham and cheese sandwich in the cabin as all the food they'll offer us on the fancy buffet line," he said.

"Are you crazy?" Ivan asked. "You can have ham and cheese any old time. They'll have all kinds of good stuff at this place."

"Little ears hear really well," Retta said.

"Yep, they do," Cade agreed.

\*　　\*　　\*

The girls were well fed but still cranky from the long day when they got home that evening, so Retta made them all take a cool shower and then join her in the living room.

"I bought each of you a little present today." She brought out a journal for each of them in their favorite color. "You can write anything you want in it but make an effort to write something once a week. When you get to be my age, you'll be glad that you did." Then she handed them a matching address book. "This has each of your addresses in it plus Mavis's so you can write to each other when you get home.

There's twenty stamps in the little pocket in the back so you can send letters."

"Oh, my gosh!" Faith gushed. "This is wonderful. Thank you so much, Retta. But I don't have a thing to give you."

"I'll expect a hug from each of you when you leave and no tears. Because if you cry I will too, and we don't want those boys to see us carryin' on like babies. Remember we almost whipped them at football." Retta then opened up her big plastic bag and gave them each a small box of pretty stationery with matching envelopes. "Don't tear pages out of your journals. Use this."

Alice ran across the room and threw her arms around Retta. "This is like Christmas. Thank you so much."

"You are all very welcome. But there's one more little thing I wanted you to have before you go in a couple of days." She brought out a brand-new hairbrush, each in the color that matched their other items. "This is to remember all the fun we had braiding and fixing hair while you were here. I'm going to miss you girls."

Tears ran down Gabby's cheeks when she marched up to Retta and hugged her tightly. "I wish I never had to leave. This is the happiest I've ever been in my whole life."

"Pay it forward," Retta said.

"What does that mean?" Sasha asked.

"It means for you to be nice to others, like Cade and Mavis and everyone has been nice to you," Retta explained.

"That won't be easy," Faith declared.

"No, but it's not impossible." Retta stood up and bent to hug her. "You've got goals. Don't let anyone stand in the way, but don't be hateful or mean on the way to doing great things."

"Yes, ma'am." Faith grinned.

"Now." Retta took a deep breath. "Tomorrow we get

all your things packed up. Your new things will be folded neatly and what you brought with you will be washed and put in suitcases, boxes, or sacks. And before you ask, you can pick out a new outfit to wear home on Thursday morning."

Alice went back to her original spot on the sofa. "I bet you're going to tell us that we need to clean this place and leave it as nice as when we found it, right?"

"Yes, I am. So take this stuff I've given you to the bedroom and yes, you can write in your journals tonight and tomorrow as well," she said.

Sasha looked up from her address book. "And where do we send letters to you, Retta?"

"I'll give Cade my address soon as I get settled and he'll send my mail on to me. So just send them here to the ranch and I'll answer every one of them," she promised with a huge lump in her throat.

# *Chapter Twenty-Nine*

Somehow Tuesday slipped right through Retta's fingers and then it was July Fourth and the last day and night she'd spend on the ranch with her girls. They arose full of energy and they couldn't wait to get dressed and get up to the big house to help Mavis with breakfast and then there would be games all day and people. The whole county was invited to the Longhorn Canyon Ranch party on the Fourth of July.

Everyone would start arriving at midmorning, and they'd put more food on the tables under the shade trees than the kids had seen at the buffet on Monday. There would be local kids for them to see and to visit with and everyone would play games and eat until dark when there would be a fireworks display.

It was going to be one of those bittersweet days for Retta. Happy that she could see Cade and yet not so much that she'd be loading up all her stuff the next morning and driving toward Dallas. Her appointment for the interview was at ten-thirty, so she would leave at the same time the kids did—right after breakfast at eight-thirty.

"So what are you thinking about?" Cade slipped his arms around her waist that morning as the kids ran here and there helping Mavis and Skip get things set up and ready for the countywide picnic.

"That I can't cry when they leave," she answered honestly. "How about you?"

"That I won't cry when you leave," he whispered softly.

"Ah, come on now. Big old tough cowboys don't cry." She fought back her own tears at the very thought of a single drop rolling down his handsome face. Reaching up to touch the cleft in his chin, she swallowed the lump in her throat. "We'll make it work."

"I know but I don't like to be away from you two hours to go plow a field much less a whole week at a time," he admitted.

She rolled up on her toes and kissed him on the cheek. "Let me get settled and then maybe I can commute a couple of days a week and have weekends here."

"Hey, Retta, guess what?" Faith ran across the yard. "It's almost time for fireworks." She tugged on Retta's hand.

"See you later. Maybe a porch visit after the fireworks?" he asked.

"I'll be the one who is worn out with scraggly hair and probably grass-stained jeans," she teased.

"The moon and stars will have a tough time outshining your beauty even if you do have on stained jeans." He smiled and waved.

\*       \*       \*

Cade waited on the porch that evening with two bottles of icy cold beer. Justin had gone into town to see some woman that he'd met a few weeks ago in a bar. Levi had met a cousin of a friend at the picnic and the two of them had left together. He didn't expect either of them home until sometime between midnight and daylight. For them it had been a long five weeks and they deserved to get away for a few hours. Truth be told, he'd love to take Retta by the hand and go find a room at the nearest motel.

He hated looking at Retta's truck, already packed with her things, so he turned the rocking chair around to face the ranch house and ignored it. When she finally came outside, he popped the tabs off two cans of beer and handed one to her. She took it from his hands and sat down in his lap.

"Thank you, and not just for the beer," she said.

"For what then?"

"Everything. Helping me get over my father's death as well as my mother's. Letting me see that there are good men like you left in the world. All of it. The girls, the boys, the fun...every single hour of it." She held up the beer. "And for this too. I've wanted one all day."

"Thank you," he said.

"For?"

"For helping me move on from Julie and for loving me," he said simply.

"I guess we've been good for each other, haven't we?"

"Looks that way." He nodded.

Putting one hand on his face, she turned it just right to kiss him. "I really do love you, Cade. Today was amazing with all the people and seeing them interact with the kids. I can't wait to see what kind of group we get next year."

"Me, either, but I wish you were the bunk mama."

"You willin' to give me up for five whole weeks?" she teased.

"Didn't think of that. Maybe not, then." He set the beer can on the porch railing and wrapped her up in his arms. Holding her for a long time without a single word between them seemed so natural and comfortable that he felt as if they were in a world of their own.

She finally pushed up out of his arms, kissed him one more time, and said, "Good night, darlin'. Those girls will have me up at the crack of dawn. They've already got most of their things ready to go. I want to keep them all but most of all, Faith."

"I know, sweetheart, but it's not possible. Finding a home for Benjy is a miracle, and that they let Skip and Mavis have him with plans for adoption is even a bigger one. We can't keep them all but we'll hope that these few weeks have given them purpose and determination. I'll see you at breakfast, then?"

"Of course." She planted one more fiery kiss on his lips.

*        *        *

Retta was determined not to get emotional as she pushed her last suitcase out into the living room and went to each of the girls' rooms to check on them one final time. Precious little Alice was going home now to a new baby in the house. Gabby smiled in her sleep, deepening the dimples on both sides of her cheeks. The moon lit up the purple streaks in Faith's hair. And Sasha, with her red hair splayed out over her pillow, had come a long way in a few short weeks.

"I love every one of you," she whispered as she crossed the living area floor and went to her own room.

She fell right to sleep but had nightmares about drowning in a dirty lake. If Cade hadn't pulled her to shore, she would have died in that murky water. At midnight she awoke in a cold sweat and went to the kitchen for a glass of milk. But the refrigerator had been cleaned completely out. There wasn't even a bottle of water left.

"When did that happen?" she wondered aloud as she drew up a glass of lukewarm water from the tap.

She went back to bed and dreamed that she was in a deep ravine yelling for help and the only person who heard her was Cade. He brought a rope and hauled her up from that miry pit with his strong arms and then held her until she could stop shaking. When she awoke that time it was to see four little girls gathered round her bed.

"You were screaming in your sleep," Faith said.

Retta yawned. "I'm so sorry that I woke you girls. Go on back to bed. It was just a bad dream."

"It's only fifteen minutes until the alarm goes off so we're going to stay up and get dressed," Alice said.

"Okay, then let's all get dressed and go help Mavis with breakfast. Y'all ready for this day?"

"I want to go home but I don't want to leave," Alice admitted honestly. "That's kinda crazy, ain't it?"

Retta threw off the sheet. "I understand so well, darlin' girl. But we'll be writing and calling each other all the time. So it's kind of like having the best of both worlds."

"Okay." Sasha sighed. "But I still don't like it. Sayin' good-bye is hard."

Retta took the time to hug her. "Yes, it is."

*       *       *

Breakfast went too fast. The last time they'd sit around the big table together as a group. Then suddenly the clock said that it was eight-thirty, which meant the vans would be arriving to pick up the children any minute.

Retta's heart stopped when she heard the engines of two vehicles coming down the lane. The kids all ran outside, started hugging each other and telling each other that they'd write every Sunday, just like always.

"Will you email me too?" Kirk blushed as he nudged Faith on the arm.

She slapped him on the arm. "Sure I will and when we graduate from high school, maybe we'll go to the same college together."

He kicked at the grass. "I'd like that. I'd know someone there even if it is a mean old girl."

"And I'll know a boy who can't throw a spiral as good as me," she shot back at him. "You better answer my emails or I'll hunt you down." She put both hands on his chest and gave him a gentle shove.

"You better email me back or I'll beat you again at football," he said.

Cade draped an arm around Retta's shoulders. "You better answer my phone calls or I'll hunt you down."

She wiggled free of him. "I might not, just so I can see you. Let's do this like adults. Give me a hug and I'm going to walk to my truck, get inside, and drive away. I'll call you after my interview."

"I'll do my best not to throw myself on the ground and have a fit like a two-year-old," he said.

Tears flowed down Benjy's cheeks and he waved until the boys' van was completely out of sight. Then after the girls had hugged every one at least three times, he stood in the yard and waved at them.

"Now can I go home with Mavis and Skip?" he asked.

"Yup. Take your things and throw them in the back of my pickup truck, son," Skip said.

"Do I get Levi's old room?"

"You sure do," Levi said from the porch. "You're gettin' some fine folks to live with just like I did."

"I know it. And I get sheep to show at the fair. I'll read books about them," he said.

"We'll definitely see you in church on Sundays," Justin said.

They drove off with him, and Cade walked Retta down to her pickup. "Don't forget to call when you get there."

"I won't." She hugged him one more time and got into the truck. No tears. No big emotional moment. This wasn't as difficult as she'd thought it would be. She was going to be fine. Until he walked away without looking back. She couldn't make herself start the engine. She didn't want to leave the ranch. The job in the city didn't seem nearly as important as it did even the day before, and her pride was gone. With her hands frozen on the steering wheel, the future flashed before her eyes and she liked what she saw. Going to sleep in Cade's arms every night and waking up with him every morning. And growing old with him right there on the Longhorn Canyon ranch.

"What in the hell am I doing?" she asked. She rolled down the window. "Hey, cowboy," she yelled.

He turned around and wiped something from his eyes. "Something wrong with your truck?"

She got out and ran toward him. "Not with the truck but with my heart."

He opened his arms and she barreled right into them. "Seems that it doesn't want to leave the ranch. And neither do I. Is that job for a bookkeeper and general helper around here still open?"

"What about your interview?" he asked.

"A *home* is way more important than a job. And remember what you told me about home? My heart is here, Cade Maguire. Or wherever you are. If you'll have me..."

"God, yes." His lips settled on hers in a long, hot kiss that made her knees buckle. "In fact..." He dropped down on his knees in the grass. "Retta Palmer, will you marry me?"

"Yes, yes, yes, a million times yes."

He stood up, picked her up, and twirled her around until they were both dizzy.

"What's goin' on out there?" Levi asked from the porch.

"I think she's here to stay," Justin said from the other end of the porch.

"Well, hallelujah! What's for dinner?" Levi threw his hat in the air.

Justin swaggered off the porch and hugged them both. "What changed your mind, Retta?"

"I finally figured life is worthless if I can't share it with someone I love," she answered, but she was gazing into Cade's pretty blue eyes when she said it.

"Welcome to the Maguire family," Justin said.

"Y'all hold down the place. I'm going to spend the rest of the day with my fiancée." He took her by the hand and led her back to the bunkhouse.

When they were inside, he sat down on the sofa and pulled her down into his lap and smothered her with passionate kisses until they were both panting.

"I'm the happiest man on the earth right now."

"Even though I'm a Sooner?" She grinned.

"Well, there is that, but no one is perfect and I love you in spite of that little thing." He held her tightly.

"Then I'll do my best to overlook you being a Longhorn because I love you that much too," she said softly.

Keep reading for a peek at
Levi and Claire's story in


*COWBOY HONOR*


Coming in Fall 2018

At the sound of heavy boots stomping across the wooden porch of the old cabin, Claire grabbed her purse, unzipped the side pocket, and brought out a small pistol. Her heart was in her throat and her pulse raced so fast that she couldn't breathe, but she held the gun steady in both hands and pointed it straight at the door. When the door flew open and what looked like the abominable snowman filled the space, her five-year-old niece, Zaylie, squealed and dived beneath the quilt they were both huddling under.

With shoulders and a chest so broad that it obliterated the blowing snow, the man just stood there, staring at her. After what seemed like forever but was probably less than a minute, he whipped off the black face mask and wiped snow from his eyelashes. Fear sent adrenaline rushing through Claire's body, but her brother had told her to never show that she was afraid—even if she was terrified.

"Who are you and what are you doin' here?" She kept

the pistol aimed at his chest. If she missed a target that big, her brother would never let her live it down.

Both of his hands went up. "Don't shoot, lady. I'm the foreman of this ranch. My name is Levi Jackson. I'm going to shut the door now and take off these coveralls. I'm not here to hurt anyone. My four-wheeler ran out of gas and I need a place to hole up until this storm is over. Why are you here?"

She lowered the gun but kept it in her lap. "Just don't get too close."

"Okay, lady. Take it easy." He bent forward and unzipped the short zippers on the legs of his coveralls and then the longer one down the front. He shrugged his wide shoulders out of the garment and hung it on a nail inside the door. "It's freezin' in here. Why haven't you started a fire? There's always wood and kindlin'."

"I couldn't find any matches."

"What are y'all doin' here anyway?"

"My van slid off the road in this awful storm and there was no way to get it back on the road. We saw this place. It was unlocked." She kept her finger on the trigger and her eyes on him. "We're not hurting anything and we'll be gone as soon as it stops snowing."

The man removed his cowboy hat and combed his light brown hair back with his fingers. "I'm glad you found shelter. It's nasty out there! Matches are here on the top shelf of the cabinet, so we can light the kitchen stove when we want to cook. I'm surprised you didn't see them."

"I'm five feet two inches. No way I could reach or even see the top shelf," she shot back at him.

He started toward the cabinet with his hands raised. "I'm going to the cabinet to get the matches. Don't shoot me."

Zaylie pushed the quilt back far enough to peek out with

one blue eye but quickly dived back under when the man started across the floor.

"It's okay." Claire hugged the child closer with her free hand. "He's going to start a fire so we can get warm."

Levi removed his gloves and stuck them in his pocket as he crossed the floor to the kitchen side of the room and retrieved a box of matches from the top shelf. "Now I'm going across the room to the fireplace. I'd sure feel better if you put the safety back on that pistol and put it away." He dropped to his knees in front of the old stone fireplace. "It won't take long to get this place warmed up. There's kindling and wood right here. Were either of you hurt in the wreck? What's your names?"

"I'm Claire Mason and this is my niece, Zaylie. We're fine except for a few bruises. We slid off the road, went through a fence, and hit a tree. My van is down there not far off the road if you need proof. My cell phone battery had gone dead and—" She shrugged.

He whipped around with a lit match in his hand. "I see blood on your forehead."

"We had the wreck sometime last night. The blood is just a scratch. I know we're trespassin' but we needed shelter. We didn't use any of your food." She pushed the safety switch to the on position but kept her thumb on it.

"We never lock the door just in case someone needs to use the cabin and you'd be welcome to whatever food you could find." He sat down on the worn sofa facing the fire, kicked off his wet boots, and removed his socks. Stretching his bare feet toward the fire to warm them, he glanced over his shoulder. "Sure y'all ain't hurt?"

Zaylie stopped shivering beneath the quilt and Claire slipped the pistol back into her purse. "We're fine. Thank you for starting a fire."

"If you'd come over here closer to it, you'd warm up quicker," he said. "Now, I'm going to reach in my hip pocket for my phone. I need to let the folks at the ranch know where I am."

Claire nodded but closed her fingers around the pistol grip again. His angular face broke out into a smile when someone answered.

"Retta, I'm at the cabin. Four-wheeler is out of gas and the battery on my phone is almost gone. Did Justin and Cade find that rangy old bull?"

He chuckled as he listened and then said, "That's great. No, we'll wait out the blizzard. There's food and plenty of wood." He drew his feet up on the sofa and tucked them under a quilt. "Okay, it's not a real blizzard but for north central Texas it sure feels like one. My phone is starting to bleep so listen up." He told her about finding a half frozen lady and a child in the cabin. Then he held the phone out and sighed before he laid it on an end table next to the sofa. "Well, that's the last of communication with the outside world. Last weather report I heard said the storm was going to hang around until tomorrow. Y'all hungry?"

Zaylie pushed back the blanket and nodded. "I'm hungry. Who is Retta?"

"You goin' to take your hand off that gun, ma'am, or do I need to verbalize every thing I'm doin' so you don't get trigger happy and shoot me? Justin and Cade Maguire own this ranch and Retta is Cade's wife. They can't come get us right now but they'll be here soon as possible." He didn't look afraid even when he tiptoed across the cold floor to the other side of the cabin.

Claire slipped the gun back in her purse but she didn't zip the pocket. "Thank you for not throwing us out."

"What are you doing?" Zaylie pushed the covers back a little more.

"I'm going over here to this chest of drawers to get a pair of dry socks, maybe two pair until this floor gets warmed up. And then I'm going to make hot soup for you," he answered as he dug around in the drawer of a dresser and brought out a pair of gray socks. "Y'all want a pair?"

"We're fine. I brought our suitcases in with us." Claire nodded toward a couple of bags at the end of the bed.

In a few long strides he was back to the sofa where he held the socks near the fire and then put them on his feet. "Ahh, that's much better. Now, let's get some food ready. Canned soup will be fast, but last time I was up here I noticed some hunters had left behind some frozen pizzas and burritos, so we'll have that for supper." He opened the top door of the refrigerator and pulled out pizza boxes.

"That sounds good." She could be polite and appreciative, but that didn't mean he was luring her into trusting him—not even with food and a sexy smile.

# About the Author

Carolyn Brown is a *New York Times*, *USA Today*, *Wall Street Journal*, and *Publisher's Weekly* best-selling romance author and RITA® Finalist who has sold more than four million books. She presently writes both women's fiction and cowboy romance. She has also written historical single title, historical series, contemporary single title, and contemporary series. She lives in southern Oklahoma with her husband, a former English teacher, who writes mystery novels. They have three children and enough grandchildren to keep them young. For a complete listing of her books (series in order) check out her website at CarolynBrownBooks.com.

## Ready for more cowboys?
### Don't miss these other great Forever romances.

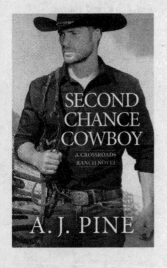

**Second Chance Cowboy**
**By A. J. Pine**

Once a cowboy, always a cowboy! Jack Everett can handle work on the ranch, but turning around the failing vineyard he's also inherited? That requires working with the woman he never expected to see again.

**Cowboy Bold**
**By Carolyn Brown**

Down on her luck, Retta Palmer is thrilled to find an opening for a counselor position at Longhorn Canyon Ranch, but she's not as thrilled to meet her new boss. With a couple of lovable kids and two elderly folks playing matchmaker, Retta finds herself falling for this real-life cowboy.

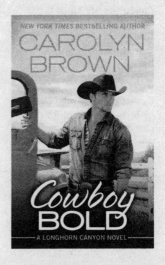

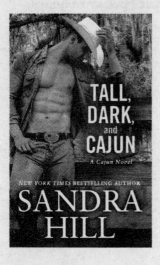
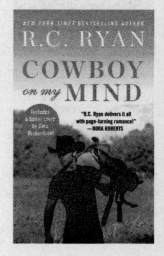

Be sure to follow the conversation using
*#ReadForever* and *#CowboyoftheMonth!*

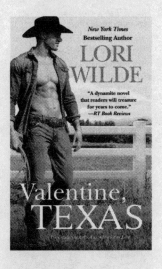

### Valentine, Texas
### By Lori Wilde

Can a girl have her cake and her cowboy, too? Rachael Henderson has sworn off men, but when she finds herself hauled up against the taut, rippling body of her first crush, she wonders if taking a chance on love is worth the risk.

### True-Blue Cowboy
### By Sara Richardson

Everly Brooks wants nothing to do with her sexy new landlord, but, when he comes to her with a deal she can't refuse, staying away from him is not as easy as it seems.

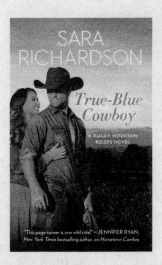

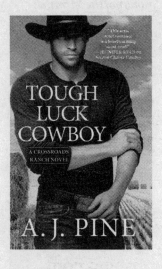
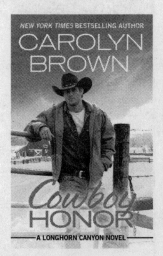